LUBYANKA

JAMES BURCH

LUBYANKA

ATHENEUM   NEW YORK

1983

I would like to thank Paul Spike, Kent McCarthy, Robert Burch, and Jan Hinson for their help in making it possible for me to write this novel.

Library of Congress Cataloging in Publication Data

Burch, James.
    Lubyanka.

    Title.
PS3552.U625L8   1983   813'.54   82-73022
ISBN 0-689-11342-0

For my mother, KATHLEEN

LUBYANKA

Quang Ngai Province, Vietnam, February 1968

An American soldier stood near the perimeter, staring off into the night. He lit a cigarette, catching his face in the glow. Though he wore the insignia of a captain, with his scraggly beard and matted hair bound in a black silk headband and the long gold earring dangling like a pendulum from one ear, he looked not at all like an officer.

He held the match for a moment after the cigarette was lit, listening in on the silence, and when it had burned down to his fingers he fanned it out.

In a bunker three men drew straws, matches. Two white hands, one black. One of the white hands produced the short match.

"Man, you waste that motherfucker tomorrow, hunh?"

"No. I'll do it now."

Without looking around, the captain listened to him approach. "Quiet," he said when the footsteps had stopped at his back. "Fuckers are out there, though. Sure I'd draw some fire."

"Perry's patrol drew too much fire."

"Some guys die, some of 'em live forever."

3

"Yeah." The soldier behind the captain, his face obscured in shadow, was momentarily silent. "Duffy? Were they drinking tea?"

"Who?"

"The V.C. in Cholon. Were they drinking tea when you zapped them?"

The captain looked back, eyes gleaming. "Yeah. They were all drinkin' fuckin' tea." He turned back toward the trees.

Behind him the soldier unsnapped his holster and took out his army .45.

Though the captain must have heard it, must have recognized the sound, he did not look around again.

1

Langley, August 1978

They were all seated at the long table when Avery Remick entered the room.

"Sorry." He mumbled something about the traffic, set his tattered briefcase on the floor, and took a seat. They were all looking at him. He took off his wire-rimmed glasses and began polishing them with his handkerchief. In his old tweed coat and broad, mismatched tie he stood out from them all. The distinction fed Remick's self-image. The maverick. Once, after returning from Eastern Bloc penetration, he'd shocked them by showing up at the conference in one of those dreary Soviet-manufactured suits and Polish button-down shirts that earmarked the men on the other side.

At the head of the table Donaldson sighed. "The matter of Alexander Terekhov." He looked at the man next to Remick. "Moscow Station?"

"Until recently," Moscow Station began, "Terekhov's status in the scientific community has made him immune to anything more than minor harassment. But in recent weeks the KGB seems to have changed its tune. And Terekhov has become increasingly outspoken. Sources say his arrest is imminent."

Donaldson focused on the face of the man across from Remick. "Science and Technology. What does he know and how bad can he hurt us?"

Science and Technology took a batch of stapled, Xeroxed pages from his briefcase and sent them down the table. "The Reisinger transcript, Mr. Director."

"Just tell us about it."

"Yes, sir. Erich Reisinger was best known here for his work on the bubble chamber experiments at Cal Berkeley. Reisinger was the particle beam expert on the project. He became friends with Terekhov when he was in Moscow on one of our exchange programs in 1974. Now, any practical charged particle beam *weapon* would of necessity be mounted on a space-based platform. The primary problem the Russians have encountered at their facility down in Semipalatinsk, Central Asia, is in finding an accelerator design that will permit construction of a weapon small enough to be launchable. That's what Reisinger claims he and Terekhov came up with in '74."

"And what the hell were *they* doing working together on *that?*" asked the director of Central Intelligence.

"They weren't working on it, sir. They were just talking. In Gorky Park. One idea led to another and before they knew it they were onto the concept. . . ." He paused and fumbled in his briefcase for a paper. "Concept of a circular accelerator principle employing controlled fusion by inertial confinement—"

"Forget the mumbo jumbo. Just tell us if it will work."

Remick finished with his glasses and set them back on his nose.

"We don't know," said Science and Technology. "Reisinger died without revealing the specific concept. He and Terekhov had made a vow to keep their discovery secret, so we can only hope the Russians don't have it either."

"And if they get it?"

"If the concept is functional they could probably launch a prototype in the early 1980s. It works somewhat like a laser, employing atomic particle matter rather than light."

"Are we talking about some kind of death ray or doomsday

device?" asked Decoding and Analysis, down the table from Remick.

"What we are talking about," said Science and Technology, irked, "is the potential for total destruction of our ICBM force in a nuclear war."

"Christ," whispered Donaldson. "Those two old codgers sitting by the lake in Gorky Park, feeding the goddamned swans!" He looked at Remick. "Avery?"

Though the image had its appeal, there were no swans and there was no lake in Gorky Park where Terekhov and Reisinger had talked. The lake and the swans were in Sokolniki Park, in the north of the city. Or perhaps, Remick thought, they were just at the Bolshoi. He wondered if he would ever see Moscow again. "Yes, sir. I've developed a contingency plan."

"To do what?"

"To remove Terekhov to the West. Or that failing, to eliminate him."

"Even assuming he'll be in custody?"

"Assuming even that." He waited, enjoying their anticipation and enjoying the special distinction he was sure he bore from all of them. For if advancement to his present rank had rendered him no longer an operative, he was still not an administrator, and certainly not a politician. And if he, as much as they, liked to use men, his men were never mere numbers or code-names, never pins or flags on the strategist's map. His pawns were real people, his people, personal and very private possessions. There were men who without ever having known it had belonged to him for years, and if ever the time came for him to move them into danger or send them to their deaths, it was never more a test of the man than a test of Remick himself.

"I want to run this one myself," he said finally. "I have a man under my thumb. An American presently residing in Paris, who spent part of his childhood in Russia. Edward Rhone. An escape artist."

2

Paris, September 1978

Until that afternoon in Paris, Edward Rhone had not seen
Avery Remick in a little over ten years, though in all that time
he'd never doubted that sooner or later Remick would turn up
again. But Rhone's day had gone all wrong even before Remick
pulled him out of the Seine.

He was out on the middle of the Pont St. Michel. While he
stripped to his swim trunks his promoter told the crowd who he
was and what he was going to do. A uniformed gendarme
pulled Rhone's hands behind his back, snapped a pair of cuffs
on his wrists, and testified they were police-issue from the
Sûreté de Paris. The leg-irons were Rhone's own, specially
made, but a Montparnasse locksmith had supplied and vouched
for the locks. His promoter got back on the bullhorn and went
into the Houdini routine. Rhone tried to ignore it. Being compared to Houdini had always made him uncomfortable, and
that day it bothered him more than usual. That day he did not
want to go down. He'd woken up with a dread and it hadn't
gone away.

The girls moved into the crowd, passing the hat and dis-
tributing fliers. There were three hundred, perhaps four hun-

dred people on the bridge, and more watching from the quays on either side. Tourists observed from the balconies and towers of Notre Dame, looming up on the Isle de La Cité. Above it the sky was gray. And the water of the Seine flowing under the bridge looked gray and cold and polluted.

Two Algerians picked him up and set him into the box. From St. Michel, the Left Bank, he could hear another, bigger crowd shouting in vague unison a series of unintelligible slogans. He'd seen them massing there, along with their complementary busloads of helmeted riot police, when he'd first come onto the bridge. He'd thought they were there to see him.

"What's happening over there?" He spoke through the side of his mouth because of the lock-pick between his teeth.

"*C'est une démonstration gauchiste,*" said the gendarme.

Rhone looked at his portly promoter, who shrugged in an expansive, uniquely French and meaningless gesture. "We thought it would increase the spectators. . . . You are ready?"

"Let's get it over with."

He squatted, then sat down in the box. Now from the Place St. Michel he could hear an orator on a loudspeaker. As they closed the lid he envisioned his audience drifting away to the call of some long-haired, ranting Pied Piper.

He leaned back, braced his shoulders against the wooden corners of the box, and planted his bare feet flat on the lead-lined floor. With the darkness and stifling closeness and the isolation made tangible by the sound of the chains drawn tight over the lid, a cold sweat broke swiftly across his face. He folded his palms and tried to pull his hands through the cuffs. They wouldn't go. He separated his wrists as widely as the short chain would allow and banged the locks hard together. They held fast. He spit out the pick and retrieved it between his toes, rocked forward onto his stomach and doubled his legs behind his back. He heard the squeak of the crane.

He started on the cuffs. Outside they hooked the cable on and the box rose up from the stones, swung out over the wall in a dizzying arch, and descended toward the water. He searched for the tumblers with the hook on the end of the pick. When it

9

caught it was somewhere between the feel of a fish getting hooked on his line and an idea clicking into place in his mind.

Rhone banged the locks again. His hands free, he rolled onto his back and got the irons off his legs. The box settled into the current and drifted free of the sling. Water spilled in through the cracks as he used one of the leg irons to chip the putty away from the hinges and the separation down the middle of the false end-board. Then he folded the manacle open and used it as a lever against the edge of the end-board. As the hinges allowed the board to fold inward, the water rushed through in a stream. The box was sinking rapidly now. He waited for it to fill. His last breath of air was the last breath of air in the box. Then he doubled the hinged end all the way open and crawled out into the murky, rushing river, clinging with one hand to the chain still locked tight over the lid.

He could see nothing for the filth. Now he was supposed to close the false-end and smear a glob of water-hardening putty, from a tiny tube concealed in the waist of his trunks, into the crack where he'd folded it open. But he felt suddenly tired. Tired of the cold and dark. Tired of the fear. Tired of holding his breath. Tired of doing for money what he'd once done for the thrill of risking his life. He was sinking toward the bottom with the box, thinking, when he should have been swimming for his life.

He turned loose of the chain and kicked off the lid with his feet. Vague light materialized gradually at the surface far above. There would be no box that day, sealed and chained and intact, just as it had been when they'd last seen it, knowing he was still manacled inside, for the divers to come down and retrieve. There would be no one-man Paris show, no German and Scandinavian tour. Just that weighted trick box with the hinged false-end exposed for all to see. But, as it turned out, that didn't matter.

He broke the surface gasping for breath. His audience had disappeared.

Rhone was fifty yards downstream from the bridge, where

the remnants of his audience and the crowd from St. Michel were being stampeded by baton-wielding police. There were more police chasing more of Rhone's spectators, the students, Arabs, Africans, and the screaming Parisian tourists, along the quay away from St. Michel. He was treading water, spitting water from his lungs. The pennant announcing his escape hung by one end off the side of the bridge, flapping in a breeze. They hadn't sent the Arabs in the rowboat to pick him up.

He swam the thirty yards to the bank of the Isle de la Cité, clung to it, shivering in the chilly water, momentarily so exhausted that he was incapable of even lifting himself out. He remembered a story he'd read when he was a boy, when he'd been ten or eleven, after his father had been transferred to the Paris Embassy, about a hanging from a bridge over a creek that ran through a small midwestern town. The rope snapped tight, unraveled and broke, and the condemned man fell to the water and swam or drifted to safety downstream, got his hands untied, and made his way home where his wife came running out to meet him. Then the noose snapped his neck and everything went dark. Rhone coughed. He'd swallowed a lot of water coming up. Somebody, of course, had made the story up. But he momentarily forgot that; he closed his eyes, still clinging to the embankment, and imagined he was still in the box, sitting on the bottom of the Seine. He imagined that all the pandemonium he'd discovered upon reaching the surface had merely been a dream. Imagined the crowd still there on the bridge, scanning the current, whispering in the hush; imagined his fat promoter, pacing on the bridge, shouting finally, too late, for the divers to go down. Imagined himself still in the box, spewing water like a whale, choking until all went dark.

A hand was clutching at his arm. He looked up. The face of the middle-aged man with the thin-trimmed moustache and wire-rimmed glasses perched far down on his nose came gradually into focus. With his graying hair curled fashionably over his ears and his tweed coat fashionably out of style, he could have passed for a university professor on sabbatical or an out-of-uniform priest. Rhone hadn't seen Avery Remick since Saigon, 1968. But he'd always known that sooner or later he was bound to see him again.

The American Embassy in Paris is situated in a large, shaded building surrounded by an iron-barred fence, on the Rue de Rivoli just off the Place de la Concorde. The office where Remick had been temporarily lodged was little more than a cubbyhole at the end of a narrow corridor somewhere in the sequestered third-floor maze that was Paris Station. Rhone, having had a shower and a fresh change of clothes at his place near the Metro St. Jacques, and a warm meal at a Right Bank brasserie, was ushered in by a clerk a few minutes after the 5 p.m. meeting time they'd agreed on.

Remick waved the clerk out and motioned for Rhone to sit down. He searched the clutter on the desk, selected a folder, and opened it and thumbed through at his leisure.

Rhone lit a cigarette.

"You're an odd bird, Rhone. You know that? Diplomatic brat, raised in ... Turkey, Russia, India, here in Paris. Never lived stateside between the ages of three and sixteen. Fluent in Hindi, French ... Russian. Full scholarship to Stanford. Then, from campus radical to Vietnam war hero." He smiled. "But we both know all about *that.* Discharged 1969, resided in Asia and Europe since then. See you started the escape thing here as a kid, under the tutelage of an old French anarchist. Challenge escapes from ... Santé, Brixton, Scotland Yard ... Spandau."

He closed the folder abruptly, produced another, and opened it to an incomplete set of architect's drawings, extensively annotated. He pushed them across the desk. "Tell me, do you think you could get out of there?"

Rhone leaned over the drawings. He didn't like giving Remick even the satisfaction of seeing his display of interest, but the man had touched his weak spot. He was fascinated with jails and prisons and the theory and science of escape from them. Perhaps it was his hatred of being locked up, just as he escaped from manacles and straight jackets because he did not like to be bound, or escaped from submerged boxes because he could not stand to be enclosed. But he knew there was more to it than that. When he broke out of a prison it was not merely that prison he was escaping from, but something it symbolized, within himself, or in life itself.

The structure in the drawings was an old six-floor building built around a courtyard. Adjoining it was a newer annex, actually somewhat larger than the prison, which, according to the annotation, consisted of administrative offices and was sealed off from the prison at its accesses by armed guards.

Inside the jail crooked corridors seemed to course and wind in a random and disorganized maze. Some cellblocks consisted of several tiers located around rectangular halls. Others were enclosed within a single, sealed corridor. Cells ranged in size from tiny "boxes" to large communal cells with as many as six beds. But each cellblock, an annotation specified, was individually sealed off from the rest of the prison by a four-inch steel door with two armed guards outside. Guards did not take arms inside the cellblocks except in an emergency, and in such a case the precautions prescribed were elaborate.

An elevator gave access from the ground floor of the prison to the exercise yards on its roof, which were guarded by a machine gun tower and enclosed by fifteen-foot walls topped with barbed wire. A separate elevator system served the administrative annex, where prisoners were sometimes taken for interrogation. Vents inside the cells were four inches by six, covered with metal gratings. The elevator shaft gave no access to the ventilation system, which was powered by a squirrel cage blower situated in a housing unit on the roof. Several ground level entrances led through sealed corridors directly into the inner prison. Passage in and out of the administrative section was available to the public, though there was a guard table at the entrance. Prison personnel consisted of guards and wardens, kitchen and maintenance workers, scrub women, etc. There was no inmate labor.

Rhone looked up.

"Could you get out of there?"

"It's the Lubyanka."

13

"I didn't ask you where it was. I asked if there was a way out?"

"I think there is. If I was in there. But I'm not."

"Would you rather try Leavenworth?"

Rhone said nothing.

"There's no statute of limitations under military law. You'll be tried in civilian federal court, but you'll be in jail stateside waiting for that trial by this time tomorrow."

He'd known it was coming, had known it the minute he'd recognized Remick bending over him on the embankment of the Isle de la Cité. Remick removed an unmarked file from the folder and opened it on his desk. Though it wasn't labelled, Rhone knew it was his M-file. Remick had access to it; he couldn't have seen it himself with an order from the Supreme Court.

"Quang Ngai. February 1968. You remember Lieutenent William A. Duffy."

"That was dismissed, Remick."

"It was dismissed. But that doesn't mean it didn't happen, doesn't mean it just went away, forever. Besides, I'm the one who got it dismissed in the first place. And don't tell me you didn't know that all along."

Of course he'd known, just as he'd known all along that someday, somewhere down the line, it was bound to come to this. "They couldn't have made it stick then. You can't make it stick now."

"You haven't bothered to say you didn't do it."

"Why waste my breath?"

"But whether you did it or whether Jackson or Corporal Perry did it, or whether some fucking slope sneaked in and did it, somebody blew Lieutenent Duffy's brains out and I can prove it was you."

He withdrew a couple of official-looking documents from the unmarked file and pushed them across the desk.

Silently, and now almost without feeling, Rhone read the two depositions, signed respectively by Corporal Thomas G. Perry and Private First Class David T. Jackson. They had both been,

14

he remembered, good men. They'd been grunts, draftees, victims of the war just as the civilians and the children and the thirteen-year-old kids from the North had been victims. And that was a luxury he'd never been able to allow himself. He had been no victim. He'd been drawn to the war and after he'd gotten there, even hating what he saw, he had not been sorry that he'd come.

Bill Duffy had not so much been a victim of the war as a product. They said he'd once been left for dead after an ambush. He'd held his breath while the Viet Cong picked over his body. He'd worn a gold ring in his left ear and kept his long knotted hair tied up in a black headband torn from a dead Viet Cong's pajamas. His eyes had looked at you from a place you'd never been and hoped you would never go, eyes they said could see like an animal's in the jungle night. Duffy had been a killer through and through, but nobody understood how he'd ever become an officer.

"Where are they now?"

"Jackson's a staff sergeant, stationed at the Presidio in San Francisco. Perry's running his father's café back in some little town in Illinois. Must be a hell of a cook. He lost a hand while you were cooling your heels at MACV.".

"How did you get to them, Remick?"

"They both *say* you did it. At least neither one of them wanted to take the fall."

Rhone pushed the papers back and Remick returned them to the file.

"There are two FBI agents out in the corridor. When I give the word, you'll be arrested, flown back to the States, and remanded to the custody of the federal marshal for trial in U.S. federal court.

"Can it."

"On the other hand I have authorization here for a Swiss bank deposit in your name in the amount of two hundred thousand dollars."

The figure hardly registered. Rhone looked back at the plans of the prison and traced imaginary lines to the various dead-ends of the maze. But there would inevitably be one line that did not lead to a dead-end. That was what the old Frenchman had always said. *"If the vessel has a leak, fill it with water and the water will find this leak. That is the great escape artist. He is like water. And every prison has a leak somewhere."* And even as he searched the maze he remembered the headline he'd seen on the cover of that morning's *Herald Tribune:*

NOBEL LAUREATE FATHER OF RUSSIAN ROCKETRY ARRESTED

Beneath the headline had been a picture of Alexander Terekhov with his head shaved and a number-tag hanging around his neck, a blown-up mug shot taken somewhere in the halls of the Lubyanka. The caption explained the photograph had been published in yesterday's edition of *Pravda* and, in a rare move for the Soviets, released officially to the Western wire services.

"How would you get me in?"

"What?" Remick was taken aback.

"Do you have a gambit in mind? Or do I just hop a plane to Moscow and surrender to the KGB when I land?"

Remick took a long, slow breath. "I've got a Russian expatriate in my pocket. I knew I had to have him the first time I saw him and I've been waiting for years to use him. He looks like you." He smiled. "His sister in Moscow has agreed to verify your cover. You'll undergo three weeks of intensive training at our estate in Staffordshire, England: Russian language review, English with Russian accent, integration into your Russian identity and what information we can provide you with about the interior of the prison itself. . . . We'd hoped to have you part way through . . . before he was arrested."

Now Remick had said it himself. Maybe it wasn't even a slip.

16

3

Moscow, September 1978

It was five o'clock when the Aeroflot Ilyushin turbojet banked and started its descent toward the runways of Sheremetevo Airport.

His name was Andrei Petrovich Davilov. He wore a conservative, gray three-piece suit, tailored on Savile Row. His hair was cut shorter than he'd had it since his freshman year at Stanford. He'd grown a thin moustache. He'd long had a trace of gray at his temples, which had been slightly augmented. "After you've had your head shaved it will grow back darker. But no one will notice the difference," Remick had assured him.

"We are landing soon," remarked the bulky man beside him, one of his constant shadows during his last days in London, who had since Stockholm, where they had both transferred from SAS to Aeroflot, officially or unofficially become his KGB escort home.

Moments later the turbojet touched down and taxied to a stop. The passengers gathered their carry-on luggage and headed for the exits. As they started down the ladder, Rhone donned the Russian fur hat which had been among the things

17

Davilov's wife had packed for him. The KGB man behind him, he descended the ladder into the bone-chilling cold, trudged through the frozen slush that covered the runway, and boarded the shuttle bus for the terminal. Across the front of the building spread a huge red and black banner that read:

LENIN ZHIL. LENIN ZHIVYOT. LENIN VSEGDA BUDET ZHIT.

Lenin lived. Lenin lives. Lenin will always live.

Once inside they were directed to a row of immigration booths. Rhone presented Davilov's passport to the uniformed frontier guard and the KGB man flashed his card. The passport was stamped and they were waved through. At the baggage area his escort beat him to Davilov's suitcase and carried it through customs unopened.

"Come. Your sister will be waiting for you."

He led him down a stark, polished corridor. Another KGB man waiting at the end opened a door to a bare little room. A woman stood with her back to him, just inside. She wore a fashionable fur-collared coat, a dark scarf over her hair, and fur boots. Even the heavy coat did not completely hide the shape of her graceful dancer's body.

"Alisa?"

She turned at the sound of his voice. A gloved hand was lifted to her cheek. Then, as if in nervous afterthought, she hastily removed both her gloves and stuffed them into her handbag. She bit her lip, her black eyes searching his face. "Andrei? Andryusha?"

She took a hesitant step toward him, then another, and rushed suddenly into his arms.

He wrapped his arms around her, squeezing her and kissing her cheeks. He lifted her from the floor and turned in a little circle before letting her easily down. She laid her face against his chest, then drew back to look at him. There were tears in her eyes. And she was lovely, more beautiful than he'd ever imagined from the photographs they'd shown him in Staffordshire.

A Volga was parked outside the terminal. Rhone got in the

18

back with Alisa Petrovna Belova and the two KGB men took the front. As she chatted about happier times, about their parents, now both dead, and her husband, an Air Force test pilot who'd been killed flying an early Mig 25, Rhone watched the frozen land slide by in the light of an early rising moon. She should have been an actress.

They entered the drab suburbs. The lighted skyline with cranes looming above it like giant preying insects gradually materialized. Soon they were on a wide traffic artery that led toward the hub of the city.

Her apartment was situated in a twelve-story brick building on Komsomolsky Prospekt. The driver parked in front and the agent who'd accompanied Rhone from London turned and looked back over the seat. "You will present yourself at 10 a.m. tomorrow at number two, Dzerzhinsky Square, the office of the KGB."

They waded through the snow and went up the front steps to the entrance. She found her key and let him into the building. They rode the elevator up to the fifth floor in silence. Then they were inside the little two-room apartment, that was saved from utter sterility only by the fact that the furniture ranged from old to antique, and by the photographs of Alisa performing with the Bolshoi that decorated the living room walls. She went straight to an old American-made mono hi-fi set and put on a record Rhone recognized as a selection of highlights from *Swan Lake*. She turned the volume to a deafening blare, removed her coat, and took his coat and fur hat and hung them on a rack. When she removed her scarf her black hair fell loose over her shoulders. She faced him in the center of the room, a terrible urgency in her eyes. When she spoke it was in a whisper, barely audible against the roar of the Tchaikovsky:

"For a moment, there at the airport, I thought you *were* Andrei. Have you seen him? Is he all right?"

He shook his head, feeling completely inadequate to the moment. "I've never seen him," he said finally.

From the look in her eyes he would have judged that just in

19

back of them something very heavy was slowly falling. She turned abruptly and walked to the window, where the snow had begun to fall, and looked out over the lights of Moscow. He walked over and stood beside her, also gazing out.

She turned away. "I think I have frozen my feet. I'm going to heat some water and try to thaw them."

She went to the kitchen. When she returned, fifteen minutes later, she was barefoot. She turned the record player down immediately, signaling she had nothing more of importance to say. When she looked him in the eye, he realized that during the quarter of an hour she'd been out of the room she'd made up her mind to hate him.

It was late afternoon, twilight in Moscow, when he emerged from KGB Headquarters in the New Lubyanka and started back around Dzerzhinsky Square with the statue of Felix Dzerzhinsky, the founder of the Soviet secret police, standing ominously in the center of the traffic circle. By the time he reached the pay phone in front of the Dom Plakata poster shop he'd spotted his two shadows, sticking out like sore thumbs in the crowd streaming in and out of Detsky Mir, the children's department store situated across the street from the Lubyanka.

He dropped two kopecks into the phone and dialed the American Embassy. When the ringing ceased there was a brief pause, punctuated by the familiar series of clicks that indicated the bugging device had tapped in. Then a female voice answered. Rhone gave a code name and asked to speak to Brown.

By the time he'd finished and hung up, his shadows were far enough around the square that they wouldn't have to chase him openly to keep up. He turned his collar up against the cold and started away.

There was a Russian joke, or at least a joke about Russians, which Rhone could remember his father telling in the Moscow Embassy when he'd been there as a boy. The joke went something to the effect that two Russians are walking along side by side; one, bearing a load that would break a donkey's back, is bowed and stooped beneath his burden, staggered by the weight, taking each step as though it would be his last; the other, bearing nothing but the clothes on his back, is bowed and stooped, staggered by his burden, taking each step as though it would be his last. Leaving Dzerzhinsky Square Rhone, who'd spent the last four hours of his life with a battery of hawkish KGB interrogators hashing over the best five years of Andrei Davilov's, walked like a Russian.

In front of the Bolshoi, where Alisa Belova had been a rising star before her husband had been killed and she'd made the mistake of applying for a visa to follow her brother to the West, he descended into the Sverdlov Square metro station with its white marble walls and glittering chandeliers. He positioned himself against a marble column and watched the long, sleek trains roar in, unload their passengers, and streak away into the dark tunnels. Hordes of long-suffering Muscovites streamed up and down the escalators running in and out of the station. Somewhere in the crowd on the platform were the two KGB men who'd followed him from the Lubyanka, but now he'd lost sight of them.

He'd stood there perhaps twenty minutes when the short, plumpish man in the billed cap with the fur ear flaps appeared on the escalator and took his place with the people waiting to board the next train. In moments it came hurtling into the station and Rhone strode forward and pushed on just behind the plumpish man. Shoved against him by the crush of the crowd as the buzzer sounded and the electric door slid shut, he palmed the small capsule Brown pressed into his hand, then made his way through the passengers up the aisle to the middle of the car. Just as he'd stepped through the door he'd seen his KGB shadows getting on the next car back.

At Mayakovsky Station Rhone stepped down from the car, walked away from the tracks and into the arcade at the rear of the platform. Momentarily the plump little man, who'd also disembarked, joined him there. Rhone moved back out of view of the two KGB men watching from beside the tracks, and examined the microfilm capsule.

"Is something wrong?" asked Brown.

"I just wondered what was in it." He slipped it beneath his overcoat and into his jacket pocket.

"Nothing you would find at all interesting. Trade data. Computer tech exports to the satellites. Relatively benign in fact."

"Benign?"

"Don't worry. You're already so hot they'll burn their fingers trying to put on the handcuffs. And it's not even you they want. But to put Yaroshenko away they have to have you."

Rhone stepped out where he could observe his shadows.

"I mean, if something goes wrong," Brown continued, "and you find you *can't* get out of there, there's no reason for you to end up spending ten years in a labor camp. The best we can hope is you'll get a wrist-slapping and be home in a year or two."

"They said you'd been in contact with my 'sister'."

"Who said that?"

"The KGB at the Lubyanka today."

"They were just trying to get a rise out of you. I did *meet* her. I did a profile on her when Remick was setting up your Davilov cover. But I'm not in contact with her. I didn't recruit her."

"That's good." Rhone was looking him in the eye. "She's not cut out for this. And if it starts to stink, I'll scrub it."

Brown looked depressed. Then, as though he'd decided to ignore the remark entirely, he said: "Yaroshenko has lunch reservations at the Rossiya at one. He's expecting a brush contact in the lobby, so you might as well set him up there."

Rhone nodded.

Brown extended his hand. "Good luck. I hope they're not too hard on you in there."

He turned and waddled away. Rhone crossed to the eastbound platform and got on a train back to Sverdlov Square. As the train was pulling out of the station he saw Brown, still on the opposite platform, dialing a pay phone.

* * *

Alisa Belova, wearing a black leotard, was seated on the couch when he let himself back into her apartment that evening. After a breakfast that morning which had been less chilly than their meal together the night before, she'd left him a spare key and taken a train to a painter's loft across the city. She said she was working with an amateur troop there consisting mostly of former professionals like herself who for one reason or another had fallen into official disfavor, and found themselves either out of the theater entirely or at least out of the spotlight. Once she was gone he'd dug the things he'd brought her from London out of his suitcase and left them for her to find. Now they were spread out on the coffee table before her. A couple of bottles of perfume, a few pairs of nylons, and three pairs of women's jeans.

"It was very thoughtful of you and I love them all," she said. "And you must have thought I was terribly rude last night. It's just ... the KGB ... seeing you ... worrying about Andrei. ..."

He silenced her with a look, went over and selected an album at random, placed it on the turntable, and carelessly dropped the arm. There was a loud scratch when it hit. He looked at her, looking back at him without expression, and turned the volume up loud. It took him a moment to recognize the selection, the clock scene from *Boris Godunov*, Feodor Chaliapin, "Ah, I am Suffocating."

When he turned back she was laughing at the irony of the selection, an irony which she, being unaware of his mission, could not possibly have fully appreciated.

Seeing his face, she ceased the laughter. "I'm sorry. I wasn't thinking."

He walked back to the table and leaned over it toward her. "You've *got* to think. The worst thing that can possibly happen is for the KGB to find out I'm not exactly who I'm supposed to be. And understand this: no matter what happens, I mean, no matter *what*, don't ever forget that I'm you brother and that you've got to act exactly as you would if what happens to me

23

had happened to him. Even if I'm arrested." He took in a long, slow breath. Boris Godunov filled the room, reaching the pinnacle of his despair. For the first time in the entire aria his deep, bass voice found a semblance of a melodic thread. Then it cracked, broke, and was silent. "If you don't do as I've told you," Rhone said, "you'll be much too old for the ballet when you get back from wherever they send you."

She nodded, swallowing. She got up suddenly, brushed past him and went out, to the bathroom, he presumed. When she returned she'd almost managed to compose herself. She resumed her place on the couch, sticking her lip out in a pout. She crossed her legs in something less than a half lotus. She shifted on the couch, squirmed, movement without destination. She knew exactly what the leotard did for her.

He turned the volume down. He walked through the bedroom to the window and gazed out over the lighted skyline of Moscow. He'd been four when his father had been transferred there from Ankara; seven when they'd left Moscow for New Delhi. Remick's files said Rhone's study of escapology had begun in Paris, where they'd moved when he was eleven. But Remick's files were wrong. On a single day in Calcutta he'd seen an old woman die of starvation on the street and an Indian fakir roll himself in a ball, tie his body in a knot, and disappear before his eyes.

Edward Rhone was eight then and that day, though he could not have put it into words at the time, he'd consciously begun the quest that he led him through his apprenticeship with the old Frenchman and later led him to Vietnam and, after the war, back to Bombay and Calcutta. In Europe he'd merely performed, marking time. And now, back in this often dreary, often magnificent country, that in its vast entirety was a prison unto itself, he'd returned to the quest where really, he now knew, the quest had first begun.

He walked back into the living room and looked at Alisa seated cross-legged on the couch.

"I shopped and there's a little meat for our dinner," she said.

"No. We have to get out and be seen together. Dress up. I've made us reservations at the Metropole."

She smiled, but was deeply thoughtful. "It took me four hours. The meat." Her black eyes twinkled. "You'd never believe what I went through to get it."

4

At the Hotel Metropole modern glass doors opened onto a pseudo-Egyptian lobby crowded with foreigners and the grim-looking police their presence required. Alisa wore a lacy black blouse and a sleek ankle-length skirt. Her hair was drawn partially back in a bun, though she'd left a few loose curls around her forehead. She looked not remotely like the drab women, or even the pretty ones, who crowded the Moscow streets, looked rather like she'd come from another place, another epoch. Escorting her to the table in the crowded, noisy restaurant, Rhone had the feeling all eyes were on her. And he was proud. And at the same time he felt strange. She wasn't his woman. She wasn't even his companion for the night. She was just his sister. But she wasn't really even that.

When he tried to explain it to her she laughed, stopped laughing, and looked at him with a kind of wonderment.

"What?" he asked her.

She glanced about to assure herself no one was listening and said, "I was just trying to see if I might figure out who or what you really are. I mean, I can't be sure you're even Russian."

"Does it matter?"

"To me?" She shook her head. "Of course not. Will it matter to the KGB?"

He made his face a blank.

"You can't tell me, can you?"

"No. You know I can't."

She smiled, thoughtful. "You must think you already know *everything* about me. So do you mind if I try, just for myself?"

"Try what?"

"To figure you out."

Afterwards they went to a place called the Café des Artistes, with marble floors and tables, packed wall to wall with people. They stood at the bar, pressed close together by the crush of the crowd. She looked at him and smiled. Something had changed. Their bodies touched; awareness tingled between them.

The KGB men were standing across the street blowing into their hands when Alisa and Rhone emerged. Bundled in their overcoats, they walked along in the cold of the night. He put his arm around her. It would have been natural enough even if she really had been his sister.

"You're some sort of a spy, of course," she said after they'd gone a small distance. "I'll never know why you came here, or who you really are. And you're so much like Andrei. Yet really nothing like him at all. . . . I wanted to hate you." She was momentarily silent. Then she looked up at him and asked, "You really never saw him?"

"No. But I'm sure he's all right." He told her about the place in Staffordshire, without giving its actual location, and explained that they would have to keep her brother somewhere and that he thought it would probably be there. He wondered if there was a chance that what he was telling her was true.

They were coming up on Sverdlov Square. She looked back at the two men following them. "I *hate* them. I wish we could leave them behind. Just for tonight."

At the entrance to the metro he stopped, his arm still around her. The two men were just reaching the edge of the square. He looked down at her face, radiant in the soft light of the night.

"Can we?" she said. "Just for fun? I thought that was the sort of thing people like you were always doing?"

He shook his head.

27

She turned away. They stepped onto the escalator and started down into the station. They heard the train just as they were reaching the platform. Suddenly she pulled away from him and started to run toward the tracks. The train was coming into the station.

She stopped and looked back. "Come on. It's not our fault if they can't keep up."

She ran toward the train now pulling to a stop. He looked back up the descending escalator as the two KGB men stepped on. Alisa entered the train and turned back, waving at him through the open door. He ran toward the tracks and pushed through as the buzzer sounded and the doors were sliding shut. Looking back through the window he could see the two KGB men running down the descending escalator. The train moved out. Alisa was laughing, in hysterics. The two men glared at him through the glass windows. The car was empty except for a lone old woman bundled in black. As the train entered the tunnel Alisa, still laughing, hugged him and kissed him on the lips.

Rhone wondered how many times during the weeks to come in the Lubyanka he would try to explain to his stony-faced interrogators that they'd meant no harm, that they were just a brother and sister together after many years apart, pretending to be kids again, playing hide and seek with the KGB.

It was snowing when they emerged at midnight from the Komsomolskaya Station. He gazed up and down the wide, divided avenue lined with old brick apartments and the newer prefab structures, and here and there the ruins of an older building under demolition. The street appeared deserted. They crossed with the traffic light in the silent, falling snow. They'd walked a block and still had three blocks to go when he saw the shadowy figure moving parallel to them along the divider among the short linden trees. A little Moskvich turned off a side street, framing the man momentarily in its headlights, and Alisa saw him too.

"Is that another of them?"

He nodded, scanning the avenue for the second man he knew

had to be there somewhere. But he saw no one, only a stooped old man with a cane, in a broad tattered hat and long overcoat, hobbling across toward their side of the street far up at the end of the block. He looked again at the divider. Now he'd lost him in the trees. A moment later he spotted him again, a tall kid with the blond hair of a Volga German, who emerged and crossed the street at an angle thirty yards behind them. Rhone observed the shell of a partially demolished building at the end of the block, where the old man, suddenly spry, no longer needed his cane to dance across the last two lanes of the thoroughfare and bounce onto the sidewalk before him. So they weren't there to tail him at all, but to teach him not to lose his tails. The kind of toughs who made their living slashing paintings at underground exhibitions and beating up elderly dissidents. But from everything Rhone had learned about Andrei Davilov, he was anything but a fighter.

The blond kid stalked him from behind. The one in the long coat, hollow-eyed and skeletal, pitched his cane in the air. It turned end over end, like a baton, and when it came down he caught it by the butt-end so the handle would serve as the head of a club. Beside Rhone, Alisa gave a muffled cry. Both thugs were moving toward them. A siren screamed back up Komsomolsky Prospekt, an ambulance flying up the avenue toward them.

He caught her by the shoulders, pushed her to the curb, and held her, waiting until it passed.

When it did he gave her a shove off the curb. "Run! Run, damn it!"

She stumbled into the street, caught her balance and turned back, wide-eyed and distraught.

"Run!"

She ran, now stumbling and clumsy, graceless as a new-born foal who'd tried to race before it could walk. Watching her go, Rhone retreated back across the sidewalk toward the demolished building. The two thugs moved in to cut him off from her. They wanted it in the building; he wanted it in the building.

Alisa achieved the tree-lined divider, stopped and looked

29

back. Rhone found footing on the snow that covered the shattered bricks piled before the crumbling shell. The one with the cane took a couple of long steps forward, like a fencer, and swung. The club-end, passing inches from Rhone's head, cut the air with a hollow whoosh.

He backed up on the bricks, ankle deep in snow, and ducked into the rubble-strewn entrance. Through the wide door he saw Alisa step off the divider and start back across the six traffic lanes. The blond kid whipped out a big switch-blade he couldn't have bought in Russia and clicked it open. Distracted, Rhone took a glancing blow from the cane handle on the side of his head and heard that cracking sound in his ears that comes when your mind lights up with stars.

He had to shake his head to clear it.

He was all the way back across what had once been the foyer of the building, reclined back at a forty-five degree angle on a pile of broken stones, bent iron, and shattered glass. Overcoat was standing before him, the cane held high above his head in both hands, like an ax.

Rhone rolled over as the cane, crashing down on the rocks where his head had just rested, shattered with a crack. And then Alisa came through the door, screaming and thrashing, her nails leaving jagged lines of blood where they tore into Overcoat's cheek. He hit her in the face and she fell face-down on the floor.

Rhone rolled over again and came up. When Overcoat turned back Rhone hit him in the groin and he doubled over like a pocketknife closing up. Rhone caught his head as he was going down and gave it a twist. There was a crack. When he turned him loose he dropped in a heap in the trash.

The blond kid had already started a forward lunge with the knife, now thought better of it, and tried to check himself. Rhone stalked him, cutting off his path. Cornered, he slashed and Rhone caught his wrist and elbow and turned the knife back up into his belly.

He left him propped in the corner, shivering and crying and bleeding, and turned and knelt over Alisa. Her eyes were open, slightly glazed. There was a rustling sound behind him. The kid, with the knife still stuck in his belly, staggered past him through the door and out. A trickle of blood came from the corner of Alisa's mouth, but when he wiped it clean he could see it was from a nick inside her cheek.

He stood and caught his breath. The dead man lay on his belly, his head turned back over his left shoulder, his eyes wide and blank, directed far up into the wrecked and hollowed reaches of the building.

He dropped two kopecks into the pay phone outside the Komsomolskaya metro and dialed the special twenty-four hour number for Moscow Station which Remick had given him in Staffordshire. After the ringing stopped and the tapping system clicked in, an American answered. Rhone gave his code-name and asked to speak to Brown. The American told him to leave his number and Brown would call him back as soon as he was reached. Rhone read the number off the phone and hung up. He looked at his watch. It was 12:24. He wondered whom he would hear from first, Brown or the KGB.

Overcoat's neck had been snapped like a doll's. Rhone had just stood there, looking down at him, for a long time. Alisa sat up, still dazed, and asked what had happened.

He told her.

It was enough to bring her out of it. He helped her to her feet and dusted the snow off her coat. She would have some swelling in her cheek and his head was already pounding but other than that, the dead thug, and his partner out trailing blood around the street, they were all right.

"We've got to hide him," she said, surveying the place with an uncanny composure.

"Yes."

Rhone knelt over him and went through his pockets. He found a hundred and eighty roubles, but no identification, and a rolled-up envelope with a small amount of white powder. Thoughtful, he took a little on the tip of his finger and touched it to his tongue. It tasted slightly bitter. He closed the envelope and put it with the roubles in his pocket. Alisa, who'd already started moving bricks from the pile where Rhone had fallen earlier, had noticed nothing.

Together they displaced enough bricks to make a kind of burrow. The body was half frozen by the time they shoved it in, forcibly curling the legs up to make it fit, then piled the bricks back on it, scattered some broken glass to make it look good, and sprinkled a layer of snow over that. They both looked up at the wrecking ball hanging from the crane, visible through a gaping hole in the rear wall of the second floor, and at the snow floating down through the open shaft of the structure.

"If they cover him up," Alisa said, "it will be months before they dig him out."

He shook his head. "It's too dangerous."

Outside, the trail of blood led into the street but already it was disappearing in the falling snow. He told her to go back to her apartment, then walked alone back to the metro station.

When the phone rang and Brown identified himself he told him: "I've killed a KGB man."

"I see. Perhaps you'd better tell me about it."

"Are we bugged?"

"I don't believe so, not really."

Rhone capsuled the incident and described how they'd lost the other two agents in the Sverdlov Square Station. "Something else. I found an envelope on him with a couple of grams of what looks like heroin."

There was a slight pause, just nasal breathing over the line. "Oh, really?" Brown said finally.

"Can you get somebody to clean it up?" Rhone said after another short silence.

"I could. But if *they* sent them, I don't think you have to worry. They'll just look at it as one of those things."

"God damn it! It's not myself I'm worried about."

"I see. I'll have it taken care of tonight."

"I still don't understand it," Rhone said.

32

"Don't understand what?"

"Why they tried to *kill* me."

"Yes . . ." Brown sighed. "Well anyway, Yaroshenko's world should fall in on schedule tomorrow. You *are* planning to keep your appointment with Yaroshenko?"

"Yeah."

He hung up. He took the envelope from his pocket and shook it out. The white powder disappeared on the snow. He threw the empty envelope into a waste container, kicked at a mound of snow, and started back up Komsomolsky Prospekt.

5

Alisa was seated on the couch when he let himself back into the apartment, on the table before her a half-filled bottle of vodka and two empty glasses. He took off his coat and hat as she poured the two glasses. She handed him one glass, took his things, and went to hang them up. Then she came back and retrieved the other glass and together they drank, solemn.

"What will happen now?" she said.

"It will be taken care of."

"They were KGB?" she said, a whisper.

"I don't know." He shook his head. "I thought so. Now I don't know."

They stood where they were, looking into one another's eyes. It seemed there was nothing to say.

"Before that happened," she said finally, to break the silence, "I was having a wonderful time with you."

"I was too."

Again they were quiet.

"Good night," she said.

"Good night."

She lingered for a moment, then stepped forward, kissed him tenderly on the lips, and went through the door of the bedroom.

She came back with his extra blanket and pillow and put them on the couch. He watched her go back out and close the door behind her.

He filled his glass and drank again and looked thoughtfully around the room. He walked across to the pictured-over wall and studied the photographs. Her body lithe and graceful in tights. The pirouettes. The pas de deux. The leaps. Her body held high on the arms of her partner. A close up of her lovely face. He heard the door open and looked back.

She stood in it, wearing a see-through negligee her brother must have sent her from London. It hid nothing and she wore nothing underneath.

"I don't want to sleep alone tonight." It was a whisper, so soft he could only read her lips.

She turned and went back in, leaving the door open behind her. He put the glass unfinished on the table and followed. When he got to the door she was still walking toward the bed, shedding her negligee as she went. At the bed she stopped and turned back. There was a soft light on the nightstand and in it her small firm body was amber. She got in, waiting beneath the covers as he undressed. Then she pushed the covers away and he knelt over her and kissed her on the lips and touched her and then suddenly, as he was pressing closer, she slipped from beneath him and got up from the bed.

He looked around, confused.

She was smiling. "The microphone," she whispered. "You don't want the KGB to hear this?"

He smiled also and shook his head.

She went out. She put on *Swan Lake* and turned it to a roar, then came back to him in the bed.

He stirred and awoke. Sunlight poured through the window. The traffic was heavy outside on Komsomolsky Prospekt. He could feel her body warm beside him. He rolled onto his side and looked at her face. She was sleeping with just a hint of a smile on her lips.

After they'd made love he'd fallen asleep with her snuggled

35

in his arms. Later he'd awakened alone in the bed. *Swan Lake* still played, but at normal volume. When he'd rolled over he'd seen her standing naked beside the bed. Then she'd begun to dance, the pas de deux at the end of the "Black Swan." Remembering that, remembering their bodies together, himself inside her, and remembering what day it was today, he was filled with a terrible dread.

She opened her eyes and he leaned over and kissed her on the lips.

"Now I know," she whispered when he drew back.

"Know what?"

"That you are not a Russian." She'd mouthed the words, silent.

He watched her without expression and said nothing.

"Don't worry." She smiled. "As long as you stay out of their bed, the KGB won't find out."

He rolled onto his back and stared up at the ceiling. Beside him, for a moment, she did not breathe.

Then she touched his shoulder, tentative. "Does it worry you so much? That I know?"

He looked back. "It's not that."

"Then what? You're sorry we—"

"No." He covered her mouth with his hand and whispered, "You're leaving Russia. Today. Tomorrow at the latest. I have a special American Embassy telephone number. I'll leave it before I go out. Call after two today. Ask for Brown. I'll have arranged it with him already and he'll have his instructions for you."

"But . . ."

"No arguments. Just do as I say. Promise me."

She was silent.

"Promise me, Alisa."

She nodded. "All right. I promise."

It was a little past noon when Rhone emerged from the crowd streaming out of the Sverdlov Square Station. It was clear and cold. The sun glared off the fresh snow that had covered the city during the night. Shivering tourists inspected the Grecian portico façade of the Bolshoi. Brown sat on the top step in his billed hat with the flaps down over his ears. He held up his right hand, his index finger and thumb forming a circle in indication that everything had been taken care of. On the street and the square bundled Muscovites trudged back and forth like drugged ants.

Rhone crossed the square and started up the steps. Brown watched his ascent with a frown.

Rhone stopped before him. "You're going to get a call from the girl. I want you to use one of your safe channels to get her out of this country."

"But . . ."

"Don't argue with me, Brown. Or I promise I'll blow this whole fucking thing wide open."

"You've got it bad, hunh?"

"Are you going to do it or not?"

"Okay. I'll get her into a safe house. As soon as you're in the Lubyanka I'll ship her out."

He turned and started back down the steps. He crossed the square, passed the Karl Marx monument, and continued by the Metropole toward the entrance of Red Square.

At the corner of the Lenin Museum he paused to light a cigarette, turning his back to shield the flame from the wind blowing up from the river. His shadows lingered at the Marx monument to keep the distance between them. He took a drag off the cigarette and continued into the square.

The line outside Lenin's tomb stretched almost to the middle of Red Square. An army drill team goose-stepped back and forth before them, turning the snow to slush. Rhone finished the cigarette and tossed it away.

The Rossiya Hotel is an enormous ultramodern tinted glass box situated on the bank of the Moskva River opposite the Kremlin and to the rear of the onion-domed St. Basil's Cathedral. Rhone entered the posh, modernistic lobby. Vasily Yemelyanovich Yaroshenko sat on a sofa opposite the reception desk, reading the day's edition of *Pravda*. Tall and delicately featured for a Ukrainian, he appeared to be in his mid-fifties, distinguished looking, probably once a very handsome man. His hands were slender, his fingers long and manicured. His hair was slightly gray, cut in western style rather than shingled in the more usual style of senior Soviet officers. Just above his collar Rhone could see a scar that indicated he'd once taken a large caliber bullet through the neck. He wore his dress uniform, tailored to his angular frame like a Western-tailored suit, with the baby blue shoulder-boards and the insignia of a lieutenent colonel in the KGB.

Rhone surveyed the lobby and spotted the well-dressed young Russian accompanied by the older man with dark, Georgian features who stood at the entrance to the dining room.

Yaroshenko looked at his wristwatch, abruptly folded the newspaper, and tucked it under his arm. He removed a cigarette case from his uniform pocket, took out a cigarette, and put it between his lips. He replaced the case in his pocket, took out a lighter, and snapped it several times without success.

Rhone hurriedly lit another cigarette of his own and strode across toward the colonel. Yaroshenko tried the lighter one last time, thrust it back into his pocket, and rose as Rhone was coming up to him.

"Sir." Rhone held out his own burning cigarette.

Yaroshenko stared at the cigarette and then at Rhone's face. Loftily he took the cigarette, lit his own, and handed it back.

"We are being watched," Rhone whispered.

The colonel glared at him. His eyes quickly searched the lobby. He saw the two men at the entrance of the dining room. The din in the lobby had been replaced by a hush.

Yaroshenko looked fiercely back at Rhone. "Who are you and what do you want?"

"My name is Andrei Davilov."

The colonel absorbed the name as though it were cyanide. His hand brushed the breast pocket of his jacket. A light sweat had appeared on his forehead. He took out a handkerchief, delicately dabbed at his brow, and replaced the handkerchief in his pocket. He took a step backward, made a motion of smoothing down his uniform, and again brushed at the pocket. He looked scornfully at Rhone, stepped past him, and started toward the exit. He walked slowly, erect and dignified, his severe gaze wilting the select unfortunate few on whom he chose to cast his eyes before he was gone.

The well-dressed Russian and the Georgian went out after him.

It was snowing again when Rhone walked from Komsomol-skaya Station back to Alisa Belova's apartment. It was dark, a little after six. Just before he entered the building he noticed the Zil limosine parked on the near side of the street a half block up. As he fitted the key into the lock he experienced a mingling of relief and sheer panic. He'd never escaped from a prison, as a prisoner, though he thought he must always have known that sooner or later it would have to happen. The toy soldier's compulsion for battle. The arid throat of fear.

The foyer was dark. He walked past the staircase and pushed the elevator button. He sensed the presence behind him too late. His mind was still telling his elbow to strike when he heard the click of the safety and felt the silencer on the end of the gun barrel nudge his temple.

"Three steps back," said a voice he found familiar but couldn't quite identify.

He stepped back.

"Now we walk very slowly around the stairs."

With the pistol still at his head, he let himself be guided around the staircase to the little alcove beneath it. Out of the corner of his eye he could see the shadowy outline of a tall man in a heavy fur coat.

"Now sit on the floor."

He sank to his knees and sat carefully down.

"I think you have some microfilm, no?"

Rhone reached into his overcoat and took out the capsule. He held it up and it was removed from his fingers.

39

There was a brief silence. Then his captor said: "Now tell me who you really are."

"My name is Andrei Petrovich Davilov."

"You lying shit." He felt the silencer jammed hard against his temple. "Don't tell me again your name is Andrei Davilov. Now why did this bastard Remick send you to double-cross me?"

In reflex he turned his head to stare up the barrel of the Makarov semi-automatic pistol at the lean angular face framed beneath the Russian fur hat. Vasily Yaroshenko smiled, alternately contemplating Rhone's head, at the end of the silencer on the pistol barrel, and the capsule of microfilm, which he held carefully between the thumb and index finger of his left hand.

"Don't you know that if I am arrested you must be arrested also?"

Rhone didn't answer. Yaroshenko regarded the capsule as though within it, if he could only have seen, lay the secret of eternal life. Abruptly, he thrust it back down toward Rhone, who took it. Yaroshenko removed his handkerchief and handed it to Rhone.

"The fingerprints."

Rhone carefully wiped the capsule clean, slipped it back into his coat, and handed back the handkerchief.

"Now," Yaroshenko said, "let's see if we can beat Remick at his little game. Up. Very slowly. And turn around."

Rhone did as he was told.

"Hands behind the back."

He crossed his wrists behind his back. He heard the rattle of the cuffs, felt the gun nudge the base of his spine as Yaroshenko stepped forward and clasped them onto his wrists.

"Now out the door."

Rhone turned his back to it and found the handle with his manacled hands. He pushed it open and backed out into the bitter evening cold. Yaroshenko stepped out after him and released the door to swing shut. Cautiously, they descended the steps, Yaroshenko prodding him with the barrel of the gun.

Steam rose from the exhaust of a Pobeda parked across the street, visible through a gap in the linden trees that lined the divider. The doors opened and two men got out and started across the traffic lanes. At the divider they both drew their pistols and shouted a challenge, then started on across the pavement.

"I am Colonel Yaroshenko and I order you to return to your automobile."

One of the men crouched, aiming the pistol with both hands, arms extended in classical form. "Throw down your weapon."

Working his hands in the cuffs, Rhone took three quick steps, lost his footing on the ice, and went sprawling headlong down the slippery stone steps toward the frozen sidewalk below. The sudden burst of automatic rifle fire from the street cut the two men down like feeble blades of grass, ripping bark from the linden trees behind them and peppering the Pobeda beyond.

Rhone skidded belly-down to a stop on the sidewalk. Up and down Komomolsky Prospekt curtains were drawn back from windows in the apartment buildings. The silence that followed the rattle of the gunfire was ghostly. The two dead KGB men lay still, contorted bloody heaps in the falling snow. Standing beside the Zil parked up the street, the chauffeur held an AK-47 still leveled at his hip. And kneeling over Rhone, again shoving the silencer hard against his ear, was Colonel Yaroshenko.

Yaroshenko jerked Rhone to his feet and marched him to the Zil. The driver was waiting beside the open back door. Rhone turned and looked back at Alisa's apartment building, up at her darkened windows. Then the door opened at the entrance. She emerged, carrying a light bag, and stopped, staring at him, ghastly pale. Yaroshenko shoved him into the limousine and ordered him to lie face down on the floor, and slipped in behind him, still holding the gun at his head. The door slammed shut. The driver got into the front, started the engine, and pulled out into the street.

Twenty minutes later they stopped, somewhere in the inner

city he guessed from the increased traffic noise. A metal gate clanged shut behind them. The door opened and Yaroshenko slid from the seat, seized him by his coat collar, and pulled him out.

"On your feet, you fucking scum!"

He almost slipped to his knees in the snow before he found a footing and managed to get his balance. He looked around. Though he'd never been there he had no difficulty recognizing the dark enclosed well with the walls of the old brick building looming up around it. They were in the courtyard of the Lubyanka.

Yaroshenko took his elbow and held the pistol back to his temple, guiding him slowly across the brick surface toward a small archway opposite. Then two plain-clothed men and a uniformed KGB officer with a submachine gun emerged through it and he stopped. Through a larger arched doorway on the other side of the courtyard came two armed guards and several more civilian KGB men.

Slowly Yaroshenko lowered the Makarov, clicked on the safety, removed the silencer, and dropped the pistol back into its holster. One of the civilian KGB men stepped cautiously up and took it. Another dug an official looking green document from his coat and held it up and began to read:

"I, deputy prosecutor general of the Union of Soviet Socialist Republics, do confirm the warrants for the arrest of Yaroshenko, Vasily Yemelyanovich and Davilov, Andrei Petrovich."

One of the civilians seized Yaroshenko's arm and started to guide him toward the big, arched door. He shook free with a curse and walked toward it on his own, still holding himself erect and proud.

At the door he stopped and turned back. "I am a loyal officer of the KGB, assigned as a double-agent, whose duty it has been to sabotage American efforts to penetrate our Semipalantinsk research project. Now I have been framed as a spy, by the Americans. And that traitor," he said, nodding at Rhone, who stood handcuffed but almost ignored in the center of the courtyard, "who has been sent here by the Americans to destroy me, is not even Andrei Davilov."

He laughed, a roaring, baritone, Russian laugh that, before he turned, still laughing, and stepped through the archway, had become maniacal.

6

Colonel Valeri Pavlovich Ilin was alone in his green-painted office when Boris brought him the news. And though he'd known it was bound to happen, known it had become inevitable the moment Andrei Davilov landed at Sheremetevo, he'd been far away from the Lubyanka, lost in a childhood memory.

His father had taken him once to the Carpathian mountains along the Rumanian frontier. They had spent the night in a village with mountain people who'd spoken a strange language and worn costumes that had appeared to young Valeri to have come out of an old forgotten fairy tale, spent the night drinking and dancing and playing music which had been like nothing he'd ever heard in Moscow. They'd fed them lamb cooked over a spit and his father had shared their vodka and danced with one of their women. It had been but a few months since the death of his wife, Valeri's mother, and though he had not known the steps of the dance, and had looked out of place in his drab city clothing, it had been the first time since she'd died that Valeri had seen his father happy and he'd been glad. . . .

Then he was interrupted by the knock and Boris came through the door. "They have arrested Colonel Yaroshenko."

"Where?" he asked.

"Below in the courtyard." Boris came forward and lay the

mimeographed copy of the report before him.

Colonel Ilin glanced over it, dwelling briefly on the transcript of Yaroshenko's statement. "The general has been informed?" he asked, looking up.

"Yes, Comrade Colonel. But he is at the dacha and will not return until morning. You have been encharged with the initial interrogation. Colonel Yaroshenko is down the hall. I will bring him?"

He'd known it was coming. But now, a thousand kilometers and forty years away from that night in the Carpathian village, he'd been taken by surprise.

After his father had drunk himself into a stupor a man had been killed in an ax fight—over the woman his father had danced with. It had been a warm summer night and Valeri had watched the whole thing through the open door of the tavern. And though it had lasted less than a minute and had been over almost before the dancing and fiddling and bagpipes had stopped, it had looked as though it had taken place in slow motion. The blood that had splattered the white wall as the man's neck had been cut half away from his shoulder by what had seemed but a gentle flick of the ax had appeared not to spew but to float, like mist. The music and the dancing had stopped, not suddenly, but slowly dwindled away.

Dying on his feet, the dead man remained to this day frozen in a frame in Colonel Ilin's mind.

Boris was half out the door when Ilin returned again to the present and stopped him with a grunt. He glanced again at the report, at Yaroshenko's remarks. "The other prisoner, Davilov?"

"He is being processed now."

The colonel wondered why General Drachinsky had chosen not to come immediately back into the city. "I do not want to interview Yaroshenko just yet. Have him taken to a cell where he will have some time to contemplate his situation. Bring me the expatriate Davilov when his processing is completed."

Boris possessed the kind of wide, dull eyes that seemed obliged almost to cross whenever the slow mind behind them was faced with the challenge of thought. At last they focused. "The emigré's processing may take half the night. If you would question Colonel Yaroshenko before he's had time to get a grip on himself . . ."

The colonel's laughter reduced Boris to silence. "Do you believe for a minute that Yaroshenko does not have a grip on himself? This cannot have caught him by surprise. He expects me to talk to him and he will already have decided exactly what he is going to say. The expatriate playboy traitor, on the other hand . . ." He heard the false echo of his words. Rereading Davilov's file that afternoon, Ilin, who had never been farther west than Hungary, was secretly envious. "Davilov, on the other hand, cannot possibly have prepared himself for what is happening to him here."

Boris lingered in the door, skeptical.

"That is all, Boris. I am going to get a few hours' sleep. Wake me when Davilov is ready for interrogation."

Boris closed the door. Ilin listened to his footsteps moving away down the hall. After the sound had ceased, he opened the drawer at the end of the table and took out his flask. He drank quickly, in a gulp, the aftertaste of the brandy warm in his throat, replaced the cap, and put the bottle back in the drawer. Beside it lay a pair of rachet-tightening handcuffs and a weighted rubber truncheon. Trappings of a brilliant career. Rarely had he been forced to use the truncheon, and when he had, it was always with a certain queasiness and even embarrassment. He took it out, delicately between thumb and forefinger so his palm never closed about the handle, and lay it prominently upon the table. Ilin regarded it as though it had unexplainably materialized there. He rose abruptly, removed his uniform jacket, and draped it across the back of his chair. He went over and sat down on the couch and removed his fur-trimmed boots, fluffed up his pillow, and reclined on his back. After a moment he pulled the blanket over his shoulders and closed his eyes.

The morning after the ax-killing one of the villagers had told Valeri Pavlovich's father what had happened. The man who'd

46

died had been the husband of the woman, the man who'd killed him her lover. In a shed nearby some of the women had been washing the body for burial. There would be a funeral and after the burial, because there were outside witnesses who would doubtless report the incident when they got back to Chernovtsy, the man would cross the frontier. "And if there had been no outside witnesses?" The woman would have borne her grief and married her lover.

That afternoon Valeri Pavlovich and his father had gone farther up the mountain and stood by a waterfall and gazed across the Rumanian frontier. There had been a look in his father's eyes that Valeri Pavlovich, still too young to grasp the concept of a frontier, had not understood. Two days later, back down in Chernovtsy, they had gone to the office of the militia and his father had reported the killing.

Ilin slept lightly. Once he woke with the impression of having dreamed he was Vasily Yaroshenko. The next time he woke it was after midnight. Dzerzhinsky Square was silent. Boris's big hand shook his shoulder. He said the prisoner Davilov's processing had been completed. The Colonel asked for some bread and cheese, washed the food down with brandy, and washed the brandy down with coffee. Smoking a cigarette, he braced himself. Beginning with a new prisoner was always like going on stage.

Finally he nodded at Boris, who brought the prisoner through the door.

He was in his thirties, dressed in loose dungarees with the words *inner prison* stamped across the back and laceless canvas boots, his hair clipped freshly short. His eyes, though red from exhaustion, stared back at the colonel clearly unafraid, even undismayed, offering no apology and granting not even token recognition of the disparity between their respective positions, the gulf that should have separated Andrei Petrovich Davilov the prisoner from Colonel Valeri Pavlovich Ilin, his interrogator.

The colonel motioned him to sit at the opposite end of the table, opened a folder, and studied the photos inside. He looked

47

again at the prisoner's face and again at the face in the photos. Though the two men looked like strangers, they also looked the same.

He rolled the truncheon back across the table and into the open drawer, closed the folder, and rose.

"I am Colonel Valeri Pavlovich Ilin. I am in charge of your interrogation. If you cooperate with me I can be pleasant to deal with." He walked down the table, took out a pack of American cigarettes, gave one to the prisoner, and lit it for him. "Or I can be very unpleasant."

The prisoner appeared patently unimpressed.

Ilin shrugged, walked back to the head of the table, and resumed his seat. "So why don't you start at the beginning?"

The prisoner smoked in silence.

"I am waiting, Comrade Davilov."

"I don't understand the question. The beginning of what?"

"Your association with the Central Intelligence Agency."

"I am not associated with the Central Intelligence Agency."

Ilin studied the prisoner silently. "Why did you leave Russia five years ago?"

"Because I married a woman who could not bear to live here."

"Why have you come back now?"

"To visit my sister."

"Why did you meet a man named Brown, a known American agent, in the Mayakovsky Square metro station two nights ago?"

"We met in the station because he thought it might be better for me if I were not seen with him. Obviously I was seen."

"I didn't ask you why you met him *in* the station. I asked why you met him at all."

"I had been acquainted with him in London."

The colonel smiled. "During the time you were a Russian language broadcaster for the CIA radio, no doubt?"

"My broadcasts for Voice of America are no secret. They went through all that with me when I was here two days ago."

Ilin opened the folder and glanced briefly over the account of

48

Davilov's interview upon his return to the Soviet Union. "Yes," he nodded. He closed the folder. "Why did you go to the Hotel Rossiya at lunchtime yesterday?"

"To have lunch."

"You did not have lunch at the Rossiya. Why not?"

"In the lobby I had an encounter with a colonel in the KGB. It spoiled my appetite."

"But *you* approached *him.*"

"I merely gave him a light. He took it as an affront."

"But Colonel Yaroshenko did give you a certain capsule of microfilm?" the colonel asked.

"No. He did not."

"No? You deny the existence of the microfilm that was taken from you at the time of your arrest?"

"No, Comrade."

"Do not be sarcastic with me. You were to deliver the microfilm to Brown. Am I at least correct in assuming that?"

"No, Colonel. You are still incorrect."

"Then what were you to do with it?"

"I was to take it to London."

"You were to smuggle it to London and do what with it?"

"Not *smuggle*. Take. I had no reason to hide it, certainly not from Soviet authorities. In London I was to give it to an American businessman named Ross."

"And you did not get it from Colonel Yaroshenko?"

"I've already told you that."

Ilin rose, walked halfway down the table, and stopped. "Where did you get the microfilm?"

"From the U.S. Embassy attaché. Brown."

Briefly, the colonel tried to imagine that the prisoner might be telling the truth.

The night had almost passed. Twilight glowed through the high, barred windows and a racket rose from the square. Valeri Pavlovich Ilin sipped his coffee and regarded the prisoner, still seated, exhausted at the other end of the table.

The colonel cleared his throat. "You say you did not consider that you would be smuggling the microfilm back to London. Why not?"

"Because if it had been Ross's intention to have it *smuggled* out of the Soviet Union he'd have had that arranged by the man who gave it to me, Brown, who could have sent it out through diplomatic channels."

Ilin absorbed this thoughtfully. It made sense. He had to try a new approach. "Why did you and your sister lose the KGB in the Sverdlov Square metro station?"

The prisoner laughed and again Ilin was conscious of the defiance, of his refusal to accept the role in which he was cast. "I wanted to see if they were worth their roubles." He shrugged. "It wasn't my fault they couldn't keep up. Now I'm sorry I did it."

Ilin smiled. "I'm afraid there is much you are going to be sorry for before this is over. Now where did you go after you lost them?"

"Back to my sister's apartment."

"The next day," said the colonel, "after the shooting incident outside the apartment, why do you think Yaroshenko brought you here?"

"Why don't you ask Yaroshenko?"

"Because I am asking you."

"I don't know why."

"At that time, why do you think Yaroshenko said you were not Andrei Davilov?"

"Did Yaroshenko say that?"

"Yes, he said it. But what do you have to say about it?"

Davilov hesitated. "If our present positions were reversed and I told you there were those who said you were not Colonel Ilin, what would you have to say about it?"

There was a brief silent staring match between them. The colonel laughed softly in appreciation. "All right. Can you think of any reason why Brown and . . . Ross would conspire to have you carry their microfilm to London rather than sending it safely through diplomatic channels?"

"It thought that was obvious."

50

"I fail to see. What is so obvious?"

"They did not want Brown's fellow staff members here at the Moscow Embassy or someone on the staff at the American Embassy in London to see it."

Ilin nodded. "And of course you do not know what the microfilm contained?"

"But I do."

"You do?"

"It contained data on our computer technology exports to the satellite countries."

Ilin laughed, a rolling boisterous Russian laugh that split his mouth from ear to ear. Then he stopped, clapped his hands, and Boris appeared in the door.

"Take him to his cell."

As he watched the prisoner being led out, the colonel congratulated himself. It was a good beginning. Not that he had really learned so much. But he had learned one thing he was sure would be very, very important.

7

Moscow, October 1978

General Oleg Drachinsky was seated with the obese prosecutor Zverev when Colonel Ilin entered the cafeteria, and though Ilin tried to retreat, the general waved to him before he could get out the door. Left no choice, he made his way among the tables, almost all occupied at this hour, to join them.

"Valeri Pavlovich. You are acquainted with Prosecutor Zverev?"

Ilin nodded. The prosecutor touched Ilin's shoulder with his left hand and rubbed his own full stomach with his right. On the table before the fat man were two clean, wiped plates and an empty bread basket. A trail of congealed egg yolk plotted a course from one of the plates to the edge of the formica. On the general's side of the table was a lone egg cup containing half an empty shell.

Though they barely knew one another, Zverev was smiling at Ilin with broad familiarity. Drachinsky, always aloof, took out an American cigarette, inserted it into his holder, and lit it before Ilin could find a match. As though it were an afterthought, he offered Ilin one from the pack and held up the flame before he barely had it between his lips. That General Drachinsky had risen from obscure Stalin era origins to official acclaim for his part in the November banquet in Budapest in 1956 was a matter of record. That in the Balkans in the latter fifties he'd acquired the nickname "Dracula" was Lubyanka legend. That he was still bitter over his transfer out of the fifth department was widespread rumour. The fact was, though there were probably few but the general and himself who knew it, that Drachinsky had handpicked Valeri Pavlovich Ilin some years before, as a protégé. That he'd never been anything but a disappointment to his mentor was for Ilin a source of chronic dread.

But he'd felt so secure, optimistic even, only a few moments before. His interrogation had been going on for two weeks and it was almost six A.M. when he'd ordered the prisoner Davilov taken back to his cell. After he'd gone he'd opened the folder and taken out the London Resident's personal character survey (with biographical data from the eleventh department). He'd read:

London, England
October 21, 1978

Davilov, Andrei Petrovich

Born Kuibyschev, May 10, 1944. Father Major General Pyotr Yakovlevich Davilov. Mother Yekaterina Anatolyevna Davilov. Sister Alisa Petrovna Belova. Komsomol member, Moscow, 1958–62. University of Moscow, 1962–67. Employed Sovexfilm, Moscow, 1969 (traveled extensively, Siberia and central Asia, 1971–72). Dismissed, 1972. Application for permission to marry non-Soviet Citizen denied, May 1972, June 1972, September 1972. Arrested for suspicion of slandering Soviet State, June 1972. Released September 1972. Permission to marry non-Soviet citizen granted, October 1972. Married British subject Joanna Elizabeth Starkey, November 1972. Permission to emigrate with spouse granted, January 1973. Emigrated to London, England, March 1973. Published for *Reader's Digest* magazine, series of eight articles slanderous of Soviet rural life, "Eye Behind the Curtain," September 1973–May 1974, in English language translation. Recorded Russian language version for Radio Liberty broadcasts July 1974. Associated with anti-Soviet emigré organizations London and Paris, 1974–76. Has lived extravagantly on wife's family fortune during five years in London. Frequents West End discotheques. No indication of homosexual activity. Resides with wife in Hampstead, maintains separate apartment in Kensington with current mistress Dorothy McGuiness, 19, of Brooklyn, N.Y., U.S.A. Developed friendly relationship in 1976 with American businessman Jacob Ross, alias Avery Remick (Executive Assistant to the director, Covert Action Staff, Directorate of Operations, Central Intelligence Agency). Applied for permission to visit U.S.S.R., September 17, 1978. Reply pending.

After he'd finished reading the paper, Ilin had returned it to the folder and returned the folder to his drawer. Though he'd been awake since early the previous morning and by rights should have deserved a long sleep, a brief nap on the couch had served to revive him. He'd wakened rejuvenated. He'd dreamed about the Davilov file and he'd dreamed about Davilov himself. A dichotomy. Feeling himself on the verge of revelation he'd stood at the barred windows of his office and watched the first morning sunlight creep over the city. Below, a monotonous army of black dots had marched in every odd direction across the snow, along the swept sidewalks, in and out of the metro entrances, all trudging to their jobs miserable as ants suddenly enlightened to the changeless drudgery of their existence. Watching them through the bars he had luxuriated in the distance that separated him from them. And told himself he had done enough for the time being. The day was his own.

Then he'd walked into the cafeteria and seen Zverev and General Drachinsky.

"Comrade Zverev has been assigned to the Yaroshenko affair," the general was saying. "I presume he will also be in charge of your man."

Zverev raised his eyes. The waiter appeared and Ilin, though he'd been ravenous moments before, ordered only toast, marmalade, and a cup of coffee.

"The returned emigré," the general prompted.

"Yes. Davilov, wasn't it? I've read his file. What the world must think of us when they see these dupes we allow to travel abroad." He looked at Ilin. "You also interrogated Yaroshenko before Gorsky was assigned, no?"

"No," Ilin said. "I had Yaroshenko but I did not speak to him."

"A clever interrogator, Gorsky," said the general. He looked at his watch. "I must go."

He rose suddenly and Zverev followed suit. Though his cigarette was hardly finished he removed it from the holder and put it out in the ashtray on the table. "You have had a long night, Valeri Pavlovich. You will go to your apartment now and sleep?"

"Yes. I will go to my apartment now and sleep."

"Good day, Comrade." He turned to the prosecutor. "Valeri Pavlovich was a friend of Yaroshenko's." Zverev waddling beside him, Drachinsky started away.

Ilin watched the waiter coming back up the aisle with his coffee. He looked as though he were far away, as though it were not the length of the cafeteria but a football field he had to cover, and he seemed to come so slowly. Ilin rose, nodded for him to leave the coffee, and turned and went after the general and the fat prosecutor Zverev. He called to them as they were reaching the exit and they stopped and looked back.

"If I had still considered myself a friend of Yaroshenko's . . ." he began and stopped himself as he heard the din of conversation falling off all around him. He walked to them. "If I had still considered Yaroshenko my friend," he whispered so softly the general had to lean into his face to hear, "I would have interviewed him first, as a friend. I did not choose to interrogate him first, as an enemy of the State because . . ."

He faltered. There was something he still hadn't put into words in his mind, that he needed in order to force himself onto the limb. The dichotomy. Davilov as he'd been observed for five years in London. Davilov the prisoner as he'd observed him night after night in his office. It came to him, absurd in its sheer simplicity: he could not imagine Andrei Davilov, the Da-

vilov he was getting to know here in the Lubyanka, in a disco-
theque.

"What is it, Valeri Pavlovich?" the general coaxed.

"I did not interrogate Yaroshenko first because I do not believe he is the key element in this affair."

He did not go back to his apartment to sleep.

Two men from Surveillance were sitting in a Pobeda across
the street, running the heater off the idling engine contrary to
the latest energy conservation directive, when Ilin eased the in-
conspicuous old Volga he'd requisitioned into the open space
before Alisa Belova's building. One of them recognized him and
immediately the vapor ceased to pour from the exhaust.

He'd been waiting half an hour when she came out of the
door and descended the steps toward the sidewalk. And though
he'd seen her on stage at the Bolshoi, had studied her photographs, and thought himself prepared for her loveliness, for the
classic delicate features so atypical of the Russian woman, she
possessed in person a strength and scorn for which no photograph could have prepared him. In her bearing there was more
than the mere ballerina, something regal, uncrushed and un-
weighted, as though even now she somehow walked with her
head above the communal burden that lay forever upon Russia.

He realized that he'd been staring and that she had been
staring back. She stopped just beside the car, raised her eyes
angrily to the men across the street, and turned and started
away up Komsomolsky Prospekt. Ilin watched in the rear view
mirror until she reached the first intersection, got out, and
started after her. Though she never looked back he was sure she
sensed him behind her. As she neared the metro station he
rushed to close the distance. He was less than half a block behind when she stepped onto the descending escalator and once
she had disappeared from sight he broke into a run.

He heard the train pulling into the station as he reached the
entrance. He pushed his way down the escalator. But a trickle
of people were coming up and the platform, when he reached it,
was almost deserted.

He looked one way, then the other. Andrei Davilov's sister was nowhere to be seen. He had to hurry to slip through the closing doors onto the crowded car. As the train was pulling out of the station he turned and looked back out onto the platform.

Alisa Belova stood just at the edge, watching him through the window with all her regal scorn.

He had to go back to the Lubyanka to check the files for the address of the loft, and it was almost noon when he pulled off Leningradskoye Chaussée and found his way to a narrow potholed back street lined with old dilapidated structures of wood and tin. He stopped outside a wooden gate with the number 13 painted on the post, got out, and locked the doors of the Volga.

Through the gate a trail shoveled out of last night's snowfall led to an oblong two story building of gray wood with walls hung with frozen ivy. A curtain on a lower window was drawn back, revealing the face of an aged woman, and was just as quickly closed. Upstairs a piano played, a piece from Stravinsky's *Firebird,* he thought.

An exterior wood staircase ascended the end of the building to the second story entrance. At the top he tried the door, found it unlocked, and stepped in quietly.

The loft was open to the rafters and, devoid of furniture, except for an old upright piano and the stool upon which the pianist sat, a couple of straight-backed wood chairs, a mattress with a feather comforter on the floor in one corner and an old-fashioned wood stove. Alisa Belova, in a black leotard, was dancing in the center of the floor with a young man the Colonel recognized as Valentin Semyonov, a former member of the Bolshoi who'd been ousted for his efforts to emigrate to Israel. An audience of perhaps ten men and women, most of them also in ballet tights, observed from aside. And Ilin observed also, unnoticed for several minutes.

It was Alisa in mid-pirouette, who first saw him, acknowledging him with but the slightest raising of her eyebrows as she moved gracefully on through the dance. Then someone else saw him. A buzz went through the audience. Valentin Semyonov heard it, looked around, and ceased his dancing. The pianist ceased to play. In the hush that followed every eye was on him, the intruder, and the moment filled him with the familiar sadness of his eternal isolation. How nice it would have been, he thought, merely to stand unnoticed and watch and enjoy this remarkable talent which, due to outrageous circumstance, would, most likely, be denied to the Soviet public forever.

She walked up to him. "You have been following me. Who are you and what do you want?"

He took off his fur hat. "I am Colonel Valeri Pavlovich Ilin—of the KGB. I am your brother's interrogator."

She watched him silently and without a visible trace of emotion.

"I want to talk with you, alone. I want to help your brother."

She laughed briefly and bitterly. He heard the echo of his words. Nothing could have sounded more to her like a lie, and though he too had intended it as a lie, he realized that somehow it was the truth. He liked Andrei Petrovich Davilov. He respected him. In a way, he realized, he was *attracted* to him. Not that he wanted him, as he now wanted her. But Davilov, who seemed to the colonel to epitomize so much of what he himself was not, appealed to him.

"Can we go some place?" he said. "I do not want to take you to the Lubyanka. Your apartment, perhaps."

"You say you want to help my brother," she said. "Why?"

Now he did lie. "Because I do not believe he is a traitor to his country."

"And how can you help him?"

"I don't know." The truth. "Perhaps I can learn something that will prove his innocence." The lie again.

He realized that he was staring at her breasts, and looked up again at her face.

"You want to sleep with me, is that it?"

"No." It was a whisper, for suddenly he had no voice.

Aloof as a prostitute she said, "Because if you can *prove* to me that you will help him, I don't mind."

"No," he lied. "I don't want that. I just want to talk."

She nodded. "But not now. And not at my apartment. Tonight at the Café des Artistes. You know it?"

"Yes."

"Now go. We must finish our rehearsal and I guess they're all afraid of you."

She turned and walked back toward the others. He put his hat back on and went out the door, back into the cold.

He called home when he got back to the Lubyanka and said he would be working all day. Her silence on the line transmitted her image, the buxom woman he'd loved, watching the last of her life passing by, enduring without complaint or accusation, sad Katusha, long suffering Mother Russia. "It's the truth, Katusha. I've been assigned to something very important, very serious."

"Yes. I believe you. You have no reason to feel guilty because of me."

He hung up. If they had not been childless, he thought. He wondered when he'd last made love to her. Not so long ago. They still did it. Making love with Katusha he always imagined she was someone else, young, and slender. And on those rare occasions when he slept with someone else, young and slender, he always imagined it was Katusha.

He took the elevator up to his office, plugged in the cassette recorder, unlocked a drawer of the file cabinet, and sorted through the stack of cassettes he'd had copied from Surveillance's original tapes until he found the one dated October 21, the day before Andrei Davilov's arrest.

He fitted the cassette into the machine and pushed the *fast forward* button. He ran off half the tape, stopped it, and pushed *play*.

"What will happen now?" Her voice.

"It will be taken care of."

"They were KGB?"

The men they had lost in the Sverdlov Square Station.

"I don't know. I thought so. Now I don't know."

59

Andrei Davilov. Why, Ilin wondered, did he lie to her?

"Before that happened, I was having a wonderful time with you."

"I was too."

"Good night."

"Good night."

In the silence that followed Ilin imagined a continuing communication between them, and though there was not a clue on the tape, he thought nonetheless he clearly perceived its drift.

Her laughter. *"The microphone. You don't want the KGB to hear this?"*

At full volume the Tchaikovsky pierced his ears. He turned the cassette machine down to a level that allowed him to appreciate the music and leaned back to listen. After half an hour he had to change the tape. The ballet played through and was followed by silence. After a few minutes, a soft rustling was heard. There was the scratching of the needle drawn across the grooves. The music resumed, much more softly, at another point in the ballet. He turned it up. The pas de deux at the end of act two.

The way they were lined up outside, shivering in the cold, it could have been the Lenin Mausoleum on a Sunday afternoon. He used his KGB card to gain quick admittance, pushing his way through the door into the crowd. There was a loud buzz of conversation. A jazz combo led by a saxophonist blared from stereo speakers on the wall. It could have been Charlie Parker or John Coltrane, or someone he'd never heard of. Ilin didn't care for American jazz and knew very little about it. Alisa Belova was seated with two long-haired young men at a table against the wall.

He got a beer at the bar. The two men abandoned the table as he moved to join her. He sat down, sipping his beer, and admired her hostile beauty.

"Would you care for something?" he said, nodding at the empty tumbler before her.

"I don't care. Some brandy."

He snapped his fingers for the waiter, who came and took the glass.

For a moment neither of them spoke.

"You said you wanted to talk to me. Why don't you get on with it? You must know it embarrasses me to be seen with you."

He smiled. "You're not afraid of me, are you?"

"No."

"And you're not afraid I might make things worse for your brother?"

"Yes," she said. "I am afraid of that. But I could deceive no one by trying to conceal the way I feel about you. About you people."

"He *is* your brother?" the colonel asked, laying a rouble note on the table as the waiter set down the brandy.

She lifted the tumbler and drank. As she lowered it he noticed the slightest trembling of her hand.

"Of course he's my brother. What kind of question is that?"

"Tell me about the two of you."

"Tell you what about us?"

"Were you close, as children?"

She shrugged. "Like any brother and sister."

"You wanted to emigrate to England to be with him. You threw away a magnificent career for that."

"I wanted to emigrate to England to get out of the Soviet Union."

"You are not happy in the Soviet Union?"

"No. Are you?"

It almost stopped him. He waited for a moment before pushing on. "The day of your brother's arrest, you made a telephone call to a man named Brown, your brother's contact at the American Embassy here. Later you went to GUM, the state department store, to meet him. But you did not meet him. Why?"

She shrugged again.

"Was Brown going to get you out of Russia? We have that on tape. You must have known there was a microphone in your apartment? You see, I am very fond of *Swan Lake* myself."

"I love my brother. After I saw he'd been arrested, I couldn't leave."

"That was noble of you. But ... he's been in the Lubyanka two weeks now. Why have you made no attempt to visit him?"

Her face was momentarily white. She drank the rest of the brandy. *"Can* I visit him?"

"Yes. I will make the arrangements."

"Is that all?"

He drank down his beer. "Yes. That is all now." He started to rise, then lowered himself back into his seat. "Just one thing. You love your brother?" He paced the delivery. "Enough to commit incest?"

He heard the crack of her hand across his face before he felt the sting. It closed his eyes momentarily and by the time he'd opened them again and looked around, she was on her way out the door.

8

The cell was painted chalky white, four and a half feet wide by approximately eight feet long. But for six feet of its length nearly half its width was sacrificed to a bed of iron slats mounted to the wall, covered with a thin mattress, and a blanket stamped, like Rhone's dungarees, *inner prison*. Another few feet of floor space were given up to the low, square table and matching wooden chair which sat beside the bed. A radiator, enclosed in a metal grating, gave off a trifling amount of heat. On the table was a tea mug with a wooden spoon. There was a small, hard pillow on the mattress. Above the door was a 200-watt lightbulb, also enclosed in a grating. High up the wall toward the twelve-foot ceiling was a grated vent, four by six inches. Posted on the wall opposite the bed a copy of prison regulations. In the center of the door was a cone-shaped peephole with a closed shutter. A covered latrine bucket sat beneath the table. Stacked on the lid were a few pages of *Pravda,* torn in handy squares.

After a morning ration of soggy, dark bread and thin, tasteless gruel, with tepid tea and three lumps of sugar, Rhone sat on the end of the bunk with his legs arranged beneath the table on either side of the latrine bucket, leaned his back against the wall, and propped his head in the corner. As he did every morning, he forced himself to retrace his footsteps from the time he'd first entered the prison. From the courtyard, double steel doors manned by two armed guards had opened onto a long, stark corridor that led past what appeared to be a guards' lounge and locker room toward the interior maze of the Lubyanka. At its end, where a large arrow on the wall pointed back toward the steel doors and a sign in red letters said "North Exit," they'd ascended a narrow staircase and turned left, or east, down a darker, narrower corridor lined with tiny olive doors. One of them had been opened and he'd been placed in a tiny holding cell and left there briefly before he'd been removed and marched down another corridor, now north again, he thought, to a bare, dingy room where he'd been stripped and searched by a boyish guard under the leering eyes of a middle-aged KGB matron. After he'd exchanged his clothing for a pair of prison-issue dungarees, an old man with a set of barber's shears had come in and clipped his hair to the scalp. In the infirmary, back down another flight of stairs, he'd been marched along an immaculate corridor, past guarded wards that echoed with moans and coughing, to another bare room where he'd again been stripped and examined and grilled about Andrei Davilov's medical history.

His processing completed, he'd been returned briefly to the tiny holding cell, then taken out, back along another corridor, and put with his guard onto a caged elevator that had carried them up to the fifth floor—though he couldn't be certain, for the buttons were unnumbered—and marched east to another set of double steel doors with two armed guards at a table. The guard escorted him through and handed him into the custody of a plain-clothed gorilla of a man who'd taken him through yet another maze of newer, brighter corridors that had led finally to the door of Colonel Ilin's green-painted office.

Rhone sat propped in the corner of his little cell, one of about twenty situated along the bullwalk of a completely enclosed cellblock on the second or third floor of the inner prison. He tried to reconstruct what he'd seen into a clear pattern that could fit over the broader scheme of Remick's floor plans, so indelibly etched into his mind in Staffordshire. But the picture blurred. His eyelids drooped and fluttered shut.

He was in a limousine speeding for an airport. Outside—the frozen wasteland of Anatolia.

"Where are we going, Papa?"

"Didn't your mother tell you?"

"She told me, but I guess I forgot."

"We're going to Russia, Edward. Russia, Russia, Russia . . ."

"Eyes open!"

He woke, shaking his head. For a second he wasn't sure where he was. Then he recognized the voice of the guard, speaking through the peephole shutter on the door.

"It is forbidden to close one's eyes or to sleep except at night. If you sleep you will be sent to a punishment cell and you will be sorry you didn't stay awake."

Again he constructed the picture in his mind of what he'd seen of the prison and moved it like a transparent diagram over the firmer image of Remick's blueprints. In those drawings no two floors were quite the same and only on one of them could he make his pattern fit.

He smiled.

He knew where he was.

The shutter closed and he heard the guard's footsteps retreating down the bullwalk. In Staffordshire they'd hypnotized him so Edward Rhone wouldn't dream in Andrei Davilov's sleep.

His father had been an OSS officer stationed in London. In mid-1942 he'd got his back broken during an air raid. He married his second wife, Rhone's mother, while convalescing in an American military hospital. The daughter of a retired British army officer, she was breaking family tradition merely by marrying outside her father's old regiment. But she'd been seeing Rhone's father for several months before his injury and neither of them ever denied that was when their son had been conceived. Rhone was born in Washington, D.C. the following spring. By the time the War in Europe began to draw to a close, the family was back in London and his father was attached to the American Embassy there.

Rhone's own first memories dated from Ankara, where they were stationed briefly after the end of the war, followed by a longer residence in Moscow. When Avery Remick approached him in Saigon a decade and a half later, Rhone couldn't remember ever having seen him. But Remick left no doubt that he had, and that during their time in Moscow, and later Paris, he'd known Rhone's father well.

After Moscow came New Delhi, then finally the good station in Paris. By that time Rhone had already seen enough to set him permanently apart from people destined to lead more ordinary lives. The oppression and suffering of post-war Russia. The magic and mysticism of the Orient. That was what Jean-Pierre Duval had perceived that first day, hanging by his feet in chains and a straightjacket from a tree on Boulevard Montparnasse, the minute they'd looked each other in the eye. Edward Rhone was fourteen then and the old Frenchman, who'd been a human fly, sleight-of-hand artist, and professional daredevil, who'd performed challenge escapes from half the prisons in Europe, and who claimed to have escaped for real from a Gestapo prison in Nice in 1943, was by that time just a washed-up carny bum who knew he'd found the protégé he'd been looking for.

Rhone's father died of spinal cancer in the American Hospital in Paris in the fall of 1959. Drawn and pale, he stared up from his deathbed at a sixteen-year-old boy who was no more American than your average Parisian Gypsy. Somehow he'd failed to notice during healthier times that he was raising a son without a country. It was his dying wish that Edward spend the last few years of his adolescence in the United States and, though she longed to return to England, Rhone's mother honored it.

He graduated from high school in Santa Barbara, California, where his father had relatives, and enrolled at Stanford. Rhone spent the next three years studying Russian history and language, which he already spoke with near-mother tongue fluency, knowing all the time his studies were no practical preparation for his future.

After the third year he dropped out. He drifted for a while. In Tucson, Arizona, he almost married a singer with a rock and roll band. They both backed out at the last minute. He moved on to Hollywood, where she'd always thought she was bound. He got a letter from her there telling him she'd been pregnant when he left and that she'd had an abortion in Tijuana.

By the time the draft notice came he was picking up steady work as a stunt man. He sometimes imagined that Jean-Pierre Duval would recognize him one day in a dubbed American film. Rhone went to Fort Ord in the fall of 1966. By spring the next year he was overseas, but in Germany rather than Vietnam. He lasted a few months in Frankfurt. Then he volunteered for ranger training. He landed in Vietnam the summer of 1967, and first encountered William Duffy in the central highlands about three months after that.

Each afternoon he was taken from his cell for his exercise in one of the small solitary pens on the roof. He was issued what appeared to be an old Red Army artillery jacket, which would be taken from him before he descended back into the prison. The first thing he saw as he stepped out of the elevator cage was the high wooden gun tower and the guards with their machine guns trained over the yards. Mounted on the tower was a large spotlight. Behind the concrete superstructure that housed the elevator's big electric motor was the smaller housing for the squirrel-cage blower. There were ten meters of open space between the two structures, in clear view of the tower. Though Remick's blueprints had contained no precise drawings of the ventilation system there was only the one blower, and Rhone knew it had to serve for both the inner prison and the office area of the New Lubyanka; some of the air ducts had to lead over there.

He breathed in the fresh cold air and looked up at the sky. He walked or trotted in figure-eights around the enclosure with its walls three times his height, topped with tangles of rusty barbed wire. After a few minutes he stopped to catch his breath, then began again.

By the time his half hour was up he would be exhausted, freezing cold, and ravenously hungry. His escort guided him back into the cage and they descended into the prison. Marching him to his cellblock, the guard made clicking sounds with his tongue against his palate before each bend in the corridor. Once the sound was answered. Just before the corner there was a narrow door. The guard opened it and pushed him into a dark closet with just room for a man to stand. There were more clicks, back and forth, like a primitive Morse code. Then the clicking ceased and Rhone listened in the stifling darkness as another guard came around the corner and passed in the direction from which he and his escort had come. The guard's boots clicked on the parquet floor and like an echo of the click Rhone heard another, softer sound, the swish of his unseen fellow prisoner's laceless canvas boots dragging along the floor.

Evening ration was at six. More watery rice soup, sometimes with a few bits of sausage or a pair of fish eyes staring up at him from the bottom of the bowl. He ate slowly and scraped the bowl clean with his last crust of bread.

His nights were spent in interrogation. Sometimes they summoned him before bed call. The next time they would wait until the guard had announced it and he'd removed his dungarees and crawled in his long underwear beneath the blanket. Those nights he thought the guard must wait at the peephole until just the moment sleep overcame him. Then he banged open the door and stormed into the cell. "Out of bed! Get dressed! Upstairs for interrogation!"

Ilin was seated at the head of the table; Rhone, by his order, at the corner near him. The colonel sugared his coffee, stirred it, and drank. On a tinny-sounding transistor radio he'd tuned in the broadcast of a live performance from the Bolshoi. Tchaikovsky's *Sleeping Beauty*. They were alone.

"I saw her dance that role in 1974," Ilin said. "She is a rare beauty, that sister of yours. But why would a woman with such a bright future wish to throw it all away?"

"Our parents had died. Then her husband. I was the only family she had. If she'd been anyone else they would have let her go."

"But instead they cancelled her contract." He beamed with sympathy. "Would you like some coffee? I'll get it for you myself."

Though he would have liked some, Rhone shook his head.

Ilin shrugged and lit a cigarette. "You're so very proud, aren't you Davilov? And you have the will to stand by your pride, at least up until now. I admire that. I do not know that I could have been so strong myself. And this must be even harder for a man who has lived as you have, for a man so handsome . . . magnetic, should I say?"

Rhone said nothing.

"Were there a lot of women in your life? Other than your wife, I mean? Tell me."

"There were a few."

He laughed. "Yes! I know from your file. You were a regular Casanova. I was never so lucky with women myself. Oh, I have my wife and I have had my mistresses. But my wife is fat and unattractive and I've never trusted the sincerity of the others. I envy you your talent with women, and I'm sure you must have your own personal vision of the two of us." He paused, listening to the Tchaikovsky. "The Frog. And his counterpart, the Prince." He smiled. "That is to say, I would envy you if you were not in your present fix. That must be the most horrifying thing of all for a man like you, though I dare say you're still too numbed to grasp your situation fully—that it will be years before you fuck another woman. That by the time you are free, you may prefer men."

Ilin fell silent, his sad eyes staring into the corner, or off far away. Rhone wondered fleetingly if by the end Ilin might not have been talking to himself.

9

He'd showered and shaved off his second ten days' growth of beard. He'd been issued clean dungarees. At the guard table beside the double steel doors, his escort produced Davilov's KGB card, in its protective laminated casing with the small black and white mug shot, and they were ushered through into the administrative block. The guard marched him along a bright, polished corridor and locked him in a little room, bare except for a table, a couple of folding chairs, and the inevitable portrait of Lenin.

He sat down and stretched out his legs. An eye regarded him through the peephole. The peephole closed and Rhone looked around. At floor level in the wall behind him was a vent twice the size of the vents in the inner prison.

The door opened and Ilin came in. "I have a surprise for you, Andrei Petrovich. You have a visitor."

The door opened again. Standing in it looking lost and afraid was Alisa Belova. Ilin beckoned her in, then went out, and closed the door behind him.

She came to him hesitantly. "Andrei?"

He heard the click of the shutter and saw Ilin's shaded eye at the peephole. Clutched to Alisa's breast was a package wrapped in *Pravda*. She held it out tentatively. Then she put it on the table. There were tears in her eyes. When he put his arms around her, her body shook with sobs.

She drew back and wiped her eyes. "What have they done to you? Oh, Andrei!" She looked at him as if he were a stranger, shaking her head with anger and disbelief. Again she was racked with sobs, once more controlled herself, and wiped the tears from her eyes. "I shouldn't have said that."

"It's all right." He held her again and gently stroked her back. He could feel her breasts, her body fitted against his. He smelled the perfume he'd brought her from London, incongruous with the antiseptic stench of the Lubyanka. He remembered the smell of her nakedness, let himself remember it consciously and without restraint, remembered her body moving beneath him, her soft cries, remembered lying with her afterwards. Remembered her dancing the pas de deux naked beside the bed.

He kissed her on the lips, then suddenly took her arms, pushed her back, and whispered: "What are you doing here?"

She shook her head.

"What are you *doing?* You were supposed to contact Brown. He promised me he would get you out."

"I couldn't go. I saw them take you away."

He thought he would burst. He wanted to shout and slap her and all he could do was hold her, digging his fingernails into the flesh of her arms, and whisper: "You promised. You promised!"

He shook her. For a moment she let him, almost limp in his hands. Then again she shook her head. "Andrei!"

"You've got to get out!" He was still shaking her furiously. "You hear me, you've got to get out!"

"Andrei, you're hurting me!"

He released her and she sagged toward him. Then she stood on her tiptoes and whispered very softly and plaintively to his face: "I couldn't go when my brother had just been arrested. Don't you remember what you told me, that night before we went to the Metropole? I couldn't go and leave you here. My *brother?*"

Now he shook his head. "Oh Christ! Call him again. Don't you understand you could end up in here too?" He put his hand on her cheek. "You still have the number?"

She nodded.

"Promise me you'll call him again."

The door opened and Ilin came back in. She looked at him urgently, then back at Rhone, then turned suddenly to the table and started to rip open the package. "I've brought you food: sausage and smoked fish, white bread, some cheese, and some jam. And cigarettes."

He stared at the food.

She looked at him. Then with a sudden fearless contempt at Ilin. "He's starving you, isn't he?"

She tore off a piece of white bread and started to roll it around one of the sausages.

Ilin stepped over, took it out of her hand, and put it back on the table with the other food items. "I told you it would have to be brief."

"But I only just arrived."

"I told you. You can see him again before his trial."

She looked at Rhone. He nodded for her to go, but she stood where she was. Ilin clapped his hands. A guard opened the door and, at the colonel's nod, stepped in, took her by her arms, and started to guide her out. At the door she stopped, looking back.

"Alisa?" Rhone said. "Have they been hard on you?"

She shook her head. The guard tugged her gently but she stood rooted.

"Tell me the truth."

"They wrecked the apartment. They broke my records. Each one separately. This big bear. He just broke them over his knee and threw them around the room. Then the turntable and.... Oh God, you don't think I care about that?"

As though with a sudden loss of will, she let herself be guided out. The door swung shut behind her.

Rhone turned to Ilin. "Bastard."

He ignored the remark and said: "Why were you angry with her?"

72

"I told her that if something happened I didn't want her to come here."

Ilin beamed. "So you knew you might end up in here?"

"I knew it was possible."

Ilin was deeply thoughtful. Rhone looked back at the food on the table.

"Food parcels must be earned," said the Colonel. "Tell me: the microfilm? Is that all you were supposed to do for Ross while you were in London?"

"Yes."

Rhone took a last look at the food and followed Ilin out. Though distracted by his hunger and by his shock at seeing Alisa, he took careful note of their course as they made their way back through the maze, and was not surprised when he found himself back at the door of Ilin's green-painted office. Inside, several civilian and military KGB men sat smoking at the table. Taking note of the ranks of the uniformed officers, Rhone wondered vaguely what their appearance might signify to him. Ilin left him, went over to the file cabinet, and produced a folder. He came over and opened it on the table. Along with the papers were a number of photographs of Andrei Davilov and Avery Remick taken in various London restaurants and pubs.

Ilin held up one of the pictures. "Is that your Mr. Ross?"

Rhone nodded.

"And who is that?"

"That's—" He broke off. He picked up several of the pictures and studied them, then looked up at the colonel. They locked eyes. Rhone stacked the pictures in both his hands like playing cards and held them in his left hand out toward the colonel, thrusting them almost into his face. "It's me, of course."

Ilin smiled, stuffed the photographs back into the folder, and returned the folder to the files. He locked the drawer and took his seat at the head of the table. When he looked back Rhone was still standing at the opposite end, his hands crossed behind his back. One of the photographs remained in his right shirt sleeve, slightly bent, held in place above his wrist by its own resilience.

"How many times did you meet with Ross before you left London?" the colonel asked him.

"Several times."

"Several? How many?"

"I don't know exactly. A few."

"All to discuss the smuggling from Moscow to London of one harmless capsule of microfilm?"

"I have said again and again that I didn't think of it as smuggling. And we only discussed that once. Or twice. Just before I left London. The other times we met socially."

"Socially? Then you must have known his real name?"

"Ross was his real name."

"No, Andrei Petrovich. His real name was Avery Remick and he is the CIA case officer in charge of American efforts to penetrate our Semipalatinsk research facility. You were photographed with him in London on thirteen separate occasions during the month before your return to Moscow."

"He told me his name was Ross. He told me he was exporting a new kind of computer chip manufactured by his company in California."

"If that is true, he lied to you. But then if you are telling the truth, explain to me why it was worth twenty thousand dollars to the CIA for *you* to smuggle that one microfilm capsule from here to London when Brown could have transferred it much more easily and safely himself?"

"I don't know what you're talking about."

"That is the amount that was deposited in your Barclay's account the day after you left London. And the microfilm does not contain trade data. It contains classified military data regarding the solution, at our Semipalatinsk facility, of certain technical problems the CIA once deemed insoluble. If you got it from Brown, Brown could only have gotten it from Yaroshenko. You see, Andrei Petrovich, your story makes no sense."

The timing couldn't have been more convincing if he'd faked it. But he was not faking. The sudden cramp that knotted his stomach was all too real.

"Does that information give you indigestion?"

Rhone gasped. His stomach was convulsing. "I have to shit, Comrade. Dysentery. I can't wait."

One of the civilian KGB men guffawed. Ilin shook his head and clapped his hands for a guard, who appeared immediately at the door. "Take him and let him have a shit."

Half doubled-over by the cramp, Rhone followed him down the corridor to a little door with a peephole. Inside was a Turkish toilet. He dropped his dungarees and squatted over the hole. Through the peephole a single eye observed. A handful of torn sheets of *Pravda* were stuck onto a nail driven into the wall. He ripped one of them loose, still watching the eye in the peephole. *Pravda* means *truth,* he thought. He used the paper. For a moment the eye disappeared. By the time it reappeared in the peephole he was standing up, pulling up his dungarees. The photograph of Davilov was safe in the waist of his underwear.

The guard marched him back down the hall to the office. They were all still seated at the table. He stopped at the end of it.

Ilin smiled. "Do you feel better?"

Rhone said nothing.

"Now, where did you get the microfilm?"

"I told you. I got it from Brown."

"Yaroshenko has confessed that he gave it to you himself."

"Then Yaroshenko is a liar."

"Do you want to stay under interrogation, in solitary, on diminished rations, for the rest of your time in prison?"

"No."

"Then where did you get the microfilm?"

"I got it from Yaroshenko."

Ilin rose and came down along the table stopping directly before him. "Why do you lie to me, Andrei Petrovich?"

"Because you don't believe me when I tell the truth."

The colonel stepped suddenly toward him, driving his knee hard up into his groin. Rhone gagged, half doubling over. He straightened up slowly, staring viciously at Ilin's froggish, smiling face.

Ilin lit a cigarette and let the smoke drift into his eyes. "How long has your sister been an agent of the CIA?"

"My sister is not an agent of the CIA! She knows nothing of my business in Moscow! *Nothing!*"

"Perhaps not. But how can we be sure of that?"

"You have no evidence against her. None at all."

"No," answered Ilin. "But we have a great deal of evidence against you."

"That is because I am guilty."

Ilin smiled, turned, walked back, and resumed his chair. "So you admit you are guilty?"

"Yes, Comrade."

"And where did you get the microfilm?"

"If you want the truth, I got it from Brown. If you want me to *tell* you I got it from Yaroshenko . . ."

"What I want is to get to the bottom of this treachery. And it makes no sense for Brown, who could easily have gotten the capsule out of the country, to have passed it from Yaroshenko to you, who never stood a chance of getting it out."

"Unless it was never intended that I get it out."

"What do you mean by that?" Ilin said after a moment's silence.

Very slowly Rhone leaned over the table. A pack of Astras and a cigarette lighter lay in front of the nearest uniformed officer. He picked them up. Looking the enraged officer in the eye, he shook out a cigarette, inserted it between his lips, and lit it. He put the pack and the lighter back on the table and looked again at Ilin, who appeared on the verge of rising, but apparently thought better of it.

Rhone took a deep drag and exhaled luxuriously. "The only visible consequence of my actions since I returned to Moscow, except for my own arrest, has been the arrest of Yaroshenko."

There were whispers up and down the table.

"But Yaroshenko was their deepest penetration in our Semipalatinsk facility. Why would they sacrifice you to destroy him?"

"How do you know that?" Rhone said. "How do you know they don't have another better placed agent down there?"

76

Though hushed, the conversation up and down the table was charged. Then there was silence.

Ilin rose. "Come with me, Andrei Petrovich. There is something I want to show you.

They rode the elevator down and got off on the third floor. The colonel marched him back to his own cellblock and, once they'd entered it, toward his own cell. Ilin stopped at the cell just before it, bent and looked through the peephole, stepped back, and motioned for Rhone to look.

The cell was identical to his own. The prisoner sat in the chair, his elbows propped on the table and his chin resting in his hands. His dungarees, stamped like Rhone's with *inner prison* across the back, hung shapelessly on his emaciated frame. He shifted in the chair, glanced up at the peephole, and rose. His cheeks were hollow, speckled with thin gray whiskers. Dark circles spread like bruises beneath his vacant eyes. His head was shaved and his long ears stuck out comically. His eyes were bloodshot, filled not with despair, but rather with emptiness, with nothingness, as though the spirit that might once have shined the light from behind them had retreated far into the bony naked skull, or flown or died. Even as they met Rhone's single eye in the peephole they betrayed no flicker of light.

"His story is essentially the same as yours," Ilin said. "But you are both traitors. So how can I dare to trust you?"

Rhone closed the peephole shutter and straightened up.

"Did you know, Andrei Petrovich," the colonel continued, "that if I fail in my investigation of this affair my own life could collapse as surely and drastically as yours has?"

Rhone regarded him without sympathy.

"And do not concern yourself with the possibility that Yaroshenko might be *innocent*. He is not. We have evidence that he planned to defect, and recently an enormous sum of money was deposited for him in a Swiss bank." He paused. "You will be tried publicly as co-defendants. You will be the primary witness against Yaroshenko. You will confess that you are a CIA spy, that you got the microfilm from Yaroshenko to pass to Brown at the American Embassy."

"My sister knows nothing of my connection with Ross, or Remick."

"We have no reason to bring any charges against your sister now. . . . Come. I will have the stenographer take your statement."

Rhone stepped away from the door and stopped as a loud knocking was heard from inside.

"Andrei Davilov, as you call yourself," Yaroshenko shouted through the door. "We are both going to the Gulag. I have sent many others there myself. But I also have many friends there. And I promise you, if I do not have the opportunity to kill you, before you leave there, one of them surely will."

A strange smile crossed Ilin's face. They moved away down the bullwalk. "An empty threat," he said. "Yaroshenko is not going to the Gulag. He is useful only if he is sentenced to death."

10

General Oleg Drachinsky occupied a plush modern office on the third floor of the New Lubyanka annex. On one wall hung an oil painting of Felix Dzerzhinsky, on another a portrait of Lenin. A large antique mahogany desk, imported from Germany at the end of the war, sat in the center of the room. Carpets from central Asia covered the floor. Two embroidered sofas lined opposite walls. Adjoining the office was a bedroom with a shower and toilet. Half of Moscow would have given blood to have the place as a lodging.

Yaroshenko's interrogator, Gorsky, and the fat prosecutor, Zverev, were seated on one of the sofas when Ilin, the transcript of Andrei Davilov's confession folded beneath his arm, arrived. He declined their offer to make room for him between them and sat alone on the opposite sofa.

He was half through his first cigarette when the General emerged from the bedroom and sat down behind his desk. "Well, Valeri Pavlovich. Tell me how you have fared."

The colonel rose and put the transcript on the desk. "Andrei Davilov's last interrogation and subsequent confession." He retreated to the sofa.

"So you have a confession?" Drachinsky thumbed through the transcript, scanning, and finally looked up. "Intriguing.

Very interesting. A better-placed American agent in Semipalatinsk. If that is true we must launch an immediate investigation of the facility and everyone associated with it." He looked at Gorsky and held out the transcript. "You have read this, Major?"

"Not the confession," Gorsky said, moving to the table. "Though I was present along with the comrade prosecutor at the prisoner's last interrogation." He took the papers and returned to the couch. With Zverev he looked them over.

The general looked back at Ilin. "I am pleased with you, Valeri Pavlovich. You have gotten to the bottom of this matter much more swiftly than I would have dreamed possible." He waited until Gorsky had finished studying the transcript and said, "What do you think?"

Gorsky folded the papers and squinted through his wire-rimmed spectacles. Though he was young for his rank, there was a sterility about him which made him look much older. "Excellent. Excellent."

"Prosecutor?" said the general.

"Yes. Excellent. With this testimony I should have no difficulty obtaining the death penalty for Colonel Yaroshenko."

"And that," Gorsky went on, "will give me the leverage I need in his continued interrogation. It is not impossible that Yaroshenko might *know* who the other American agent at Semipalatinsk is."

Though aware of the unlikelihood of that, Ilin said nothing.

"Then we are all in agreement," the general said. "The matter is settled. Valeri Pavlovich deserves our gratitude and congratulations." He beamed at him. "That is all."

Gorsky and Zverev started to rise, but Ilin remained where he was.

The general's beam became a leer. "Colonel?"

He cleared his throat and tried to summon a few drops of saliva to his arid mouth. "I am not satisfied."

"And why are you not satisfied?"

"It is hard to explain. The Davilov character."

"The Davilov character?" asked the general.

"I do not think him legitimate, as he has thus far revealed himself to me. He has confessed to being an American spy, which I am certain he is. But in confessing that, he has also confessed to being a fool, which I most definitely believe he is not. And I am sure that all these weeks he has been *leading* me to the exact conclusions I have now pretended to reach."

"You believe these conclusions are wrong?"

"I believe we are all on dangerous ground."

The general looked at Gorsky. "Major?"

Gorsky shrugged. "Comrade Colonel has offered not one fact in support of his misgivings. And he has certainly proposed no alternative explanation for the affair."

"Valeri Pavlovich?"

"It is a question of instinct. I have no concrete facts. Only unanswered questions. Why did Yaroshenko say that Andrei Davilov was not who he claimed to be? Why would a man of the prisoner's obvious intelligence allow himself to be so easily duped? Why would the CIA give up an agent of Yaroshenko's stature to protect another agent whose existence we did not even suspect?" He shrugged. "As for an explanation of the affair itself, I don't know. Perhaps they intend to trick us into launching a witch hunt at Semipalatinsk. Can you imagine the effect a full scale committee investigation would have on their progress down there?"

The general pondered. "A fascinating concept, and certainly not beyond the scope of Remick's vision." He looked back at Gorsky. "Major?"

"These questions can all be asked after Yaroshenko is convicted and sentenced." Beside him Zverev nodded in agreement.

The general thought it over and looked back at Ilin. "The sooner this matter is officially resolved, the better. Yaroshenko is a blemish upon us all. We will proceed with the testimony and the Davilov confession as it stands. In the meantime I will initiate a limited and secret investigation of the possibility of another American agent in Semipalatinsk." He sighed. "That is all, comrades."

Back in his office Ilin drank a glass of vodka and chased it with black coffee. He told Boris to get him a cell by cell roster of the prisoners occupying communal cellblocks. When the list arrived, he spread it on the desk before him. It took him an hour of studying it before he made his decision, picked up the telephone, dialed an inter-prison number, and ordered that Andrei Davilov be transferred to the communal cell occupied by Vladimir the Ingush, the dissident Grigori Gertsenberg, and the stoolie Ivan Ivanov.

Snow fell on the roof of the Lubyanka. Twenty prisoners in hand-me-down greatcoats marched in the shadow of the gun tower. Beside Rhone was Gertsenberg, a Jewish activist whose arrest almost a year before had been reported in the western press. Before them marched the two other members of the cell, Ivanov, a great Russian bear of a man, and Vladimir the Ingush, a native of one of Stalin's "lost races," who'd served over thirty years in the camps and had taken his very nickname from a hell-hole called Vladimir prison.

"There is a tradition in the Lubyanka," Gertsenberg said as they neared the far turn, away from the guard. "In every communal cell there is at least one informer."

They moved into the turn, walking in silence along the short wall and back toward the guard, who looked at his watch, announced their time was up, and hurried them back toward the lift.

They rode down in fours and were marched back to the cellblock. Inside, in his brown uniform with the baby blue shoulder-boards, was a blue-eyed kid who looked hardly old enough to shave. That morning as he'd first ushered him to the cell, something in his clear blue eyes had haunted Rhone. It wasn't until later that he'd identified it in his mind: humanity, his first glimpse of it during his three weeks in the Lubyanka. Walking along the bullwalk the young guard bounced on his toes and whistled a familiar classical tune. Incongruous with the place, the melody struck a chord in Rhone even before he'd recognized it. A theme from *Swan Lake*. The pas de deux at the end of the "Black Swan."

The cell was fifteen feet deep and perhaps twelve feet across, with double bunks on each side. Cut high into the wall in one corner was a small window. In the center of the floor was a table with a chessboard, surrounded by four wood chairs, where the Ingush immediately sat and started setting up a chess problem.

Ivanov sat down on the lower bunk, took a pack of Mahorka from beneath the mattress and started to roll a cigarette. Gertsenberg climbed laboriously to the upper bunk opposite, and Rhone ascended onto the upper bunk above Ivanov.

He leaned back against the wall. Tired and famished from the walk in the cold, he thought he could almost imagine himself out of the cell, could walk the streets of Moscow in the snow, or Paris in those first few weeks of spring when the women sit with their skirts pulled high sunning their legs at the sidewalk cafés in St. Germaine. Sometimes it was Vietnam which would seize him and transport him away. Vietnam, which had seemed muddled and murky as a dream when he had been there, now returned in a vivid montage of chopper landings and lift-offs, tracers and ground fire, of incoming artillery, of booby traps and land mines, crying civilians and burning hamlets, of rain and mosquitoes, of the dying and the dead. And cut through all this like vast ragged gaps, the boredom, the interminable and terrible boredom. He remembered his first day on the line, the looks in the eyes of the men already there.

He remembered Duffy especially. Looking at Duffy for the first time, who stared back at him from across that boundless gulf between the place Rhone had just come from and the places Duffy had already gone, Rhone found himself trying to affect, not Duffy's look, for that was far beyond him, but at least the look of some of the other men he'd seen.

Bill Duffy just stared at him and after a long time turned his head sideways and spat into the bushes and said, "You're green."

He couldn't have guessed that within a few weeks they would almost become friends. On their first R & R in Saigon he'd met a girl named Phuong. Right out of Graham Greene. The Tet

Offensive broke out the next time they were there. It was three days before Rhone could get out to Cholon and when he did he found her dead with all her sisters in her mother's house. He didn't see Duffy again until he got on the chopper to go back up on the line. He said he'd found an AK-47 and a couple of banana clips cached in the whorehouse and that single-handedly he'd knocked out a whole Viet Cong sapper squad. Rhone knew he'd enjoyed that more than he would have the whores. But by then Duffy had already started going off the end, as if he'd decided to take personal responsibility for seeing America didn't lose the war. The next week he sent Perry's squad out after two snipers at dusk and Perry and Jackson were the only ones who came back. They hadn't been snipers, but point men for a battalion. In the darkness you could see nothing of Jackson but the whites of his eyes and his teeth, and already there was murder in his eyes.

Something snapped him back. It was Ivanov standing up beside his bunk, holding out the cigarette he'd rolled. Rhone accepted it, took a drag and handed it back.

"The scum one is forced to spend his time with," Ivanov said. "That's the worst thing about this place. First an enemy of the state. And now an American spy."

"Ivanov, you are a big stupid bear," the Ingush said from the table. "But that is not why I loathe you."

"Vladimir the Ingush. Thirty years in prisons and he thinks he's Czar of the Gulag." Ivanov turned back to Rhone. "Sincerely, Davilov. We are all in this together. So why don't you tell us how you got involved with the likes of Colonel Yaroshenko?"

Rhone saw the glance that was exchanged between Gertsenberg and the Ingush. Saying nothing, he dropped down from his bunk, brushed past the big man, and went over and sat at the table.

Ivanov followed, towering over him. "I may be a criminal, but at least I am a Russian patriot."

"Ivanov is the most pathetic kind of criminal," the Ingush said.

84

The big Russian glowered. "You know nothing about my case."

"You are wrong, Ivanov. I am on the telegraph and I know everything about it." He looked at Rhone. "Ivanov was an ambulance driver. And he was also a drunkard. One day when he did not have to work he drank a bottle of vodka, beat up his wife and kids, went to Botkin Hospital, and stole his own ambulance."

Ivanov's face flushed red. Beside his left eye a small spot of flesh jerked in rapid palpitations. Very slowly he opened and closed his hands, extending the long fingers stiffly, and tightening them deliberately into two giant fists.

"He ran a red light in full view of a police car, which then pursued him down Leningradskoye Chausée. Just past the Belorussian Station he ran a second red light. In the middle of this intersection was an old woman from Kiev carrying the boxes and bags of all the things she'd accumulated in her miserable life, too decrepit to get out of the way. She was dead and Ivanov was in jail for a year before they got around to sentencing him to the camps for twenty-five. But they never sent him to the camps. Instead they moved him here."

Ivanov was still towering over the table, glaring down at the Ingush. There were tears in his eyes. The Ingush, again intent on the chessboard, seemed no longer aware he was there. Something seemed to drain slowly out of him. He stepped back to his bunk, sank down and buried his face in his hands. His big beef-rack of a body shook with his sobs. When he wiped his eyes and again looked up, he appeared sullen, withdrawn.

The door opened and the young guard stepped in, in his hand a ballpoint pen and four sheets of stationery.

He placed them down on the table before Rhone. "Colonel Ilin has instructed that you be permitted two letters. One to your wife in London and one to your sister here."

He wrote the letter to Andrei Davilov's wife first. It would go, of course, to Remick. But the content had to be convincing enough that Ilin wouldn't suspect the code when he read the

Russian translation. And though the code was still clear in his mind, he had difficulty working the message into the context. Writing to Alisa in Russian he could say nothing of what he wanted to say, though if she had done as he had told her she would never get it anyway. But the fact that he'd been given permission to write her was a source of gnawing apprehension to him. She was supposed to be out of the country already.

Finishing the second letter, he sensed something and looked around and saw Ivanov, leaning forward on his bunk, trying to read over his shoulder. Sulking, the big man reclined back.

Rhone finished the letter and signed it. He left the pen and the two remaining sheets of stationery on the table, rose, and went over to stand in front of the door. When he heard the shutter open over the peephole, he knocked.

The guard took the two letters and closed the door. Rhone turned back to the table. Gertsenberg was looking at the two remaining pieces of stationery.

Then the Jew lifted his eyes to Rhone. "Our guard has been careless."

Rhone picked up the paper and the pen and held them up toward him. "They're yours if you want them."

Gertsenberg hesitated, then reached out to take them. He stuffed the pen into a hole in the end of his mattress, folded the two sheets of paper, and fitted them between the pages of his book, *A Year in the Motherland,* by Georgi Valininovich Plakhanov.

Gertsenberg placed the book back under the end of his mattress and looked again at Rhone. "So you have a sister? And a wife in London?"

Rhone nodded and resumed his seat at the table.

"Your sister is in Moscow?"

"Yes." He was lonely for her. And it seemed now that the loneliness was only worse because he could not really talk about her, for his having to pretend she was his sister. And it seemed almost bad luck for him to say she was in Moscow. "She was allowed to visit me once. She's very worried."

"And is her situation secure?" asked the Jew.

"No." He told him about Alisa Belova's attempt to emigrate after her husband's death. "Her contract with the Bolshoi was canceled." He told him about the amateur group she worked with.

"Yes," Gertsenberg said. "I am acquainted with that group." He paused. "And your wife is a British national?"

"Yes. Her father was once a British vice-consul here. Otherwise I would never have been permitted to marry her. Now I doubt if I will see her again."

"How many loved ones I've had whom I'll never see again."

"In Israel?"

"Yes."

"You were also refused an exit visa?"

Gertsenberg smiled. "I've never applied for an exit visa. I am a Jew and I love the state of Israel. But I love Russia too and, though the KGB might disagree, I am, like Ivanov there, a Russian patriot."

Ivanov looked up fiercely and the Ingush, bent over his chessboard, chuckled.

"I am not so brave," Rhone said. "And you could never call me a patriot."

"Do not call me brave," said Gertsenberg. "And as for your patriotism, that is something for which you need not answer to me."

There was a hush over the cell. Then they heard the creaking wheels on the bullwalk. The door opened. Outside stood the young guard and a flat-faced Mongol pushing the mess cart.

The Ingush moved to the door as the Mongol ladled out the soup. He took the bowls and passed them back, saving the last for himself. The door closed and the wheels creaked on down the walk. Each of the other men moved to his respective bunk and dug what remained of his morning bread ration from under his mattress. Rhone sat back at the table and stared into the watery liquid, broth rather than gruel. But it was only midday and in the solitary cell he'd received nothing between morning and evening. He dipped his spoon into the soup and sipped the soup off without actually putting the spoon into his mouth.

He sensed Gertsenberg was staring at him and looked up. "You have finished your bread ration?"

He shook his head. "I missed rations this morning."

The Jew contemplated his own half loaf of bread. Slowly he started to tear it in half again. The other prisoners were staring at him. He held one piece toward Rhone.

Rhone shook his head. "I can't. No."

"Please take it."

He took it with a trembling hand. He broke off a piece of crust and dunked it into the broth. He was overwhelmed, unable even to voice his thanks.

11

The Ingush took his place at the door as morning rations were delivered, passing the bowls of gruel and then the bread loaves back one at a time as they were delivered to him. As the men took their bread, each paused to balance and weigh the loaf in his hand. It was automatic, ritualistic. After bed call the night before, Rhone had waited until the snoring of the other men became rhythmic, then taken out the small torn-out photo section of Andrei Davilov's face, ripped open the seam at the end of his mattress, and slipped it in.

In the evening Gertsenberg had talked. He'd been born in Kiev in 1920, the son of a career officer in the Red Army, a devout Marxist who at seventeen had been drafted into the Czar's army and had been a first-hand witness to the debacle of 1915–16, when thousands of Russian soldiers had been sent to the front with neither arms nor ammunition. Shortly after Gertsenberg's birth the family had moved to Moscow, where his father had survived the Kremlin intrigues of the 1920's and advanced to the rank of major. Gertsenberg had been fifteen when his father'd been dragged from their home one midnight. Six months passed before the family learned he'd been shot.

The death of his father had instilled in Gertsenberg a fanatical hatred of Stalin but Marxism had been a second religion in the household and he'd retained his Communist convictions. He'd completed his primary and secondary education, and in 1938 enrolled in the university as an engineering student. In 1940 he'd been drafted into the army. He'd endured an enlisted man's life for six months. Then he'd entered officers' candidate school. Six months later he was in a tank brigade in the Ukraine. Wounded severely at Dniepropetrovsk, he'd been evacuated to Kharkov and, after a hasty convalescence, transferred to the rear, only weeks before that city had been encircled. The Soviet government had been transferring its heavy industry to the east of Moscow and as a former engineering student Gertsenberg had been assigned a desk job in Kuibyshev.

After the war he'd returned to the University and completed his studies. Moscow was being rebuilt. He'd prospered as a construction engineer in the post-war years in spite of a rash of anti-Semitism inspired by one of Stalin's whims.

Gertsenberg's Marxist fervor had been jaded by his World War II experience, but after Stalin's death in March 1953 he'd enjoyed a period of renewed hope. And for a few years conditions had improved. Hundreds of thousands had returned from the concentration camps. In 1957 his father had been posthumously rehabilitated. Had she not died the year before, his mother would have been eligible for her husband's pension. Gertsenberg's wife, a gentile, had borne him his first son in 1958. Two years later she had died giving birth to a stillborn girl.

By the early 1960s the liberal tide had been turned back. Russia was reverting to Stalinism and Gertsenberg had been completely disillusioned. His association with other Jewish malcontents had become exclusive. He'd gotten fewer and poorer work assignments and finally found himself out of a job entirely. He'd been arrested and questioned several times, though he'd never been held for long. He'd been forced to accept menial labor to survive. Many of his friends had applied for permission to emigrate to Israel. Some actually had received it. Other had been fired from their jobs, or been tried and imprisoned. The Helsinki Treaty had been passed in 1974. Gertsenberg had been a charter member of the monitoring group. Briefly it had again appeared that conditions would improve. Then a new wave of arrests had occurred.

Gertsenberg had been arrested in December 1977. He'd endured nine months of solitary confinement and interrogation that had left him near death. He supposed that he might inadvertently have implicated others, but he had denounced no one. He'd confessed to his own "crimes," but what his interrogators had been unable to make him admit was remorse. In the end they had given up. After almost a month in the infirmary he'd spent three months in various communal cells. He was slated for a show trial, he was sure, but as yet no date had been set.

After they'd finished their tea, Rhone was summoned from the cell and escorted upstairs and across into the administrative section. Ilin awaited him in the company of a fat Russian in a drab Soviet business suit and a little man with a tape measure, who quickly took his measurements and left.

"A suit," Ilin explained. "For your trial." He smiled. "I know we have the suit you were wearing when you were arrested. But you will be presented in court as traitorous scum who has sold out Russia for money. We don't want you looking the successful western playboy." He introduced the fat man as Comrade Zverev, his prosecutor, and told him to have a seat and tell the man his story. When Rhone got to the part about Brown having given him the microfilm, Ilin stopped him. "I thought we had agreed. Yaroshenko gave you the microfilm."

"We agreed I would *testify* Yaroshenko gave it to me. We never agreed he *gave* it to me."

"But when you go on trial for your life before the Supreme Court of the Soviet Union you must be ready to *believe* that he gave it to you." The colonel smiled. He reached down and placed his hand on Rhone's shoulder. Rhone looked at the hand as though it were leprous and he withdrew it. The smile was replaced by a scowl. "Don't be concerned. Only Yaroshenko will receive the maximum penalty. But we must take advantage of all the dramatic potential, if only for the benefit of the CIA."

Rhone finished his story. Ilin clapped for the guard and told him to take Rhone back to his cell. At the door Rhone paused and looked back. "I have been told I have the right to buy cigarettes from the prison commissary."

"Do you have the money?"

"There were three hundred roubles in my pocket when I was arrested, not to mention the pounds sterling."

Ilin removed a nearly full pack of Astras from his pocket, walked over, and pushed them into Rhone's hand. "I will make the arrangements. In the meantime you may smoke these."

Rhone regarded him silently, crossed his hands behind his back, and preceded the guard into the hall.

Back in the cell he shook one of the Astras out of the pack, fitted it between his lips, and lay the pack on the table. The Ingush watched him silently, his dark eyes weighing and balancing him. Rhone met his gaze, held it for a long time, then shifted his own eyes to Gertsenberg, watching him from his upper bunk.

"I was measured for a suit for my trial today," Rhone said. "I demanded my right to buy cigarettes and the Colonel forced me to take these."

He was distracted by the abrasive sound of the Ingush striking a match on the iron rail of his bunk. He held it up toward Rhone, who stooped slightly to receive the light, then shook out a cigarette for himself, and lit it. Rhone looked at Gertsenberg, who shook his head, and at the big Russian bear, who'd been watching all this eagerly from his lower bunk but now averted his eyes, sulking. "Ivanov?"

The big man looked back sullenly. He tried to meet Rhone's eyes but his own eyes kept straying toward the cigarettes, which the Ingush had returned to the table. In a sudden, impulsive movement he stepped forward, took one of them without a word, and retreated back to his bunk. He lit it himself and smoked rapidly in sulking silence.

A light snow fell on the roof of the Lubyanka. Two abreast, the twenty prisoners marched about the yard. "I must talk to you about something," Rhone whispered to Gertsenberg as they made the turn and started away from the guard.

"Yes?"

He waited until they were nearing the far end of the yard. "Alexander Terekhov. You must have known him on the outside."

"Yes. Though not intimately. But Terekhov is the spirit and the inspiration of the movement for freedom in this country."

"Is it possible for me to contact him?"

"Contact him? I don't understand. Contact him where?"

Rhone glanced sideways at the Jew and spoke in a whisper. "Alexander Terekhov is here. You couldn't know. He was arrested two months ago."

Out of the corner of his eye he saw Gertsenberg turn to stare at him. Quickly he caught himself and again looked straight ahead, but as they made the next turn and faced back in the direction of the guard, Rhone saw the gesture had attracted attention. They completed the next two rounds in silence.

"I would never have believed they would go so far as to arrest Terekhov," Gertsenberg whispered as they again started away from the guard. "But why do you want to contact him?"

"It's personal. Believe me. It's very important."

"I don't know. I almost trust you."

They completed the walk in silence. Out of the corner of his eye Rhone could see Gertsenberg's chiseled face, grim-set, rigid. He did not look him in the eye as they rode the elevator down. Back in the cell, he opened the book to the two pages of stationery Rhone had given him, took up the pen, and began to write, rapidly, feverishly. As he wrote, the tears filled his eyes and spilled down his wrinkled cheeks.

The shower compound was at the end of the cellblock. Inside was a row of tin washbasins and a single concrete shower cubicle with four heads. They waited in line as other naked, emaciated prisoners vied for places under the meager trickles of lukewarm water. The young guard with the haunting blue eyes watched, tossing and catching a fifty kopeck piece. Then he turned the water off and ordered them to get dressed. An old woman orderly piled fresh dungarees and underwear on the floor for them and took their dirty clothes away. They dried with ragged towels, supplied by the guard from a locked cabinet, and took turns shaving over one of the washbasins with cold water, using a razor with a locked-in blade. Rhone's group started to get undressed as four more naked men moved into the shower ahead of them. As the Ingush stripped off his undervest, Rhone started.

Tattooed on his broad muscular back was a portrait, three times bigger than life, of the smiling moustached face of Joseph Stalin.

Back in the cell Gertsenberg climbed onto his bunk, opened the book, and took out the two pages of stationery, now covered on both sides in a fine cyrillic hand. Ivanov watched curiously as he somberly read them over, then folded them and slipped them back into the book. He closed it and lay it aside. He looked up, his eyes briefly meeting Rhone's. He looked away. Then he looked back again. They stared at one another in silence for several seconds. Rhone lit the last of the Astras the Colonel had given him. Gertsenberg sighed. He climbed down from his bunk, walked over to the table, and leaned over to whisper something in the Ingush's ear.

The Ingush looked up and spoke unintelligibly. Gertsenberg nodded and walked back to his bunk. He climbed laboriously up. The Ingush looked at Rhone, that same balancing, searching look, then returned his eyes to the chessboard.

Rhone finished the Astra. Ivanov was watching him like a vulture. He handed Ivanov the half-inch butt. Oblivious to the burning of his fingers, the big man took several rapid drags, then crumbled the last bit of tobacco into his dwindling supply of Mahorka.

"There is a tradition," the Ingush said to Rhone after they'd finished their evening rations. "A man can discuss anything but the circumstances of his own arrest. But I want you to tell me, Andrei Davilov, how you were arrested and why."

Rhone, glancing over at Gertsenberg first, began. The Ingush listened in attentive silence until he had finished. Then, for a long time, he stared at him, weighing and balancing. Rhone dropped down from his bunk, walked over to the table, and leaned over him. "At least that is the story," he whispered, "as Colonel Ilin now sees it."

A faint smile crossed the Ingush's wrinkled, leathery face. He nodded at the chair across from him and Rhone sat down.

The Ingush leaned forward over the table and spoke in a whisper. "So tell me. Why do you wish to contact this other prisoner?"

Rhone glanced at Ivanov. "It's personal."

"That is not enough."

"I have a message from the outside." He hesitated. Ivanov was straining so hard his ears twitched, but from the look on his face Rhone could see he could hear nothing.

In the Ingush's eyes the balance tilted back and forth. "A message is not so difficult. It has to pass through a few hands, but it will eventually reach its destination."

"No. It can't pass through any hands. I have to give it to him personally."

"That is more difficult. I think the only possibility is the infirmary. I have heard on the grapevine that Alexander Terekhov is very ill."

"Can he get himself transferred there? Can you get word to him to try?"

"He should *be* in the infirmary. He has tuberculosis. But to get there he would have to give something up."

"What?"

"Something of whatever he's managed to hold back. Perhaps only a scrap of pride. You are a different matter. You are scheduled for public trial. So it will not be so difficult."

"And getting word to him?"

"It is possible. But you must give him a reason to believe it is important."

Ivanov, though he made a point of not looking in their direction, could hardly sit still.

"Gorky Park," Rhone said. "June 1974. He'll understand."

It meant nothing to Rhone, but Remick had assured him that was all the introduction he would need.

Ivanov could stand no more. He rose suddenly and stalked past the table to the door, turned and stood staring down at them in seething rage. The Ingush looked back down at his chessboard. His concentration seemed to close out or negate the rest of the world around him. Finally the giant walked back past the table and sat down again on his bunk. The guard rapped on the door and announced bed call. The Ingush glanced briefly at Rhone, a twinkle in his eye.

Crawling beneath his blanket, Rhone remembered his history. Stalin had deported the entire Chechen-Ingush nation in 1944 for their desire to collaborate with the Germans, whose invasion had already been stopped nearly a hundred miles short of their northern Caucasus homeland. They had never returned, never been reunited. As he drifted off to sleep, Rhone wondered what kind of man wore a portrait of Stalin on his back, and what stories the Ingush could have told. And remembered the day in 1947 when his father had taken him to the Kremlin to see the man with the moustache for himself.

12

They were stopped by the guards at the Troitskaya Gate.
After a phone call they were waved through. His father held
him in his lap in the back of the big Zis. On the other side the
ambassador. They stopped again in front of the palace and the
driver opened the door for them. He recognized him when they
started up the steps, from a newsreel, in his brown uniform
with all his ribbons and medals. His eyes were dark, shining;
when he smiled they were almost lost in the wrinkles that sur-
rounded them. He shook hands with the Ambassador and then
with Rhone's father but all the time he was looking down at
Rhone. His father said, "This is my son, Edward." Then he told
him who he was. The old man bent down and said in Russian,
"Come to Grandpa." He picked him up and held him before his
wrinkled face with the eyes almost lost in the smile. His mous-
tache was bushy and his breath smelled like onions. His smile
became a laugh. And there on the steps of the Kremlin palace
Joseph Stalin pitched Edward Rhone up in the air, and caught
him and pitched him and caught him and pitched him. . . .

He opened his eyes. It was half dream, half conscious recol-
lection. He could hear Ivanov laboriously snoring below. He
listened to the footsteps of the guard. The peephole opened and
closed and the footsteps moved on down the hall, away into si-

lence. He lay still, staring up at the bright white ceiling. He rolled on his side and peered down over the cell. The Ingush was sitting up on his bunk. He held a stubby pencil in his thick hand and scribbled something onto a scrap of *Pravda* from the latrine bucket.

After morning reveille they were marched single file to the latrine, next to the showers at the end of the cellblock. The Ingush led with the bucket, dumping it and passing it back. The stench was nauseating. One by one they took their turns over the hole.

Back in the cell there was nothing to do but wait for morning rations. It was the longest two hours of the day. Gertsenberg opened his book and took out the two pages of stationery and began to read over what he'd written. His lips voiced each word silently. After a moment Rhone realized he was repeating the lines, over and over, memorizing.

They heard the clang of the cellblock door, the creaking wheels of the mess cart. The Ingush took his place at the door. When it opened, an old gray-bearded orderly looked in. Rhone saw the brief glance between the Ingush and the old man. The guard, standing just beside the door, tossed and caught his coin, seeing nothing. Rhone observed the careful motions with which each loaf of bread was passed between them. When the mess cart returned it was the Ingush who gathered the empty bowls and passed them back out, with the same precise deliberation.

The mess cart rolled on. The guard closed the door. When the Ingush turned back his eyes met Rhone's. They flicked from side to side, with the merest suggestion of a negative shake of the head.

After the midday cup of broth was delivered, he gave Rhone the same negative signal. And again after evening rations. Rations the following morning were delivered by the flat-faced Mongol. He regarded the Ingush with no sign of recognition. The guard watched them carefully, hovering. The Ingush passed the bowls back one at a time, to Ivanov, Gertsenberg, and Rhone. He took the fourth bowl for himself and started to turn. It slipped through his hands and clattered on the floor. The Mongol cursed and the guard cursed. The Ingush dropped to his knees in the doorway and tried frantically to slosh the thin soup back into the bowl. But it was almost all liquid. He asked for more. The guard shouted for the Mongol to move on. He handed the four soggy brown loaves past the Ingush to Ivanov, sloshed another ladle of soup into the bowl and moved away, pushing the mess cart before him. The guard glowered into the cell and jerked the door shut. When the Ingush turned back to the table, the vertical bob of his eyeballs in the affirmative was so subtle Rhone almost missed it.

Though it was only mid-afternoon the sky through the high barred windows was dark as at the crucifixion. Valeri Pavlovich Ilin drank his brandy and wondered if *that* could have really happened. He contemplated the outrageous circumstance: that he could have become a Chekist. Not by choice and not against his will either, merely a turn in the road of his life that he had not resisted and hardly regretted either. Just the dreamer in him who thought he should have made a choice. He was quite drunk, he realized. Boris, in his drab suit and button-down Polish shirt, observed disapprovingly as he refilled the glass. At the other end of the table, Ivan Ivanovich Ivanov licked his lips as he raised it. Ilin drank and lowered the glass and slid it toward him.

Ivanov caught it and, at the colonel's nod, eagerly drank what remained.

Ilin took out the bag of Mahorka he'd had Boris bring from the commissary and slid it toward him. "We are both Chekist, you and I," he said with a smile. In the eyes of the big Russian bear not a glimmer of comprehension. But it was true, the colonel thought, and in the case of Ivanov due to circumstances far more outrageous than his own. And Andrei Davilov, what circumstance or choice had brought *him* here, made him who and what he was, whoever he was, whatever he was?

"Now tell me, Ivan Ivanovich," he said when the stoolie had

finished rolling the smoke, "everything you can tell me about the new man in your cell."

At midnight the halls of the inner prison seemed hallowed and quiet as a cathedral. Their boot heels echoed like blasphemy. Lenin. To name a Russian child Vladimir Ilich would be like naming an American baby Jesus Christ. The colonel had a hangover. Headache. Sour stomach. Bowels rumbling like a dysenteric prisoner's.

At the cellblock door a guard turned a key in the lock. The unarmed guard inside met them and led them along the bullwalk. He stopped at the door. Ilin eased the shutter silently aside and peered into the cell. The four of them slept on their bunks in the glare of bright light, the cacophony of snoring. He stepped back and nodded at the cellblock guard, who unlocked it silently with his key.

The colonel kicked the door open and two of the guards rushed through. On his upper bunk Gertsenberg sat up, blinking. On the lower bunks Ivanov and the Ingush struggled into their dungarees. Davilov pulled his blanket up over his head. One of the guards struck him at the base of his spine and he threw the blanket off and dropped down. Gertsenberg and Ivanov let themselves be hustled through the door past Vladimir the Ingush, who stood looking back at Davilov. One of the guards gave Davilov a shove and he stumbled into the table and sent the chess pieces flying. The Colonel caught his brush contact with the Ingush as he came through the door. Ilin shoved past Davilov toward the Ingush, who'd dropped to his hands and knees and was pawing about for the chess pieces on the floor, and sent a kick to his belly that half flipped him to his back. As the Ingush scrambled up, Ilin caught both his wrists and held them until he opened his hands.

They were empty.

The two guards on the bullwalk lined them up. They started with Davilov. The Colonel stood aside and watched. One guard in front of Davilov, one behind him, they felt up his thighs, up his torso, around the waist of his underwear, inside the sleeveless undervest. They opened his mouth and looked inside. One of them took his hands, checked the back of each of them, then the palms, spread the fingers, and checked between them.

They repeated the process with Ivanov and Gertsenberg, then moved on to the Ingush. The colonel saw Davilov watching out of the corner of his eye as they searched up and down his body, inside his underwear, inside his mouth, in his hands, which Ilin already knew were empty.

Inside the cell one guard was tearing the padding out of the hole in the end of Davilov's mattress. Another found the pen Ivanov had told him about under the end of Gertsenberg's mattress and held it up triumphantly. Ilin dismissed it with a nod. They had finished with the body searches on the bullwalk. They had finished inside the cell. After all the bustle and racket it was as if the driving spring had wound down, to stillness or slow motion. Ilin walked restlessly back and forth before the four men. He looked each of them over, looked into each of their eyes. He entered the cell, littered with their scattered pillows and blankets and mattresses, the padding from Davilov's mutilated mattress, the chess pieces.

He stooped and picked up a black knight, examined it briefly, and placed it on the chessboard. He walked over and lifted the lid of the latrine bucket, holding his breath against the stench, and peered inside. A Lubyanka wishing well. He picked up Gertsenberg's prison library edition of *A Year in the Motherland* and thumbed casually through, pausing now and again to read a few lines.

He glanced up at the Jew, whose face was beaded with sweat, turned a few more pages of the book, and found the two sheets of stationery, written over on both sides as Ivanov had told him, and began to read. After a moment he stopped, folded them, and stuffed them into his uniform pocket.

He strode through the door and stopped directly before the Jew, who was visibly trembling. "You are a madman, Grigori Mikhailovich," he said after a moment.

He ordered the guards to return the prisoners to the cell. After the door had been locked he motioned them away down

101

the bullwalk. Listening to the click of their heels, he stooped and, easing the shutter aside, peered through.

Davilov had gathered up his mattress stuffing and was pushing it back through the tear in the end. The Ingush was gathering his chess pieces from the floor. Ivanov replaced his mattress on his bunk and slid beneath the blanket. Gertsenberg merely stood at the end of his bunk, staring blankly at the door. His face was ghostly pale and he was shaking, shaking all over as though it derived from some great cataclysmic inner palpitation.

Andrei Davilov picked up Gertsenberg's mattress and laid it on his bunk for him, then retrieved his pillow and blanket. He helped him gently up onto his bunk and laid his blanket over him, then climbed onto his own bunk and pulled the blanket over his shoulders. As he let the shutter slide closed, Ilin heard the Jew weeping softly on his pillow. He walked away down the bullwalk.

Back in his office, he took out the stationery and read Gertsenberg's statement over carefully. It was not what he'd been looking for. He had not found what he looked for, had not known what he looked for.

What he had found, he was sorry he had ever seen.

They heard the cellblock door open and close, in a moment the squeak of the mess cart. The guard looked in through the peephole and opened the door. Pushing the cart, the same flat-faced Mongol. The Ingush was already at his place. He took the four bowls of gruel and passed them back one at a time. Then the bread. Gertsenberg, Rhone noticed, accepted his without the customary ritualistic weighing in the hand. The guard closed the door and the cart squeaked on. The Ingush looked at Rhone and shrugged almost imperceptibly. Rhone sat down at the table across from him. They ate in reverent silence.

The orderly had just come back and taken the bowls when they heard the key turn again in the lock. Rhone saw Gertsenberg's face pale. "Ivanov! Upstairs for interrogation."

The big man rose, crossed his hands behind his back and walked out. The door was pulled shut behind him. Gertsenberg

102

sighed. His emaciated body seemed to sag, as though last night the life force had almost seeped out of it. He climbed shakily onto his bunk and leaned his back against the wall, staring blankly away.

"What they found," the Ingush said, nodding at the Jew, "was not what the *nasedka* had them looking for."

The cellblock door opened again. Gertsenberg's eyes widened and again he shook as though from violent palpitations within. They heard boots on the parquet walk, drawing closer, stopping outside the cell. The key turned in the lock and the door opened. Framed in it was Colonel Ilin. Gertsenberg stared at him, shaking. With a deliberate downward flapping of his thick fingers, Ilin motioned him out. "Come, Grigori Mikhailovich."

"Where?"

"Away."

He hesitated, lingering on his bunk. Then his shaking ceased. He calmed himself and lowered himself to the floor, and as he walked out the door it was even with a certain dignity and poise.

"Where will they take him?" Rhone asked the Ingush after they were gone.

"I do not know. But it is a bad sign that the colonel came for him himself." He took his half loaf of bread over and slipped it beneath his mattress, then resumed his seat at the table. He removed the black king from the chessboard and twisted the base, which proved to be a hollow screw. When the base separated from the figure, Rhone saw the tip of the rolled-up photograph protruding from the opening. The Ingush took it out, folded it open on the table, looked at the picture carefully, and then looked at Rhone's face.

Rhone picked up the photo, walked over, and replaced it in the hole in the end of the mattress.

"How old do you think I am?" the Ingush asked after he'd returned to the table.

"I don't know. Fifty. A hundred."

"I was twenty-one in 1944, when the man with the moustache deported us to central Asia."

"Where did you get the tattoo?"

"In Alma Ata, in 1948."

"Why did you get it?"

He shrugged. "It appeared that I would spend the rest of my life in the camps. They said he was the greatest Stalin tattoo artist in the Gulag." He paused. "You should hide the photograph outside the cell, somewhere in the office of your interrogator. Then you can always get yourself taken there when you are ready to retrieve it." He leaned forward. "Are you also going to have a photograph of Alexander Terekhov?"

Rhone stared silently back.

"You came in for him, didn't you? I am helping you, so do not lie to me. The Yaroshenko affair was just a means to get you in here. And now you intend to get Terekhov out. But you couldn't have engineered Yaroshenko's arrest without help from outside Russia, which means you probably have a way to get him *out* of Russia." He was briefly silent, weighing Rhone with his penetrating eyes. "I do not deceive myself. Whether they hang me or not, my next sentence will be my last. . . ."

"Don't say it." Rhone rose abruptly, stepped to his bunk, and removed the photo section from his mattress. He slipped it into his left boot, and walked over to the door. When he heard the peephole shutter open, he knocked.

Ilin had just finished making himself a cup of coffee when Rhone was led in. "You have something to say to me, Andrei Petrovich?"

"Gertsenberg."

"Gertsenberg?"

Rhone sat down at the table, crossed his left leg over his right and removed the photo section from his boot. "I want to know what you have done with him."

"You are making a joke?"

"No, Comrade Colonel. I am making no joke." He reached up beneath the table and felt along the under edge until he found the cross-brace that supported the leg.

"You worry about yourself and forget that fucking Yid!" the colonel exploded, bolting up from his chair and jerking open the drawer at the end of the table.

Rhone slipped the picture into the thin crack between the top end of the leg and the under-surface of the table. Ilin produced a thick folder and came stalking down alongside the table toward him. He opened the folder and took out the two pages of stationery with Gertsenberg's writing and threw them down onto the table.

Rhone leaned over, squinting to read the tiny hand. It was in the form of an open letter, addressed to the highest court of the Supreme Soviet. Written eloquently, it stated that the author had devoted a number of years of his life working toward an increase of personal liberty within the Soviet Union, and briefly described the fundamental idea behind the formation of the Helsinki Monitoring Group, of which he admitted being a member. He admitted that he had violated certain statutes and stated that he did not deny a certain amount of illegal activity. He said he was prepared to face whatever prison sentence was given him, that he'd known from the beginning that this was the likely consequence of his actions. He reaffirmed his Russian patriotism, then recounted his interrogation, his eventual confession, his perhaps inadvertent implication of others less guilty than himself and, finally, his shame when, under torture, he'd been reduced to admitting his remorse for his actions. *"My only remorse,"* the paper concluded, *"is for the continued suffering of my people, not only the Jews, but all the great long-suffering people of this great, misdirected nation. My confession you may have but my remorse, I recant. I recant."*

"He is a madman if he thinks he will be allowed to say that before the highest court of the Supreme Soviet."

"So what will happen to him?" Rhone asked.

Ilin picked up the papers and walked back to the head of the table. "That is still under consideration. He is in a solitary cell until I make up my mind. But I will tell you, Andrei Davilov, that there are worse places than the Lubyanka. There are worse fates than a sentence to the camps." He paused. "But perhaps you would like to help him?"

"How could I help him?"

"You could tell me what you and he and Vladimir the Ingush have been whispering about for the last few days."

105

"Bastards."

"What?"

"Bastards, Colonel. We've been whispering about the rotten bastards we've known in this world."

The colonel clapped his hands angrily. Boris appeared at the door and Ilin ordered Rhone to be taken out.

After the prisoner was gone Ilin sat back down and looked the Gertsenberg statement over one last time. What he had to do now filled him with sadness. But he'd known the moment he found it that he would really have no choice. And what choice he could have had he'd given up by showing the papers to Andrei Davilov.

He poured himself a stiff shot of brandy, drank it in a gulp, put the papers in his pocket, and went out. He took the elevator down to the third floor and knocked on the door of General Drachinsky's office.

An aide let him in and said the general was performing his morning toilet and would be out in a moment. Ilin spread the two sheets of paper on the desk and took a seat on the sofa.

13

Noon rations were cancelled. After the same flat-faced Mongol delivered their evening gruel and was gone, the Ingush turned to Rhone and nodded.

"He entered this morning," he whispered after Ivanov had taken his own bowl and sat down on his bunk.

They ate in silence. The door opened and the Mongol took the empty bowls. The Ingush reached into the left leg of his dungarees and produced a needle which had been inserted into the thick material of the cuff. He unraveled a piece of thread from above the cuff and inserted it into the eye of the needle, then took the loose end of the thread and ran it through his crooked brown teeth, working it back and forth like dental floss. When he handed it to Rhone the thread was coated with plaque.

"Through the skin, to leave the plaque inside," he whispered. "It's an old camp trick, but unless they want to see you die of gangrene there is nothing they can do but treat it."

Rhone waited until he'd heard the peephole shutter open and close, then climbed onto his bunk. He pulled the dungaree trouser and the long underwear up his left leg and pinched up the skin on his shin, just below the knee. The Ingush watched him from the table but Ivanov, still sulking on his lower bunk, was oblivious. He inserted the needle into the one layer of skin and forced the point out the other. He seized it and drew the thread slowly through. It did not hurt much and there was only a little blood. When he pulled the loose end of the thread out he could see he'd left all the plaque under his skin.

Rhone lay shivering on his bunk. There was a pounding on the door but it sounded far away. When he opened his eyes he saw it was the Ingush, in his underwear, pounding from within. Ivanov, also in his underwear, stood beside his bunk, looking at Rhone with sleep-swollen eyes.

"I have told you," said a voice outside the door. "He can see a doctor in the morning."

The shutter closed and the Ingush resumed his pounding. The guard came back and opened the door. Big and broad-shouldered, he appeared to Rhone as if seen at a great distance through shimmering water.

"He is scheduled for public trial," said the Ingush. "Do you want it on your record if he appears with one leg before the Supreme Court of the Soviet Union."

He brushed past Ivanov and pulled the blanket down off Rhone's swollen leg. The guard came in and looked and went back out.

Rhone slept again. It seemed like hours. He dreamed he was far away, but when he awoke nothing in the room had changed. The Ingush was back at the door and Ivanov still stood beside his bunk, rolling a Mahorka.

He slept. The next time he woke he was in a ward. Two rows of cots lined the walls, with an aisle between them. Patients in white gowns, sleeping or talking, ranting in feverish delirium or slowly dying of their racking, tubercular coughs. He slept and woke. It was a big white hall with a guard table and a single guard at the door. There was a needle in his arm with a tube leading to a bottle of fluid hanging from a rack by the cot. He pulled the blanket aside. His leg was still there, now heavily bandaged.

He looked up and down the two rows of cots. He couldn't see

Terekhov but at the far end of the ward, away from the guard table, a single cot was isolated behind two portable shades.

The next time he woke, the ward was dark and silent. A single small bulb burned above the door. The guard, a fat Armenian with a drooping moustache, had a magazine spread open before him on the table but his eyelids were already closing. Half an hour later he was sleeping face down on the pages.

Rhone extracted the intravenous needle from his arm and tied off the tube. He slipped from beneath the blanket and sat up on the edge of the cot. After a moment he stood and tested the knee. He turned his pillow longways and slipped the tube beneath it, then pulled the blanket all the way up over it. He looked at the guard, snoring peacefully, and tiptoed down the aisle toward the back of the ward.

Alexander Terekhov opened his eyes as Rhone stepped behind the shade. He lay still for a moment, looking up at him without fear, almost without curiosity. In Staffordshire Rhone had studied films of him, tall and handsome in spite of his age, broad-shouldered and imposing, the kind of man who had a way of filling a room when he entered it. And before him now lay a pale, emaciated shadow of that figure, gasping for his breath, pungent with the night-sweat in which he bathed. Of his former self only the eyes remained the same, bright and clear, shining out of his fever.

"I sent you the message," Rhone whispered.

"You have word from Erich Reisinger?"

"I was sent to get you out."

Terekhov was racked by a fit of coughing. After he'd controlled it, a faint smile flickered on his lips. "Get me out? Is it as simple as all that?"

"No. But it is possible."

"The Americans sent you?"

Rhone nodded.

"What makes you so certain I will be willing to risk escape?"

Rhone peered around the edge of the partition. The Armenian shifted in his chair but did not raise his head. He turned back to Terekhov and said gently, "My orders are not to leave you here alive." Terekhov said nothing, so after a moment he continued: "I'll come for you in a week or so, after you've been returned to a solitary cell."

"You have threatened to kill me," Terekhov said calmly. "How do you know I won't report you?"

"If you report me, the KGB won't stop until they find out why the other side can't afford to leave you here alive."

It was a guess, but from the look on Terekhov's face he could see he'd guessed right. They heard footsteps, a matron making her way slowly down the aisle. Silently they waited and listened. The footsteps stopped just on the other side of the curtain. They looked at her silhouette, and intently at each other. After a moment, the footsteps moved away, back up the aisle, growing gradually softer, finally silent.

"Do you really think it is possible for us to get out of this place?" Terekhov asked him softly.

"Yes." Rhone peered around the shade. The guard had woken. His chin was propped on his hands, his elbows propped on the table. Very slowly they were sliding apart and he was slumping back toward the table.

"They are returning me to my cell tomorrow," Terekhov said when Rhone turned back to him. "D-block, the ground floor, number twenty-seven."

"And the name of your interrogator?"

"Colonel Moiseyevaite."

"How often does he call you out of your cell?"

"Almost every night."

"After bed call?"

"Yes. Usually after I've fallen asleep." Terekhov paused. "If we do get out, what then?"

"Passage out of Russia has already been arranged. You'll know the rest when we get to Helsinki."

A light shone in Terekhov's eyes. Rhone managed a smile, reached down, and touched his shoulder. Then he left him, staring off into the unfocused distance as if he could see the whole world through the walls. On the nearest cot a prisoner even older and worse off than Terekhov stared at the ceiling with bulging eyes. But the guard was still sound asleep on the table.

He tiptoed back to the cot and got beneath the blanket, and hooked himself back up to the intravenous fluid. He was so hungry he found it almost impossible to sleep, and when finally he did drift off, his dreams were haunted by the vision of Alexander Terekhov's shining eyes.

The young guard with the haunting blue eyes, whistling the theme from *Swan Lake*, bounced on his toes along the bullwalk, tossing and catching his fifty-kopeck piece. Limping slightly, Rhone followed. They stopped outside the cell and the guard unlocked the door.

The Ingush sat alone at the chess table. Rhone entered and sat down across from him. "Ivanov?"

"Summoned for interrogation. You have seen Terekhov?"

"Yes."

"Now you will get yourself transferred back to solitary?"

"Yes."

There was a brief and baited silence.

"I still don't see how you intend to do it," the Ingush said finally.

"You already see too much."

Again they were silent, each staring into the other's eyes. The Ingush glanced at the peephole, reached into the left leg of his dungarees, drew out a crude prison-made knife, and started cleaning his fingernails. Then they both heard footsteps and he slipped it back up his leg.

The peephole opened and closed and the key turned in the lock. Ivanov came through the door and the guard pulled it shut behind him. The big Russian walked over and sat down on his bunk and started to roll a Mahorka.

"Gertsenberg?" Rhone asked.

The Ingush shook his head.

"Gertsenberg?" said Ivanov. "I can tell you about Gertsenberg."

The Ingush glared at him. "Where is he, Ivanov?"

111

"He is in Chernyakhovsk. He was transferred there two days ago."

Rhone looked at the Ingush.

"A special prison hospital. For the criminally insane."

The Ingush was still glaring at Ivanov, whose whole enormous body shook in spasms. "Even the sane go crazy at Chernyakhovsk." It was laughter, but that mad kind of laughter that lay just on the edge of the fine line between humor and despair.

A light snow was falling. A bundled guard escorted them to one of the smaller exercise pens and went over and stood in the corner beneath the gun tower. Rhone and the Ingush left Ivanov, lingering just inside the gate, and walked across the enclosure toward the opposite wall. White crystals of snow caught in the short man's matted hair.

"I'll be back in solitary by tonight," Rhone told him. "A week from now I'll either be dead or far from the Lubyanka."

"How will you get yourself transferred?"

"I'll send word to Ilin that I'm withdrawing my testimony against Yaroshenko."

Rhone turned his back to the guard tower and extended his hand. Absently the Ingush took it, staring past him. Rhone looked around at the giant ogre Ivanov, standing alone in the falling snow in the center of the yard, trying even now to eavesdrop.

He looked back at the Ingush.

"You don't live thirty years in the camps by always doing what is honorable," said the little man thoughtfully. "But I have a better way, for all of us to get back to solitary."

He pushed suddenly past him. Rhone turned, staring after him. The Ingush made a motion of hitching up his trousers beneath his ill-fitting greatcoat, and walked swiftly toward the big Russian standing like a statue in the middle of the open yard. Ivanov watched his approach with a frown. Though it was only fifteen feet it seemed to Rhone that it took him a very long time to get there; it seemed that on the Russian's ruddy

112

face, where the bewilderment turned gradually to surprise and the surprise became alarm, there was hint enough for him to divine the what and the why of it all.

Ivanov reached out instinctively to fend him off. The Ingush walked straight up to him, veering half a step at the last moment, brushed by him and continued on his way as though it had been no more than a brush against a stranger on a crowded sidewalk. Ivanov pivoted slowly, his mouth open wide though no sound came forth, both hands clutched across his belly, where the blood oozed and bubbled out between the fingers around the handle of the knife. He stared unbelieving after the Ingush, who had not looked back, who walked straight on as though nothing at all had happened, toward the little arched gate with the tower rising up behind it. On the tower the guards swung their machine guns across the yard. Rhone hit the snow. A bellow rose to Ivanov's lips, Ivanov still clutching at the knife stuck up beneath his ribs, which Rhone knew the Ingush must originally have intended as a defense against him.

The rapid blast of automatic rifle fire must have sounded like a jackhammer on the streets of Moscow below. The giant Russian jerked grotesquely, staggering backwards to the wall where, pinned temporarily on his feet, he continued the convulsions until the firing ceased, then sank down in a massive bloody heap in the snow.

And Vladimir the Ingush, who'd walked just beneath the line of fire all the way without ever ducking his head, passed the immobilized guard still standing in the corner below the tower and disappeared through the arched gate.

Rhone waited unmoving on his belly in the snow. Two armed guards entered the yard and warily approached him. One of them pulled his hands behind his back and slapped a pair of cuffs on his wrists. They jerked him to his feet and marched him back to the elevator, where waited another guard who delivered him below, still handcuffed, to a tiny, unfurnished box. An hour later he was moved to a cellblock on the second or third floor and locked, after the handcuffs had been removed, in a solitary cell with a chair, a table, an iron bunk, and a shitcan.

Standard solitary rations were served at six. He waited for the summons to his inevitable interrogation about the death of the *nasedka,* but the next knock on the door was the guard announcing bed call.

He took off his dungarees and got beneath the covers. He lay awake for a long time. It seemed he'd just drifted off when the door opened.

"On your feet! Get dressed!"

He pulled on his dungarees and laceless boots, crossed his hands behind his back and stepped out onto the hall. He stared automatically toward the cellblock door.

"No," the guard said. "This way."

He marched him back along the walk and into the showers. Utterly confused, Rhone undressed and stepped beneath the head. Afterward he shaved with a locking razor with a dull blade and put his underwear and dungarees back on. The guard put a pair of cuffs on his hands and marched him toward the door.

Two armed guards were waiting outside. From the bustle in the corridor he judged it must be midnight, the shift-change. They walked him along the passage, past the elevator where a crowd of guards were waiting, and down a stone staircase to another winding corridor, also bustling with guards. They turned to the right onto a straight corridor which he now remembered from the night he'd first entered the prison, past a crowded locker room and a red painted sign that said *North Exit,* toward an open set of heavy steel doors, where a line of bundled guards with passes in their hands moved in single file past the table.

One of Rhone's escorts shouted an order and the way was cleared for them. Their passes and an official paper pertaining to Rhone were checked. They passed through a second set of doors and emerged onto the courtyard, where a Zil limousine with curtained windows waited.

A driver opened the back door and the guards hustled him

inside. Seated opposite, an angry scowl on his face, was Colonel Ilin.

The driver got in and started the motor. They pulled through the iron gate, out into Dzerzhinsky Square.

"Where are we going?" Rhone asked him.

Ilin stared at him in angry silence. Finally he sighed. "To the Supreme Court of the Soviet Union. Yaroshenko has withdrawn his confession. You will be tried in camera. Tomorrow morning."

14

Rhone stood in the dock in his ill-fitting suit. On the other side of the guard Yaroshenko, looking confident, almost defiant, regarded him with an occasional ironic smile. Two older military judges sat on either side of a younger civilian on the bench, behind them an enormous hammer and sickle flag. At a long desk below the bench and just in front of the rows of empty pews sat Rhone's court-appointed attorney and the attorney for Yaroshenko. At an identical desk opposite sat the fat prosecutor Zverev and his two assistants. There was but a single observer. Colonel Ilin, in the first pew, looked very much alone.

"Tell the court why you returned to Moscow," one of the prosecutors was saying.

"Ostensibly to visit my sister, though actually I was carrying out an assignment for an American I knew as Ross who claimed to be a businessman."

"You say *claimed* to be. Did you actually believe he was a businessman?"

"No. I made the logical assumption he was a member of the American intelligence service."

The prosecutor produced a photograph of Remick, which Rhone identified as the man he worked for. Zverev identified

Remick for the court. Rhone's attorney suppressed a yawn.

"What was your assignment?" asked Zverev.

"I was to transfer a microfilm capsule from a Russian contact to a contact in the American Embassy here."

"Name your Russian contact."

"Lieutenant Colonel Vasily Yemelyanovich Yaroshenko gave me the capsule." He nodded down the dock.

Zverev nodded at the judges.

"Does the defendant wish to cross-examine?" the civilian judge asked Yaroshenko.

He said he did and looked again at Rhone with his ironic smile. "What is your name?"

"My name is Andrei Petrovich Davilov."

"Are you sure?"

"Of course I am sure."

Yaroshenko regarded him skeptically. Some color had returned to his cheeks and he appeared to have been on increased rations since Rhone had last seen him in the Lubyanka. Colonel Ilin observed with a frown from his place alone on the pew. After an extended silence, Yaroshenko turned back to the judges. "I have no further questions, Your Honors. But I submit that this defendant is not who he claims to be."

"Your Honors," said Rhone's attorney, rising. "If the man in that dock is not the man he claims to be, then he does not even belong as co-defendant in this trial."

The civilian judge pondered this logic for a moment and looked back at Yaroshenko. "Who is he, if he is not Andrei Davilov?"

Ilin had taken out his handkerchief and was carefully dabbing at his brow.

"I do not know. I merely know that he is not Andrei Davilov, and I request that the court, and Colonel Ilin, take note of what I have said." He regarded Ilin briefly, and looked back at the judges. "Someday you will all regret letting expedience deter you from seeking out the truth."

He smiled the same ironic smile, this time for the judges.

They were out for thirty minutes. One of the military men

read the espionage and treason charges against Yaroshenko. Expressionless, he listened to the sentence that he be shot.

"Andrei Petrovich Davilov. To the charge of espionage on the soil of the Soviet Union, in the employ of a foreign government, this court finds you guilty and sentences you to a term of three years in prison and ten years in a strict regime corrective labor camp." The judge paused. "Three years prison sentence is suspended in consideration of testimony and cooperation of the defendant."

Yaroshenko smiled. Ilin was already on his way up the aisle between the pews. A guard pulled Rhone's hands behind his back and snapped on a pair of cuffs. He was marched out, down a corridor to the courtyard. The same Zil limousine was waiting, standing outside it two civilian KGB men. They put him in the back seat, between them. The driver got into the front and it pulled out through the gate.

They'd driven but a few blocks before he realized they were not going in the direction of the Lubyanka. As he picked up landmarks through the front windshield, the grim realization crept over him. Somehow, during the entire comedy of the trial, this possibility had never occurred to him.

"Where are we going?"

They were silent.

Moments later the chauffeur brought the Zil to a stop outside Yaroslavl Station. Still handcuffed, Rhone was helped from the limousine. The chauffeur opened the trunk and took out a large cardboard box tied up with a string. They marched him into the bustling station, where the people took but furtive notice of his handcuffs and his grim-looking escorts. They boarded the train and entered an empty compartment. The chauffeur deposited the box on the floor and left. Moments later the train pulled out of the station.

One of the KGB men met Rhone's eye. "The far north," he said in belated reply to the question asked a quarter of an hour before. "Archangel."

Boris was waiting for him in the limousine when Ilin emerged from the court. "Back to the Lubyanka, Comrade?"

"No," Ilin sighed. "Take me back to my apartment." It had been four days since he'd been there.

He changed his mind as they were driving past the Kremlin. He told Boris to make the turn and asked him to park and wait across the street from the café. It had begun to snow and though it was not yet 5 p.m., the street lights had already come up. At this time of day there was no line.

Inside he took his coat off and sat alone at one of the marble tables. The place was half full but Alisa Belova was nowhere to be seen. Not that he'd had any real reason to expect he'd find her there now. He ordered a brandy, drank it hurriedly, and left.

Boris was running the heater off the idling engine, and the limousine, when he got back inside it, was like an oven after the cold of the street.

He saw Katusha's face in the third floor window when they stopped outside the apartment building at the end of Gorky Street. Boris got out and opened the door for him.

"I will see you tomorrow?"

"No," he told him. "Take a holiday tomorrow. I am going with my wife to the dacha."

He took the elevator up. Buxom and tall, she was waiting in the open door at the end of the hall when he emerged. She beamed, but he could see from the red in her eyes that not long ago she'd been crying.

She put her arms around him and he kissed her on the cheek. She whispered in his ear how lonely she had been. "You will be home for some time now?"

"Yes. I think so." But in the back of his mind was a gnawing dread. Andrei Petrovich Davilov. Valeri Pavlovich Ilin. Lubyanka. It was over. He hugged Katusha and hoped to Lenin, if there was a Lenin, it was over.

15

Archangel, November 1978

Half a mile past the mess tent the road abruptly ended. A crane was ensconced on a flat place on the incline. Farther down, a temporary supply shack had been constructed of wood and corrugated tin. A crude logging trail weaved out over the desolated field of stumps and disappeared three quarters of a mile on into a forest of uncut fir.

It was morning twilight, his second full day in camp.

A caterpillar dragged three heavy timbers up the trail toward the crane. In the edge of the standing forest a tall fir crashed to the ground. Bundled men in ragged jackets or coats, pigskin caps, worn gloves, and rags bound over their faces, fanned out over the grade. At the supply shack he was issued a crowbar, a shovel, a set of three twenty foot cables each with a loop spliced into one end and a metal nub on the other, and a sliding bell in the middle. Carrying the tools over his shoulder and dragging the cables behind him, he trudged out across the devastated field, sinking in up to his knees in the deep snow, and found a felled, stripped bit of timber.

He plunged almost waist-deep into the drift above it and began to shovel away the loose snow. When he hit hard ice he

120

switched to the crowbar. Around him over the site the buzz of labor blended to a din, chainsaws and caterpillars, the creak of the crane, the softer swish of bucksaws and the tap of ax blades on frozen wood.

After he'd cleared an opening beneath the log he lay on his belly on the ice and thrust the nub-end of the cable through. He got up and leaned across the log to retrieve it and snapped it into the sliding bell. Then he picked up his tools and, dragging the two remaining cables behind him, moved off in search of another log. His wet trousers had frozen stiff and crackled as he walked.

The sun rose. By noon it was a red ball on the lip of the southern horizon. A soldier blew a whistle and they left their tools, formed up in their gangs, and trudged back up the road toward the mess tent. Inside, it was crowded and steamy. Several of the men moved to secure them an empty spot at one of the tables while the others pushed through the line to get the bowls of gruel. They all crowded in at the table. He reached into his coat and took out the half day's ration of soggy dark bread, then dug his wooden spoon from his boot. Now moving through the serving line was a tall gangling fellow with a long nose and the virtual absence of a chin. Rhone had noticed him that morning as they were formed up to be searched; he'd looked entirely out of place in the army of stooped and shuffling *zeks*. When their eyes had briefly met he'd smiled with a grim familiarity.

Tsvilko, seated opposite Rhone, looked back over his shoulder, following Rhone's gaze.

"Who is he?" Rhone asked when the gang boss turned back.

"The Australian? He was caught at Sheremetevo with a false-bottom suitcase and half a kilogram of Laotian heroin. He was on his way to London. He got five years but he has almost completed his term."

Rhone dunked his bread into the gruel and took a bite, chewing slowly, savoring its faintly fishy flavor. When he looked up again the tall fellow was standing on the opposite side of the table, smiling down at him. An old Tartar from another gang scraped his bowl clean and rose from the seat beside Tsvilko. Swiftly, though another man had been waiting for the place, the Australian slipped in, oblivious to the sudden tirade of Russian curses at his back.

"Mind if I join you, mate?"

Up and down the table heads turned at the English. Rhone merely frowned, looking at him blankly.

"Don't tell me you don't understand English," the Australian said with a broad smile. He held out his hand. "Jack Carruthers. Newcastle, now South Wales, Australia."

"Andrei Petrovich Davilov," Rhone said, hesitantly taking the hand. "Moscow."

"Ah!" Carruthers shook his head. "You may fool these bleeding Ruskies, but you don't fool Jack Carruthers." He took his bread ration out of his coat, tore off a piece, and stuffed it into his mouth. "Know how I knew?"

"How you knew what?" Rhone asked in Russian-accented English.

"That you weren't one of these Ruskies. I can see in your face you weren't cut out to suffer." He smiled again, immensely pleased with himself. "Fact is, when I first saw you this morning I had the feeling I *knew* you from someplace. But I'll write that off to familiarity, like it was two members of the same species meeting for the first time in an alien region where that species didn't grow. Had you figured for a Yank, which I guess in this godforsaken place is close enough for a digger. But suffering! The bloody Russians are *bred* for it. The Russians have been suffering for centuries, and don't tell me it's any different on the outside. Their middle name is *suffering*. Ivan Suffrovich Ivanov!"

He laughed aloud. All along the table the bewildered men watched and listened. One of the most reverent moments of the day had been violated by this mad barbarian who seemed more interested in talking than eating.

Two fences topped with barbed-wire ringed the perimeter, one fifty feet inside the other. From two opposite corners of the enclosure rose tall gun towers. A sign above the outer gate read:

Directly before the inner gate was a concrete and stone building with a sign over the entrance indicating it was the headquarters of the camp commandant. Behind this building stood the old stone punishment barracks, the BUR with its heavy barred windows, a prison within the prison. Opposite was the oblong mess hall and beyond, in rows, the two lines of uniform gray barracks. Bathed in artificial light, the entire compound appeared translucent in the falling snow.

Marched between the two soldiers, Rhone dragged his feet in the snow. He was exhausted from his labor, and after the initial shock of his trial, sentencing, and transfer to the camp, he'd drifted gradually into a state of numbness at the seeming sheer hopelessness of his situation. For the Lubyanka, horrible as it had been, was still a solid entity that he could understand, a prison of locked doors and cells and walls, where the boundaries between imprisonment and freedom were clearly defined and where his own special abilities might successfully have been exploited. But beyond these barbed-wire fences lay not freedom or salvation, but merely the seemingly endless frozen taiga that served far more proficiently than the fences and the guards and the dogs to contain the miserable little island inside.

At the commandant's headquarters they ascended the steps and went in. Seated behind the desk in the anteroom was a young, immaculately groomed MVD captain. Rhone took off his pigskin cap and heavy overcoat. The captain rose and knocked on a door. From behind it came a bellow. He opened the door and motioned Rhone through.

Seated behind a desk inside the broiling office was a massive man wearing the insignia of a major in the MVD and a name tag which said *Senchenko*. He appeared to be in his fifties, with a dark complexion and a bushy black moustache. Something in his heavy-jowled face appeared out of proportion; it took Rhone a couple of seconds to pinpoint it as his left eyelid, which drooped.

"You have enjoyed your first week in camp?" The Commandant regarded Rhone with a scowl, then shuffled through some papers on his desk. "Davilov ... Andrei Petrovich," he read aloud. "Espionage on the soil of the Soviet Union in the employ of a foreign government." He scanned down the page. "Three years prison. Ten years corrective labor. Prison sentence suspended in consideration of defendant's testimony and cooperation."

He rose and came around the table and stopped directly before Rhone, now an even more imposing figure. He looked at him silently for a long time, then said with contempt: "American spy!" He made a motion of spitting, though no spit came. "You know why I summoned you here?"

"No, Comrade Commandant."

His massive hand lashed out. Rhone recoiled as the open palm cracked against the side of his face, and stared back fiercely, using all his control to restrain himself.

"Don't call me comrade, traitor." The major glowered at him. "I just wanted to see what you looked like. Captain!"

He stalked back to his desk. The door opened and the young captain stepped back in.

"Take this scum away," the major said without looking back.

The captain took Rhone's elbow and started to lead him out, but Rhone stood firm. "I have the right to correspond with my wife and my sister. They have the right to be informed what has become of me."

Senchenko turned back. He picked up some of the papers from his desk, stalked back to Rhone, and waved them in his face. "This is a strict regime camp. They have no rights! You have no rights!"

Stamped across the top of the first page Rhone read the words:

CORRESPONDENCE DENIED

The captain pulled him out the door. The major slammed it shut behind him.

The barracks was thirty feet wide and eighty feet long, open to the rafters except for a small enclosure housing the washroom and latrine situated in the center of the board floor. There were four sections of double bunks containing twenty beds each. Before the latrine was a wood stove, and before the stove a table where three men were playing cards. One was young, tough-looking, with eyes wise beyond his age. Another was very old, but fit and plump as a party bureaucrat. The third, in his forties, had dark Slavic features and wore an expensive fur hat and leather boots that looked as though they'd never been out in the snow. These were the *urki*, the "underworlders," a select and privileged class.

Rhone passed the latrine and moved down an aisle toward his upper bunk in one of the rear sections of the barracks. The gang boss Tsvilko, seated on his own lower bunk below the frosted window at the end of the aisle, was writing in a ledger. Men sat or reclined on their bunks, chatting or smoking, trying to ignore the scavengers waiting for the butts. Someone strummed a seven-stringed Russian guitar while another man sang in a mournful baritone voice. Men who'd got packages had a wealth spread out on the blankets and were surrounded by scavengers and friends. Popkov, the bespectacled old university professor who occupied the bunk beneath Rhone's, was reading a musty Russian translation of Conrad's *Heart of Darkness*.

Rhone took off his overcoat and hung it on the wooden knob in the locker he shared with the old man, then climbed, still in his jacket, up onto his own bunk. He took out the piece of cheese and the pack of Astras he'd retrieved from the orderly room, where at the expense of a daily bribe he'd stored the contents of the several food parcels from Alisa which had accumulated during his time in the Lubyanka. He carefully unfolded the white paper in which the cheese had been wrapped and ate the cheese, slowly, as *zeks* had to learn to eat, and when he had finished he shook out one of the Astras and lit it.

As he smoked he carefully smoothed out the paper, creased it in the middle, and tore it in half. One piece he lay aside; the other he carefully folded into the form of an envelope. He leaned off the edge of the bunk and looked back at Tsvilko, who was just closing his ledger, then shook out three Astras and dropped to the floor. He handed Popkov the butt from the cigarette he'd just smoked, then walked down the aisle toward the gang boss's bunk. Tsvilko lifted his stoic, chiseled face as Rhone approached.

"I would like to borrow your pen," Rhone told him, holding out the three cigarettes.

Tsvilko looked at the cigarettes, looked at Rhone, then took one of them and handed him the pen. "If it's a letter," he said as Rhone was turning to go back to his own bunk, "give it to the free worker on the crane. He still hasn't forgotten his own years as a *zek*."

A bell outside the barracks sounded reveille. He opened his eyes, curled beneath his blanket and the overcoat spread on top of the blanket. His body was covered with bites from the bedbugs. Tsvilko had told him that after a few months or a few years he would develop an immunity and the bugs would no longer bother to bite. Around him men stirred. Mother oaths greeted the day. He pulled his feet out of the sleeves of his jacket and got up. The Pole came down the aisle with a bulky bag wet with snow and placed it down before Tsvilko. Rhone wrapped his feet and put on his boots and cap. The men lined up in the aisle and Tsvilko distributed their bread.

Rhone slipped the letter in its makeshift envelope into his boot. Sensing something, he looked up. One of the *urki*, the tough kid with the wizened eyes, was watching him from the head of the aisle. In spite of the cold he was shirtless and his muscled torso was completely covered with tattoos of naked men and women entwined in various heterosexual and homosexual postures. After a moment, he turned and walked back toward the stove.

Outside, though it was still dark as night, the compound was lit up like a soccer stadium. Prisoners and soldiers and trusties moved about in every direction. There were several hundred men outside the mess hall, pushing and shoving to get in, fought back by the orderlies guarding the door.

126

Steam filled the interior. Someone claimed an empty spot at one of the tables and they got their watery soup with the bits of fish boiled off the bones and the few random pieces of cabbage, with a side place of frostbitten potatoes. They ate in silence, with reverence and deliberation.

Bent into the wind, they trudged back to the barracks. Inside, the prisoners sat or reclined grimly on their bunks. The *urki* were cooking their breakfast on the wood stove. The men waiting in line to get into the latrine observed them with hungry eyes. Rhone climbed onto his bunk and lay back on the pillow. Around him some of the men were binding masks of cloth over their faces. After a moment he closed his eyes, though he knew it was too late to go back to sleep. A whistle shrieked at the door, echoed almost instantly by Tsvilko's baritone roar for them to form up.

They got up quickly and started toward the door, carrying their heavy coats, some of them making the final adjustments to the rags that bandaged their faces.

They were stopped by the bottleneck at the door. The men moved through two or three at a time and formed up outside in groups of five abreast on the asphalt road. They made a line with the other gangs streaming in bunches out of their barracks and the other barracks on both sides.

Once grouped, they marched slowly forward, past the bakery and the mess hall and the looming BUR. Shouting wardens and soldiers moved back and forth along the line. Strains of the Soviet national anthem seemed to come and go on the wind, growing gradually more audible as they neared the Camp Commandant's headquarters. It was snowing only lightly but the snow was swept fiercely on the wind. A motley little brass band was assembled before the entrance of the building. Standing on the top step like a general reviewing a parade was Major Senchenko, on the step below him the young captain at a pose of rigid attention. Cold and miserable as the work force for whom they performed, the band labored through the song. The fingertips were cut out of the horn players' gloves. White flakes of snow caught and clung in the men's whiskers.

127

They marched through the gate into the no-man's land between the fences. The gang before them was searched and waved onto the first of the trucks lined up outside the gate. Rhone saw the Australian Carruthers, in his own gang back up the line, towering over the stooped men around him, smiling his grim smile.

They marched forward and stopped again. As an armed guard looked on, an unarmed soldier moved quickly down the row, pat-searching each man. When his turn came Rhone stepped forward and opened his coat and jacket, holding out his arms to either side. The wind seemed to blow through his bones. The guard ran his hands inside his jacket and patted down his torso. He looked him briefly in the eye and moved to the next man. He finished the row and ordered them to board the truck.

Rhone was just climbing when the armed guard said: "Davilov!"

He hesitated, looking back. "I am Andrei Davilov."

"Back here!"

Rhone's eyes briefly met Tsvilko's as he stepped back from the truck.

The guard was holding out his hand. "You have a letter. Give it to me."

16

He finished chipping through the hole beneath the ice, dropped to his knees and thrust the nub-end of the choker cable through.

"I saw the trouble you had this morning."

It was Carruthers, in his heavily accented English, standing three paces up the incline with his ax resting on his shoulder.

"Senchenko's got the bloody *urki* watching you," he continued after Rhone got to his feet. "I do a bit of business with them myself so I probably should have warned you. But what I meant to say, mate, is that I'll be leaving here in a couple of months at the most, if you want me to take word to someone when I go."

Rhone studied him in thoughtful silence. Moving swiftly down the incline toward them was a soldier with a leveled AK-47. "I'll think about it."

Following Rhone's gaze, Carruthers looked back at the approaching soldier and started quickly away. The soldier stopped. Rhone turned back to the log, hit it a couple of times with his crowbar to assure himself it was steady, then leaned across it and retrieved the nub-end and fitted it into the bell.

When he straightened up he saw Carruthers had climbed up onto the side of a caterpillar that was dragging three logs up the grade to talk to the free worker who drove it.

Two guards marched him across the compound, bathed in light in the dark of the evening. As they neared the commandant's headquarters he heard singing, an off-key rendition of "The Song of the Volga Boatmen." When they went up the steps and entered the anteroom he realized the song came from inside Senchenko's office. His deep voice seemed just on the verge of finding the range when the captain rapped on the door and he stopped.

The captain opened the door and motioned Rhone inside. Senchenko sat at his cluttered desk, his necktie loosened, his uniform wrinkled and soiled. Before him was a half-emptied bottle of vodka.

Rhone took off his overcoat and let it fall to the floor behind him. After the barracks the office was like an oven.

Senchenko lifted the bottle, drank, and slammed it back down on his desk. "That is all, Captain."

The captain lingered in the door, looking at him with disapproval.

"I said that is *all*, Captain!"

The captain went out.

Senchenko drank again, spilling the clear liquid down his cheek. "Did you know?" he said after he'd lowered the bottle, "that I hate this fucking place."

"I hate it too, Major."

He scowled. "You are ridiculing me. But it does not matter. This is my island and I will always have the last word here." He searched through the clutter on the desk and produced Rhone's makeshift envelope with the letter to Andrei Davilov's wife. "You probably think it is because of this you are here? I don't give a fuck about this, your fucking messages to the CIA. I can have you sent to the BUR for it, but I can have you sent to the BUR anyway."

He crumpled the envelope and letter in his hand and tossed them violently away, again lifted the bottle to his lips, and drank.

He rose and came around the table toward him. "I did not

know Colonel Vasily Yaroshenko. But I knew of him. He served in the battle of Kharkov. He was decorated. Hero of the Soviet Union. I also served in that battle. Tell me about him."

"What is there to tell? He was convicted and sentenced to hang?"

"Do you believe he was guilty?"

"I saw no evidence of it."

"But it was your testimony that convicted him."

"The KGB gave me no choice."

The major's enormous fist filled his eyes. He rolled and ducked and took it on the side of the head, and came back with a straight right that caught Senchenko full on the mouth.

The major staggered back, stunned, blood spurting from his lips. His hand curled around the handle of his holstered Makarov. A drop of blood landed on the floor between them with an audible splat. He looked down at it, then back up at Rhone. He removed his hand from the gun handle, wiped his mouth, and looked at the blood on his hand.

His lips relaxed into a smile. He shook his head, laughing softly, walked back, and sat down at his desk. He lifted the bottle, drank, and lowered it, still shaking his head. "You've got more guts than brains," he said, using the Russian word that meant literally *soul.* "I like that. It's more than I would expect from a traitor." He paused. "Why do you think Moscow wanted to crucify Yaroshenko?"

"At first they were convinced of his guilt. Later they had their doubts. But he had been broken by interrogation. They said he was of no further use to them except in a show trial."

"But he was tried in camera."

"Because he had withdrawn his confession."

"And your lies convicted him."

"Do you think that even if I'd wanted to I could have saved him?"

"No. You could have done nothing. You were sentenced to die here and he was sentenced to be shot. But he will not be shot, Andrei Davilov. And do you know why he will not be shot?"

131

"My interrogator told me that was the only purpose he could serve now."

"No!" Senchenko smiled. "In being *sentenced* to die he has already served that purpose. To shoot him would be to lose something he might know and still has not told, about you perhaps." He laughed aloud, bellowing. "You are trying to get a message to your employers in the CIA. But they could not help you even if they knew you were here. And they do not know and they will not find out. Sometimes the *urki* are even more valuable than the guards. And the *urki* will know, even if the guards do not, when next you try to smuggle a letter out. And do not worry, Andrei Davilov. It is not yet time for you to die. I must let you live a while longer, for the same reason Moscow must let Yaroshenko live. But you are an American spy, and you are under a death sentence, here and in the rest of the Gulag. It is my suspension of that sentence that is keeping you temporarily alive."

He gurgled down another stiff shot of vodka and bellowed for the captain.

The captain came in, regarding Senchenko with the same disapproving look.

"Take him away."

"To the BUR?"

"No. Take him to his barracks."

The major slumped forward on his desk. The captain looked at him with disgust. Then his eyes strayed to the crumpled papers on the floor. He walked over and picked them up, folded the letter out flat, and read it. He slipped the note back into the envelope and put them both into his uniform pocket.

He shouted for an enlisted man in the anteroom to take Rhone out.

On Sunday there was laughter in the barracks, comradeship. The guitar player strummed a livelier tune and an old Cossack danced. In the next aisle over from his bunk a young Jew with thick glasses was drawing a sketch, almost finished. The scene was Red Square. In the background St. Basil's was suggested in grotesque caricature, the domed towers contorted like live, writhing figures. Pointed in the direction of the Lenin tomb, a bulldozer filled the foreground, enormous beyond proportion, animated like a charging beast. The driver, in hard hat and construction clothing, was an outrageous caricature of the artist and, universally, of the stereotypical European Jew in general. Before him and his unseemly machine soldiers and police and austerely garmented mourners scattered. Across the façade of the mausoleum hung a banner with an enormous portrait of Lenin, but one end had broken loose and flapped in the wind, twisting the face into a mask of terrified contortion, the eyes rolled back like the eyes of a dying horse, mouth open wide in a silent scream.

The artist hesitated, his hand trembling. But when again he attacked the paper the trembling had ceased. The strokes came swiftly, in sure triplets. Beneath the intact corner of the Lenin banner an almost insignificant little figure took shape, his moustached face adorned by an enormous smile, his arms folded complacently across his chest. The figure was hardly more than suggested, but Joseph Stalin was unmistakable.

He finished. He lowered his pen, panting. Around him men laughed and applauded. On the other side of the barracks a group of Christians were singing a Russian hymn. Carruthers came in, took off his heavy coat, slung it over his shoulder, and started up the aisle between the first two sections of bunks. He stopped at the table by the stove and spoke briefly with the *urki* in his pidgin Russian. He slapped the man wearing the expensive fur hat on the back and the two of them laughed loudly, along with the older criminal. The young tough did not laugh. He was conspicuously sullen.

The Australian left them to their card game, came on across, and started up the aisle toward Rhone's bunk. When he reached it, Popkov stood up from his own lower bunk and held out his hand. Carruthers took it.

"You have it?" the old man asked.

Carruthers smiled, reached into his coat, and took out a book wrapped in brown paper. Popkov eagerly tore off the paper. It was, Rhone saw, a paperback English version of *Heart of Darkness*. Popkov put on his glasses, hastily thumbed through it, then sat down on his bunk, dug his hand into his boot, and produced a roll of bills. He handed them to Carruthers, who slipped them into his own boot.

"You should count them," said Popkov.

"No need to count them," Carruthers said. "I trust you, old man." He looked at Rhone. "So how's it been, mate?"

Rhone shrugged.

Carruthers looked back toward the *urki*. "I've got a deal going," he said almost absently. "I'll let you know if it comes through."

"The man in the hat," Rhone said. "Who is he?"

"Sergeyev. He was a dope smuggler too. Lucky I get on with him. Else I'd never have been able to do any business in this place. It's the old man, Kolnyshevsky, who's the nominal head of the underworld in this camp. But it's Sergeyev's got the real power."

He shrugged, smiled his grim smile, and started away.

"Carruthers."

He stopped and looked back. Rhone walked after him, stopped before him, and stared into his pale blue eyes.

"Tell me," he said finally in English in hardly more than a whisper. "Has anyone ever gotten out of here? Has anyone ever tried?"

Carruthers shook his head. "Out to where? There's nothing out there. In the winter you wouldn't last the first night. And even in the summer . . ." He shrugged.

"There must be a town where the free workers live?"

"The settlement. Just another island, hardly better than camp. No. And don't think I've never thought about it. My first couple of years. But forget it. You'll drive yourself crazy for nothing."

The Christians had stopped their singing. The guitar had stopped. All over the barracks the din of conversation was falling off. Within a moment all was quiet save for the click of boot heels on the boards.

134

Two soldiers were bringing a new prisoner up the first aisle. The *urki* watched them pass the table and latrine. They continued up the aisle toward the bunks where Tsvilko's gang slept. The prisoner wore a clean black coat with snowflakes still white on the lapels, a big ruddy-faced Russian who looked so well-fed and happy he could have come directly from a Caspian holiday. Bunched in his hands were several parcels wrapped in *Pravda* with big puncture holes where they'd been inspected. The guards stopped, the prisoner between them, just beside Rhone's bunk.

Tsvilko sat up on his own lower bunk.

"New prisoner for your gang," one of the guards said.

"I've got my new man already. My gang is full."

The guard took out a piece of paper and looked at it. "Litvenko." It was the Moldavian who occupied the lower bunk opposite Popkov. "Get your things. Transfer."

He sat up, blinking, on his bunk. He didn't know how to take it. It could be the best news or the worst. Clutching his parcels, the big Russian stepped forward and waited while Litvenko gathered his belongings from the bunk and out of the locker. The new man put his parcels on the bunk and hung his coat in the locker as the soldiers escorted the Moldavian away.

"I am Saunin," he announced to Tsvilko, who had risen and started forward. "Inoshin Petrovich." He held out his hand. Tsvilko took it skeptically. Rhone and Carruthers watched the silent, barely perceptible little struggle between them, each trying to out-squeeze the other, Tsvilko all the while looking with his changeless stoic eyes into the eyes of the bigger man and Saunin just smiling pleasantly back at him; the struggle ended suddenly as if by a mutual, unspoken consent communicated telepathically between them.

Tsvilko returned to his bunk. Saunin looked around with his smile, at Popkov, Rhone, Carruthers, and the others. At last he let his gaze fall on several of the *urki*, who stood watching from the beginning of the aisle. "I see the underworlders are not quite sure who I am," he observed, "and therefore cannot make up their minds whether to steal my parcels or not."

He stared at them, smiling all the time. After a moment they moved away. Saunin turned back to his bunk and tore open one of the packages. All around him men were watching like hungry dogs. Except for Tsvilko and Carruthers.

"If you are not from the outside," Popkov observed, "you must be one of them?"

Saunin turned back, laughing easily. In his hand was a big loaf of Moscow French bread, which he started to tear into chunks. "No, old man. I am not one of them. And I would wager I've been longer in the Gulag even than you."

"Eight years, three months, and a day," Popkov answered readily as if it had been his name.

"Then I would have won my bet," said Saunin, handing him a piece of bread. "But until now I have spent all but my initial interrogation in a place called Semipalatinsk." He laughed. "Yes. The land of milk and honey. And now, after that good life, I am doomed to spending my last three years here."

Tsvilko observed with interest from his bunk. "You are a scientist?"

"Yes. I am a physicist and my specialty, outside, was particle accelerators." He handed a piece of bread to Rhone and briefly his attention was focused on him. "For the last five years I've been working on something known as Project Semipalatinsk. All top secret, of course," he added generally, his smile returning.

He kept a small slice of bread for himself and distributed the rest. Only Carruthers declined. The Australian looked at Rhone, shook his head almost imperceptibly, said goodbye, and started away.

"Our specialty here is felling timber," Tsvilko said and reclined back on his bunk.

"I don't believe it is coincidence," Saunin said that evening as he crowded into the seat opposite Rhone in the steamy mess hall.

"What?" Rhone asked him.

"The same prison. The same *gang* even." He paused. "I know

who you are. Yaroshenko was in charge of our security too, and
his fall from grace was no secret in Semipalatinsk. And heads
are falling there. You've got to assume the same thing is happening at the test site, so it looks as if the Americans have finally done something intelligent." He fell silent, observing out
of the corner of his eye the old Tartar from another work gang
who'd already scraped his bowl clean and sat, oblivious to the
curses of the men waiting for his seat, listening.

Saunin held his silence. After a moment the Tartar shrugged,
picked up his bowl, and left. Behind Saunin two men immediately began to struggle for the place.

"I don't know what you are talking about," said Rhone.

Saunin laughed, then turned it off. "Project Semipalatinsk.
When the Americans used you to expose Yaroshenko, his un-
derlings had no choice but to begin a witch hunt for the agent
they are so determined to protect. They have destroyed a lot of
brain power and the project is falling far behind schedule as a
result."

"And you were caught in the wave?"

"Not exactly. But I am realistic enough to see it was bound to
happen. I decided to get out. You can always get out of a
sharashka, if you don't mind going some place worse."

17

Vladimir, November 1978

A brass band was playing a dirge in the cemetery across from the prison when the limousine pulled to a stop. Colonel Ilin told Boris to leave the heater running while he waited. He got out and walked along the cracked front wall to the entrance. He presented his KGB card to a militiaman in a ragged greatcoat. A phone call was made. The big doors swung open and Valeri Pavlovich Ilin entered the gloomy store lobby.

He'd left with Katusha for the dacha the day after the trial. There was a blizzard and for two days he could not even get out of the house. On the third day the snow had stopped and though it was bitterly cold, he went out. Walking alone in the orchard among the bare, frozen trees he tried again to convince himself it was really over. Andrei Davilov was gone forever from his life. Gorsky had gone with Yaroshenko to Vladimir, where he would continue his investigation. But Ilin's part in the case, General Drachinsky had assured him, was over. His interrogation, everyone said, had been a splendid success. Down at Semipalatinsk the witch hunt had already begun.

He returned to the house at dark and Katusha, sad and troubled, told him he was to return a call that had come to him from the Lubyanka. They looked at each other grimly over the distance that separated them. Once they'd loved each other so much. And though she must have known she had lost him, there, during the two days they'd been snowbound inside the dacha, if she could not touch or hold him at least she'd been able to reach toward him, or clutch at him.

It was Surveillance, calling to inform him that Andrei Davilov's sister had contacted the American agent Brown and made arrangements to be smuggled out of the country. They asked if she should be placed under arrest. He thought about it for a long time, silent on the line. He thought of her in prison, what a few years in camp would do to that lovely face, that lovely body, those scornful, defiant eyes. "No," he said finally. "Do not arrest her yet. Arrest her only if it is necessary to prevent her from leaving the country." In the silence that followed, now on the other end of the line, he discerned the disapproval. He gave instructions that he should be kept informed of her movements, and hung up.

After that he waited constantly for the phone. Katusha, now silent and moody, no longer reached for him, no longer clutched. Two days later he was informed that Alisa Belova had missed her rendezvous. They said Brown had made all the arrangements. The woman simply had not gone.

He left Katusha at the dacha and returned to Moscow that night. He found her, quite drunk, at the Café des Artistes. When he asked her why she had not gone she did not bother to deny having contacted Brown. "What would I do in England?" she said. "I don't even speak the language. Besides, how can I leave when you have my brother in that terrible place?" Becoming somber, she asked when she could see him again.

"I don't know," Ilin whispered. "Perhaps ... I can arrange it."

When he finished his beer she took his glass and went to the bar and got him another. The barman, he noticed, did not ask her to pay. Ilin's eyes were on her body as she walked back to the table.

"I know you want to sleep with me," she said when she had

sat back down. "I told you, I am willing to do it if you will help my brother."

He wanted her so bad he ached. "All right. I will help him."

"You will free him?"

"No one can free him. He's . . . he's *going* to be sent to a labor camp."

"Then you cannot help him." She rose and started to go.

"Alisa Petrovna."

She looked scornfully back.

"You would not think of doing it for . . . some other reason? You would not do it simply . . . because you wanted to?"

She laughed.

"Then perhaps there is something else I can do for you." Planning the lie, he loathed himself and loathed his pathetic longing. "I have influence with many important people. At the Bolshoi, for example."

She thought it over. Now he knew she'd only pretended to think it over. She smiled and said, "Fuck the Bolshoi. Fuck your mother."

Off-chocolate paint flaked like dandruff on the walls of Gorsky's office. Immaculate in his KGB uniform, the young lieutenent colonel looked somewhat embarrassed to show Ilin in.

"Rather more grim than we're accustomed to, I'm afraid," he said with a self-conscious shrug, and nodded toward a chair.

"For the prisoners too, I've been told," Ilin said, sitting down.

Gorsky grappled for the humor, which passed above him, and said: "I was surprised to get your wire. I thought your involvement in this affair had ended."

"Officially yes. Unofficially I still have some questions."

"Yes? What questions?"

"What, other than the destruction of Yaroshenko, might possibly have been Davilov's mission in Moscow?"

"I thought we had agreed his mission *was* the destruction of Yaroshenko."

"You, the general, Zverev, and Davilov agreed to it. I did not. But whatever his mission, it must somehow have related to the American Embassy here and it must have been accomplished, or at least attempted, during the three days he was free on the streets of Moscow. I checked on the movements of the embassy personnel during those three days. The day of Davilov's arrest the death of an American citizen, a male secretary attached to the office of the ambassador, was announced. The body was flown out of the Soviet Union the next day, through diplomatic channels."

"That is routine procedure."

"Yes," said Ilin. "What is not routine is that shipment of the casket was arranged by Brown. And Brown would not ordinarily concern himself with such trivia. Brown is not a functionary. He is a spy."

Gorsky absorbed this thoughtfully. "But I still don't see what this has to do with Yaroshenko."

"What if Yaroshenko was telling the truth? What if the prisoner I interrogated was not Andrei Davilov. A body was *smuggled* out of the Soviet Union. There are thirty minutes of 'Davilov's' time in Moscow that we cannot account for."

"But if Davilov is an impostor no one would know that better than his sister."

Ilin swallowed. "I have questioned his sister."

"You have questioned her. But have you interrogated her in the Lubyanka?"

"She has committed no crime," the colonel lied.

"But you could arrest her merely for her dissident associations."

It was true of course. And he had thought of it. Alisa Belova to do with as he pleased in the Lubyanka. He was haunted by the vision of it. That was why he had come to Vladimir. "I prefer to question Yaroshenko first. Even if Alisa Belova could tell us the man is an impostor, she would never have been informed of his actual mission."

"I suppose not," Gorsky said and picked up the phone.

They went through a few minutes of awkward silence before

Yaroshenko, in black prison pants and jacket, was delivered to the room. Though it had not been a month, he looked different than he had in the Lubyanka, and different than he had at his trial. He'd lost some of his teeth and his hair was falling out. He looked at Gorsky with a loathing and turned his eyes on the colonel.

Ilin motioned for him to sit down. "Vasily Yemelyanovich."

"Valeri Pavlovich."

Looking at him, the colonel felt a swirling dread in his stomach. They had been friends at the Academy and their relationship had remained cordial through the years. But he found it hard to accept that the human wreckage before him was really the same man he had known.

Feeling awkward, he brought the box out of his coat. "Chocolates. I brought them from Moscow. And American cigarettes." He brought out two packs of Winstons.

Yaroshenko took them, with the box of chocolates. He unwrapped the cellophane slowly from one of the packs of cigarettes. Gorsky, sterile as a surgeon's scalpel, looked on with a scowl.

Yaroshenko fitted a cigarette between his lips and Ilin leaned forward to light it.

He inhaled, deliberately, exquisitely. "Now, Valeri Pavlovich. What do you want from me?"

"I want to help you."

"Can you get me out of here?"

"No."

"Then you cannot help me."

Where, he thought, had he heard that before? "All right, Vasily Yemelyanovich. I want you to help me."

Yaroshenko smiled.

"You said the man who was arrested with you is not Andrei Davilov. Then who is he? And how do you know this?"

"Why have you come after all this time to ask me this?"

"An unopened casket from the American Embassy was flown out of Moscow the day after your arrest. There are thirty minutes of Davilov's time in Moscow that cannot be accounted for."

142

"Well, Valeri Pavlovich. You are not the fool I took you for."
Yaroshenko glanced contemptuously at Gorsky, looked back at
Ilin, and waited.

Ilin looked at Gorsky. "Colonel?"

"Very well." Silently seething, he rose and walked out of the
room.

"If you think I'm going to tell you how I know the man who
was arrested with me is not Andrei Davilov you are a
dreamer," Yaroshenko said after he was gone. "I would have
nothing to gain."

"And nothing to lose."

"But the pleasure of knowing that you squirm."

"Then what are you going to tell me?"

"If you want to know about the impostor Davilov, find out
what became of Igor Glazunov."

On his way across the yard to the gate, he passed the hospital
block, a five storied building with eighteen muzzled windows to
a floor. The top story was the administration section and the
hospital itself. Below this were the wards for prisoners under
actual medical treatment. The next two floors down were for
male political prisoners under segregation. The bottom floor
was for female politicals. The Vladimir Isolator.

18

Archangel, December 1978

He lay on his bunk, staring up at the ceiling where the ice clung white to the wood. Below, Popkov and Saunin were talking about their wives. He thought about Alisa. Wondering where she was, he was filled with loneliness. It was ironic; he'd been with her but a few days and now, in this place where a man had little but his memories, she was all he had. The others, and he supposed he could say there had been many of them, were too far away, lost, almost forgotten.

In Vietnam it was Phuong he had to remember and now he could hardly conjure an image of her face. He'd spent a week with her, the nights and the days, in a small hotel. Then he went on the line. He'd explained to her how to write him and he'd gotten a couple of letters from her, in stilted formal French.

He and Duffy got back to Saigon the first day of Tet. He saw her on the street in front of the National Assembly. She said her brother was in town and she had to spend the evening with her family at her mother's house in Cholon and that she would come to his hotel when she could. She kissed him and told him to be careful, and there was something ominous in her voice.

144

Then she flagged a pedicab and left him standing on the street. When he found Duffy in the bar of the hotel he told him what had happened and Duffy told him it wasn't a brush off, and it seemed there was something just as ominous when Duffy said that. Duffy said he was going to the whorehouses, but Rhone wasn't in the mood. Then he told Rhone to be careful, the same as Phuong had told him. Later, in the Chinook flying back to the line, he'd tell him he'd sensed the coming of the Offensive as soon as they'd gotten into the city, that he'd felt it, like it was 1964 again, that everywhere he'd looked he'd seen the little hints. And that was why *he* had been ready.

Saigon was tense, more so than Rhone had felt it the last time he'd been there. The people were groggy from the feast and the beer. By nightfall the town felt as eerie as the Highlands. The attack came at three the following morning. Nineteen members of the C-10 Viet Cong Sapper Battalion shot their way into the American Embassy compound on Thong Nhut Boulevard. Mortars landed all over the city. Rhone hadn't been able to get anywhere near Cholon.

He didn't see Duffy again until they boarded the chopper. After the ARVN had chased the Viet Cong deep into the Chinese shantytown he went back to look for Phuong. Up and down the streets he saw grieving people transporting their dead from the Cho Roy morgue back to their homes in the pedicabs. There were three dead V.C. in front of Phuong's mother's house and four more of them dead on the floor with her sisters inside. The walls and the furnishings were shot to pieces and the riddled bodies lay twisted together on the floor. He found Phuong beneath the body of a boy who was her male dead ringer, who must have dived over her to try to protect her. He wore a green shirt and slacks and a red band on his arm. Strapped to his waist was a Samurai scabbard but the sword was missing. There was a bullet-riddled Viet Cong flag on the wall, but the table where they'd all sat was miraculously unscathed. The cups unbroken. The pot still full of tea. . . .

After all these years the vision still hadn't left him. He heard the boot heels on the board floor and looked up. Two soldiers were coming across the barracks. Even before they called his name he knew they'd come for him.

He put on his overcoat and went out with them. It was snowing. They crossed the brightly lit compound and entered the commandant's headquarters. The captain opened the door of Senchenko's office and motioned him through.

The major was seated behind his desk. Though it was warm, he wore his fur hat. Seated in another chair off to the side was the Jewish artist he'd seen doing the sketch that afternoon, now working on a portrait of Senchenko.

There was an empty chair before the desk. The major motioned for him to sit down. On the desk was a flat cardboard box containing, Rhone saw after he'd opened it, an assortment of chocolates. Senchenko held it out to him and he took one hesitantly. Tasting its sweetness, he felt suddenly terribly sad, as though it were the taste of his own lost youth or his innocence or his freedom.

The major looked at Rhone thoughtfully. "What kind of a man was Colonel Yaroshenko?"

Rhone shrugged. "I didn't know him. From a first impression I would say he had a certain ... flare. He was proud, and not very much afraid. There was something almost *Western* about him."

"You speak of him as though he were already dead. But I told you: he is not." He was momentarily silent. "You saw the bullet scar on his neck. That was done at Kharkov. Do you know your recent Russian history, Comrade Davilov?"

"A little."

"But you lived in London, how long?"

"Five years."

"Five years. You were a fool to come back."

Rhone said nothing.

"You have a wife there?"

"Yes."

"Does it worry you that she might leave you while you are here?"

"I'm resigned. I'll never see her again."

146

"I had a wife," the major said. "I lost her by coming here."
He looked up at the artist, still rapidly sketching. He rose,
walked over, and stepped around behind him. "You have talent, Tubelsky. A weaker man might have flattered me. Take
this man, Comrade Davilov. The last time he was here I hit him
in the face. And do you know what he did? He hit me back." He
laughed suddenly, a bellowing. The door opened and he
stopped the laughing. The young captain stood in it, looking at
the major in silence. "Russian history," Senchenko said, looking back at Rhone. "The British and you Americans think *they*
won the war. But that is not true. We are the ones who defeated
the Germans. The Red Army. Did you know, Comrade Davilov,
that more Russians died in the battle of Kharkov alone than
the Americans lost in the entire war in Europe and the Pacific?"

Rhone had known, but he said nothing.

"And where were you then?" the major asked him.

"I was not yet born."

"Yes. I know. Neither was this boy here," he added, nodding
at the captain.

The captain said nothing. After a moment he turned, went
back out, and closed the door behind him.

The day was still, crisp-freezing, and clear. The logging site
was buried under a layer of new, clean snow. Saunin, working
thirty meters up from Rhone near the line of the standing
trees, took a breather and leaned on his shovel. He smiled at his
own fogging breath and surveyed the beauty of the forest, the
snow that dropped now and again in great scoopfuls from the
weighted branches of the firs. Bogged to his knees in a drift, he
returned to his labor with a fervor.

At the crane, the loading of a truck was almost completed.
The free worker-driver stood smoking with a guard. He wore a
fur hat, high military boots, and a black coat in almost as good
a condition as Saunin's. His helper, also a free worker, stood to
the side rubbing his hands together. His gloves were worn and
a couple of his fingers peeked through. His boots and greatcoat

147

were in hardly better shape than Rhone's, or those worn by the two *zeks* who guided the last log into place atop the load. The driver gave the last of his smoke to the prisoners. They tied the cables across the load and he and his helper got into the cab. The engine turned over, sputtered, and caught. The truck pulled away up the icy road.

"The new man doesn't ring true," Carruthers told Rhone when he joined him at noon in the mess tent.

Rhone made a question with his eyes.

"I watched him this morning. *Zeks* are wretched or they're proud. But they're not happy. Watch out for him."

Another loaded truck was rolling by outside when Carruthers joined Rhone in the mess tent at noon. They heard its brakes squeak as it pulled to a stop at the checkpoint up the road.

"Where do they go?"

"What?"

"The trucks," Rhone said in English. "Where do the convoys go?"

"They go south," Carruthers said. "But don't start driving yourself crazy with that again. Even if you could forge a card and switch places with one of the free workers, you'd be missed in the body count here before the convoy got anywhere. And there're half a dozen rats for every decent one of that lot anyway." He sighed. "I've got it on good authority of the *urki* that I'm due for early release. Just give me the message, whatever it was in the letter, and I'll get it to your people when I go."

"I told you I'd think about it."

"Look. I served my whole sentence, damned near it, because I'm a foreigner and a dope smuggler. But you're a spy. And spies get traded. Just give me the message and bide your time. You won't be here forever."

Carruthers' gang were rising to go. He wiped his bowl clean with a crust, stood, and turned toward the door.

"Aussie?"

He looked back.

Rhone could see Saunin two tables away, watching them.

148

"You've taken an awful lot of interest in me since I got here. Why?"

"Look, mate." Carruthers leaned back toward the table. "I know you're a Yank. I spent four years in Nam, as a cameraman, you know. I think I might've even seen you there."

"The Englishman seems to take a great interest in you," Saunin told him as they trudged back up the frozen road.

"Australian," Rhone said. "He's Australian."

"I see."

"And you?" Rhone said. "Why are you in the Gulag? You know so much about me. I might as well know something about you."

"I was arrested in East Berlin in 1969, attempting to escape to the West."

"And for that they gave you . . . twelve years?"

"They gave me much more than that. I was charged with attempting to smuggle classified military information to the West Germans. My sentence has been greatly reduced for my work at Semipalatinsk."

"Which brings us back to square one."

"Square one?" asked Saunin.

They passed the supply hut and waded into the deeper snow.

"If you don't think it was coincidence," Rhone said, "what do you think?"

"I don't understand."

"The two of us in the same camp."

"Oh." He was deeply thoughtful. "It was not coincidence, of course. The odds against that are almost incalculable. Certainly they wanted to observe how we would react to each other. That's why I asked about the Englishman. Australian, I mean. I thought perhaps he was observing us for the KGB."

On the eve of Western Christmas, Carruthers bribed a guard at the gate and brought in a bird and a bottle of vodka. They packed it in mud and baked it in the wood stove at the edge of the coals. The aroma permeated the barracks. A pigeon. From the crane operator, he explained.

The Australian cracked the baked mud shell and it fell away like shattered porcelain. The skin was crisp and golden, the meat inside dark and filled with juice. They ate the pigeon and washed it down with the freezing vodka, picked the bones clean and distributed them to some of the hungry men watching from all around. Carruthers sang "Silent Night" in English in a clear, tenor voice. Rhone saw there were tears in his eyes. They drank the last of the vodka and he tucked the empty bottle in his coat. The next morning Rhone heard he was in the BUR, that they'd snatched him from his bunk at midnight.

Later that morning Saunin set a choker cable on a log up the grade from where Rhone was working and lost it. Hearing it strip the bark Rhone turned and watched oddly spellbound as it bounced down the grade toward him. When it hit a stump ten feet up the incline, he dove face first into the snow and felt the snow spray over his back as the log flew over him, struck another stump thirty feet down, stood up magnificently on its end, and then toppled again and bounced away down over the stumps and gullies and drifts.

Rhone got up. All over the site men had ceased their work to watch. Two soldiers with leveled AK-47's were guarding Saunin. Tsvilko inspected the cable.

"It was an accident, Andrei Petrovich," Saunin said when he got there.

One of the soldiers inspected the cable and agreed it might have been an accident. He told them to go back to work and warned Saunin to be more careful unless he wanted to spend his nights with Carruthers in the punishment barracks.

"You almost didn't move," Tsvilko said to Rhone after the soldiers had started away. "You could have gotten yourself killed." He handed him a pouch with a few pinches of Mahorka and told him to give it to the trustee in the supply shed. "He'll let you rest a while in back."

He'd been asleep an hour when a hand on his shoulder woke

150

him. He'd been dreaming but he could not remember what. Some place warm and far away. It took him a few seconds to remember where he was.

"I know you think I tried to kill you but I promise I did not." It was Saunin, kneeling over him and holding out a bowl of gruel in one hand and a piece of cheese and dried sausage from his food parcels in the other.

Rhone sat up and took the gruel, removed his spoon from his boot and a chunk of brown bread from his coat. He spooned a piece of fish and a few grains of rice from the bowl. Only after Saunin had executed a little gesture of insistence did he silently accept the cheese and sausage.

"I will go now," Saunin said as he rose and stepped toward the door.

"Saunin," Rhone said.

He turned back.

"You say you did not try to kill me. Then you will answer this question for me. When you were at the *sharashka*, what were you working on?"

"I've already told you. My specialty is particle acceleration." He glanced back at the old man at the stove, who'd removed Tsvilko's tobacco pouch and was tailoring a thin cigarette. "And I've told you I was assigned to research work for the Semipalatinsk project," Saunin added, looking back at Rhone.

"Yes. But what specifically were you trying to accomplish?"

"You are an American spy," he said in heavily accented English. He smiled. "Yes, I speak a little bit of English. What you are asking me to do is reveal a state secret. But since we are on the same side . . ." He paused, watching Rhone's reaction as his words sank in. "Our major problem is the construction of an accelerator compact enough that the apparatus can be launched into space. But the obstacles are tremendous. Success would virtually require discovery of a new principal, the formulation of an entirely revolutionary accelerator concept."

Rhone was thinking of the code-phrase Remick had given him with which to approach Alexander Terekhov, way back in the Lubyanka. *Gorky Park, June, 1974.* He remembered the name Terekhov had associated with it. *Erich Reisinger.* He hadn't made the connection at the time. But there had been a Reisinger at Berkeley when he was at Stanford. He was the charged particle beam expert on the bubble chamber experiments there. Rhone had read his obituary in the *Herald Tribune,* before Remick had contacted him in Paris. *Gorky Park.* He could almost see it now, and he realized that before Saunin woke him that was what he'd been dreaming. The two old men. The grass and the trees. He'd dreamed their wrinkled faces, their old cracked voices talking excitedly in the language of their profession, that somehow had not been beyond his own scope, as the ramblings of their random speculation suddenly became theory, breakthrough.

"And what would be the result?" he asked Saunin, "if this country could put a particle beam weapon in space?"

"Complete neutralization of the American missile deterrent."

They'd locked eyes. "And what did you mean? About us both being on the same side?"

Saunin smiled. "Haven't you guessed? I was Remick's good Semipalatinsk contact. The man you and Yaroshenko were both sacrificed to protect."

He left Rhone staring after him, brushed past the old man, and went out the door.

Rhone was still groggy from the nap. Something bothered him. He drank from the soup and listened to Saunin's words echo through his mind. Of course if what he'd said was true it appeared sheer madness for Saunin to have told him. But something else bothered him even more, that he could not quite put his finger on.

He felt the cold as the door to the outside was opened. Past the old man he saw two soldiers enter and pause to warm their hands at the stove.

He stuffed the last of the cheese into his mouth, slipped the sausage into his coat, and drank the last of the gruel from the bowl. He wiped it with his bread crust as he moved past the soldiers and went back out the door. The prisoners were already marching back from the mess tent and fanning out over the field of stumps and saplings. All along the line the tired, hopeless eyes stared at him from their rag-bandaged faces.

19

Ilin got Igor Glazunov's name out of a computer in Registry and Archives and with it enough information to tell him where to go to learn more.

Leaving the Lubyanka, he stopped by the KGB Club and selected a bottle of imported unblended Scotch. He felt a presence behind him and turned. It was General Drachinsky, staggering drunk, accompanied by an older man the colonel had never seen.

"Valeri Pavlovich!" The general inspected the label on the Scotch and nodded his approval. "I would like you to meet State Counselor Shitkin. Counselor. Colonel Valeri Pavlovich Ilin."

They shook hands.

"I recently entrusted the colonel with the interrogation of the expatriot who was arrested in the Yaroshenko affair."

"Yes. I am familiar with that."

"He conducted a swift and thorough investigation," the General said, looking at Ilin severely. "I had the utmost confidence in him. Valeri Pavlovich has been with me since Budapest. Fifth department in those days."

Fifth department, nicknamed "wet affair." And "wet affair" in the parlance, meant bloodshed. Hungary, 1956. He'd won a medal for his part in that.

"The Budapest Banquet," said the Counselor. "The entire Hungarian government in one fell swoop."

"We had the Hungarians for dinner . . ." the General began, his gleaming eyes urging the colonel to finish the quip.

". . . and they were delicious," mumbled Ilin.

He nodded at the general, nodded at the counselor, and turned and started up the lavishly stocked aisle toward the checkstand.

The general fell into step beside him. "I have heard, Valeri Pavlovich, that you have made certain inquiries at Archives and Registry?"

"Yes."

"And that on your own initiative you have gone to Vladimir?"

"Yes."

They were almost to the checkstand.

"I would be very unhappy, Colonel, if you learned something that would prove we have been mistaken in our handling of this affair."

He stopped and turned and looked Drachinsky in the eye. "Yes, General. I would be very unhappy, too."

His old friend Yevgeny Doyarenko occupied an office slightly larger and more modern than his own in the Militia Headquarters building on Petrovka Street. A corpulent, outgoing man, the MVD Inspector had a reputation that extended from central headquarters in the Lubyanka to the seamiest reaches of the burgeoning Moscow underworld.

Doyarenko contemplated the bottle of whiskey briefly, and let out with a burst of boistrous laughter. "So, my old friend, you need my help again?"

Ilin chose to ignore the cordial condescension. Though they had been friends since their army days there'd always been a rivalry between them. A Ukrainian, Doyarenko had a political outlook that was questionable at best. A less talented man with the same point of view could never have risen to his rank.

The inspector got two glasses from the cabinet, opened the bottle, and poured them shots. "To the security of the State," he toasted.

Ilin smiled and drank.

"Now what can I do for you? You have procured this Scotch for me and that is something a humble criminal inspector could never do."

"Igor Glazunov."

"Igor Glazunov? State Security is now interested in Glazunov? I have also been somewhat curious about Glazunov." Doyarenko put down his glass and turned to the file cabinet.

"Why have you been curious about Glazunov?"

"Because he has not been seen for some time." The inspector lay a folder on the table.

"He has not been seen for three months," Ilin suggested. "Since the ninth of October."

Doyarenko raised his eyebrows.

Ilin opened the folder. Lying on top of the first page was a photograph of a gangling gaunt-faced man in a tattered hat and shabby overcoat. He studied the face briefly, then pushed the photograph aside and started to read down the subject's arrest record. The list was long and, considering the subject had received only one prison sentence and that over five years previously, almost defied belief.

"How did you know how long it had been?" asked the inspector.

"Because that's how long it's been since he was murdered."

"Murdered? Who murdered him?"

"I believe a man now going under the name of Andrei Davilov, who is serving a sentence in an Arctic labor camp, murdered him. What I want you to help me find out is why."

Doyarenko poured them two more drinks. "Something to do with his underworld connections. I don't know." He shrugged.

"Tell me about him."

"He's in his thirties. He started as a thug. Ten years ago he

156

applied to join the KGB but was turned down. He did one stretch in a camp in central Asia. The last few years he's been a henchman for the city's biggest heroin supplier, an *urka* named Sergei Sergeyev, who is now also in an Arctic camp."

"Archangel?" Ilin felt a throb of excitement in his chest.

The Ukrainian pondered. "Yes, I believe so."

"And Glazunov? With so many arrests, how has he managed to stay out of the camps?"

"Somebody keeps pulling strings." Doyarenko's eyes narrowed. "I've always thought it was one of your people. Sergeyev enjoyed the same protection until last summer. Then he was arrested and sentenced to three years."

"Only three?"

"He was not arrested for heroin. He was arrested for conspiracy to smuggle icons."

Leaving Petrovka Street in the back seat of the limousine Ilin remembered the grim walls and the muzzled windows of the cells in the women's sector of the Vladimir Isolator. He had spoken to his old friend from the Militia for perhaps half an hour in all. They had both agreed that Doyarenko, with his network of underworld *nasedki,* was better equipped to investigate the disappearance of Igor Glazunov, which he'd promised to do unofficially and with discretion until they had more information. Glazunov was a notorious pederast and during the weeks before his disappearance he'd been in the almost constant company of a Volga German boy who should not be too difficult to find.

Even given the promise of that, Ilin knew he had no choice. It was time for him to arrest Alisa Belova. She would be his, whether he wanted her or not.

But when they got back to the Lubyanka, he did not give the order.

20

Archangel, January 1979

He saw Carruthers enter the barracks just after he got back from morning mess. The Australian limped along the aisle with the aid of a makeshift cane. But there was a smile on his face, in a place where no one smiled in the morning.

Rhone dropped from his bunk and started out to meet him. Carruthers stopped by the latrine and stared back at the table, where several of the *urki* were cooking their breakfast.

For a moment he was solemn, but the smile returned as Rhone came up beside him. "Transfer! They woke me in the infirmary before reveille and told me to pack my things. Damned relieved. I was afraid they'd tag me with another fiver." He was racked by coughing. "Bastards."

"I heard about it," Rhone said. "I'm sorry."

"Across that snow without my bloody boots. Feet were frozen even before they threw me in the hole."

"How many?"

"Two off the left foot and one off the right. Leaves me a bloody gimp." Again he was briefly solemn. "So like I said. If you want me to get word to someone . . ."

Rhone studied his face and nodded. He told him the Moscow Station twenty-four hour number. "Ask for Brown. He may have been expelled from the country so if he's not there, ask for his replacement. Give them my name and tell them where I am, that I was tried and sentenced in closed court."

"I still didn't *get* your name," Carruthers said after he'd repeated the phone number. He held out his hand.

Rhone took it. "The name is still Andrei Davilov."

Carruthers smiled and squeezed his hand. Rhone felt a sense of loss. He could have counted on one hand the times he'd even spoken to him, yet by his very presence the Australian had served as a kind of anchor, a non-Russian entity, a tie to a past that belonged not to Andrei Davilov but to Edward Rhone.

Carruthers released his hand. The young, tattooed *urka,* again shirtless, had just emerged from the latrine. "That's the fag what ratted on me."

Sullen, the *urka* stared at him. Then he smiled. "Goodbye sucker."

Sergeyev walked back to the table. He put his hand on the boy's back and stroked his tattooed muscles. Rhone thought, though it was almost concealed, that he saw the cringe on the boy's face. Then Carruthers stumbled toward the table, swinging the cane like a club. The kid ducked as it whooshed past his head and Carruthers, turning in an awkward pirouette, lost his balance and went stumbling toward the floor. Rhone saw the flash of the blade coming out of the kid's boot, took three long strides, and kicked him on the chin. Blood spurted from his mouth as he collapsed. Then somebody's feet were tangled with Rhone's and his legs were suddenly swept from beneath him. He landed face first on the board floor, a knee landed hard on his back, and his right hand was wrenched up to his shoulderblades. He struggled, then ceased his struggling and turned to look up.

A crowd had gathered. An enormous man with one blind eye, open and sallow white as a milky oyster, was holding him. Sergeyev was leaning over the kid, dabbing at his bloody mouth with a handkerchief.

"*Nasedka!*" Carruthers hissed, getting shakily to his feet. "Goddamned fuckin' *nasedka!*"

"Get out of here," Rhone said to him. "Go on!"

159

Carruthers glared at the kid, then seemed gradually to become aware of Rhone's position, still pinned on the floor.

"Go on. I'm all right."

The Australian's eyes were wild and his face was ghostly white. Slowly, in silent panic, he backed off into the crowd.

Sergeyev left the kid on the floor and turned back to Rhone. He nodded at the one-eyed man and Rhone's arm was released. "What is this about?" said the *urka.*

Rubbing his arm, Rhone got up. "The Australian says the boy ratted on him."

Sergeyev looked at the kid. "Is this true? Why?"

The kid was whimpering, pathetic, grotesque with his mural of tattoos. "The captain said that he would arrange to let me see a woman."

Sergeyev dropped the bloody handkerchief. He turned back to Rhone. "Go back to your work gang. We are the underworlders and we will judge our own."

They found the young, tattooed *urka* dead in his bunk at reveille the following Sunday. His lips had turned blue and his blank eyes stared up at the ice-laced rafters. Major Senchenko looked around at the rest of the *urki,* then at Rhone, then ordered the soldiers to take the body out. They rolled it in a blanket and lowered it onto a stretcher. His locker had already been emptied. Sergeyev watched them lift the stretcher with the body and start out. His eyes glistened with tears. Senchenko took a last look around and went out after the soldiers. After he was gone, Sergeyev sat down and motioned for Rhone to join him.

"It saddens me," he said, deeply thoughtful. "But I always respected the Australian. Though he was a foreigner I thought we understood each other. I visited him in the infirmary the morning before he was released and gave him a message for my wife in Moscow." He smiled. "Yes. Outside of prison I lead the other life." He took out a pack of American cigarettes, shook one out for Rhone, and lit it with a gold-plated lighter. "I understand you are here because of your involvement with Vasily

160

Yaroshenko. That interests me. You see, I have also had considerable involvement with Vasily Yaroshenko."

He was momentarily silent. Rhone looked at his expensive fur hat, the coat, the rings on his uncalloused fingers, his dark, aquiline features.

"We had a very good arrangement in central Asia," Sergeyev said. "An import operation from Afghanistan that was very profitable for both of us, until Yaroshenko decided to take it all for himself." He paused. "It is also because of Yaroshenko that I am in this place."

21

Moscow, January 1979

The ringing phone woke Ilin before eight on Sunday morning. Beside him Katusha groaned and rolled over, still half asleep. He waited for a moment beneath the covers, listening to the harsh annoying jangles, then slipped out and crossed through in his pajamas to the living room to answer it.

"I've got him." It was Doyarenko, calling from Petrovka. "Glazunov's Volga German. He's told me everything you'll need."

"I'll be there in half an hour. Thank you, Yevgeny."

The Volga German's name was Aleksei Herman Dorn. He'd had a couple of minor arrests and he'd served one stretch for parasitism. Sitting in his little cell, barred rather than enclosed like the cells in the Lubyanka, he looked lonely and afraid. He had one black eye and there were ugly blue marks, like fingerprints, around his neck. Ilin glanced with brief wonderment at Doyarenko's strong, stubby hands.

"Open the shirt," said the inspector.

The kid unbuttoned his shirt. Running across his stomach was a purple scar, still fairly fresh, that wore a shaggy edge of nonprofessional medical treatment.

"This is Colonel Ilin, of the KGB," said Doyarenko.

The kid shuddered and appeared as if he might begin to cry.

"Tell the colonel where you got this scar."

"A knife," the kid whimpered. "A man named Andrei Davilov. He killed Igor. He broke his neck with just a twist of his hands."

"He attacked you?" the colonel prompted. "Tell me how it happened."

The kid was silent. In his eyes a pathetic gleam of hope.

"Tell him how it happened," said the inspector through the bars.

Hope faded. "We attacked him. Him and a girl, on the Komsomolsky Prospekt."

"Why did you attack him?"

"A man paid us."

"What man?"

"I don't know. A tall man with a bullet scar in his neck. A fancy dresser. I'd seen him a few times with Sergei."

"Sergei Sergeyev," Doyarenko said to the colonel. "The smuggler."

And the man with the scar, thought Ilin, was Vasily Yaroshenko. "This man—did he work with Sergeyev?"

"It looked to me like Sergeyev worked for him," said the kid.

"And you were to attack Davilov?" asked Ilin.

The kid nodded, again a gleam of hope.

"You were to kill him," said Doyarenko.

Hope faded eternally. "We were to kill him. The man said there would be no difficulty. He said he was a sucker."

"And what happened?"

"Igor went after him with his club and I had my knife. It looked like he wasn't going to fight back. Then he realized we were going to do more than beat him up. He broke Igor's neck and he turned my knife back into my stomach."

"Enough?" Doyarenko asked the colonel.

Ilin nodded. Now he understood. What Yaroshenko had known. How he had known it.

They left the kid, weeping in his cell.

163

Upstairs he used the inspector's phone to call the Lubyanka. But he didn't get the chance to tell them what he'd learned.

The Lubyanka switchboard had been trying frantically to reach him. General Drachinsky was already on his way back from the dacha. There had been a suicide on a special Soviet Embassy flight back from London.

22

Archangel, January 1979

Though it was mid-morning, the barracks was still under lock-down and no one had even been allowed to go to mess. Soldiers with machine guns were stationed at the door. Angry, hungry men milled about, cursing under their breath.

Spread out on the card table between them was a feast of the foodstuffs Sergeyev kept in his locker. A pot of coffee was brewing on the stove and the smell richened the air.

"Yaroshenko and I were in business together. The business of smuggling heroin."

"Heroin? Yaroshenko?" Rhone looked at him with incredulity.

Another soldier arrived at the door and announced that the barracks would be allowed to go to mess. The men started forming up by gangs, pushing and shoving to get to their places.

"Yaroshenko had no contact with the drug itself," Sergeyev explained as he spread butter over a slice of Moscow French bread. "I handled importation, from Afghanistan. But his guarantee assured passage at the frontier. Periodically he would fly down to Dushanbe, from somewhere in Kazakhstan. Semipalatinsk, I think. He also guaranteed transport from

165

Tadzhik to Moscow, which without him would have been even more dangerous than the border crossing."

Rhone carefully placed a piece of herring in sour cream on a thin salted wafer and fitted it into his mouth. Seated with them at the table, though he had not spoken except to be introduced, was the old man, Kolnyshevsky. The other lesser *urki* kept a discreet distance apart, a buffer against the famished men watching from all around.

"Once the shipment reached Moscow," Sergeyev continued, "distribution was my responsibility alone. But Yaroshenko claimed to have an outlet in Czechoslavakia that could more than double our market. This required giving him control of the shipment from Tadzhik. I finally agreed to this arrangement, last summer."

"And Yaroshenko sent the entire shipment to western Europe," Rhone said.

"How did you know?" Sergeyev smiled.

"Because he planned to defect."

"Yes. I suppose he did. Exporting the heroin out of the Socialist Bloc allowed for a hard currency sale. And I suppose he left the money abroad."

"He left it in a Swiss bank," Rhone said. "And then you must have been arrested for the Moscow distribution of one of the previous, smaller shipments?"

"No." Having finished his breakfast, Sergeyev lit another smoke and left the pack on the table. "I was arrested for conspiracy to smuggle Russian icons to West Germany. It was a frame-up, of course. There was not one person in the courtroom who did not know who I was and what I really did. But I received only a three year sentence, which I accepted graciously enough, because I knew that if Yaroshenko had considered it necessary he *could* have seen me tried on a heroin charge. This way, I'll be released next spring."

"But why did Yaroshenko want to send you to prison?"

"I would have killed him."

"But you could have killed him next spring."

"Yes. But he did not plan to remain in the Soviet Union that

166

long. But once he found himself in the Gulag he had no choice but to try to arrange for my death before I could arrange for his. This is a very small world and it's impossible to know when one will cross one's worst enemy's path."

Now Rhone too had eaten his fill, for the second time in the months since his arrest. The lock-down had been lifted and the gangs were forming up for mess.

"You are also a natural target of Yaroshenko," said Sergeyev. "And I have heard a rumor that a KGB agent loyal to him has been planted among the inmates here. I do not know who he is and I do not know which of us is his target."

"I know," Rhone said softly, wondering how the obvious had eluded him for so long.

"Tell me who he is and my men will kill him."

"No," Rhone said, rising. "I'll kill him myself."

He turned and started to go.

"Comrade."

He turned back.

Sergeyev slipped his hand into one of his polished boots and drew out a knife. He flipped it, caught it by the end of the blade and held it out handle first. Rhone stepped back and took it, dropped it into his own boot, went back to his bunk, got his coat, and started out.

Though the sun was up there was still a crowd around the mess hall, pushing toward the door where the cursing orderlies fought them back, periodically called out a number, and admitted a gang. Rhone spotted Saunin, almost at the door. He pushed in among the ragged hungry men and fought his way up to join the gang.

Popkov greeted him with Andrei Davilov's name and patronymic. Saunin, who had seen him at the table with the *urki*, observed him thoughtfully. Rhone looked back in silence. One of the orderlies called their number. Saunin turned slowly away and led the gang up the steps. Popkov produced Rhone's bread ration, which he'd gotten for him from Tsvilko, and held it toward him.

167

"It's all right," Rhone said, motioning for him to keep it.

The bespectacled old man stared at him incredulously.

In the steamy interior two men moved to guard an empty place at a table. Popkov got a tray. The gang was identified and counted. Rhone and Saunin collected the bowls of steaming gruel. They moved to the table.

Rhone sat at the end, next to Popkov, across from Saunin. Outside they could hear the din of the waiting crowd, the curses of the orderlies, the grumbling of the men. At the serving counter another gang were clamoring for their food. Down the table, members of two separate gangs were arguing about who should claim an empty space. But at the crowded tables where the men were eating their food there was reverent silence.

Rhone looked down indifferently at his own gruel. Across from him Saunin ate self-consciously, paused, and looked up.

"Why did you tell me?" Rhone said in English. "Knowing I could give you away? If you were really Remick's contact that would have been the most foolish thing you could do."

"I told you because I know who you are. Or at least I know for certain who you are not."

"And you could only have gotten that from Yaroshenko."

Saunin smiled. "I was going to tell you I got it from the Australian. That I read his lips that day in the mess tent when he told you he knew who you were."

"But that is not what gave you away."

"I know. I have masqueraded as a character who exists only in your own fabricated confession. And Yaroshenko was destroyed not to protect this imaginary American contact in Semipalatinsk, but as a gambit to get *you* into the Lubyanka. Are you going to tell me why?"

All over the mess hall curious eyes and ears were watching and listening to the strange confrontation in a foreign language between these two men who did not have enough intelligence to shut up and eat their food.

"If I tell *them* who *you* are," Rhone said, looking around, "you will not even live out the day."

Saunin smiled again. "And of course it would be too much

168

for me to expect you to keep my little secret until I can arrange to leave this place."

He rose suddenly, abandoning his soup and his bread on the table, and started toward the entrance. Rhone rose also, watched him push his way past the orderly and down into the crowd surging up the steps. Rhone made for the exit at the back of the long hall. As he went out he noticed a fight had broken out over the food the two of them had left.

Outside the cold air burned his face. He ran toward the front of the building. Reaching the corner he stopped, gazing over the yard where men rushed here and there in all directions. He spotted Saunin at the corner of the BUR, hurrying toward the commandant's headquarters building.

Rhone ran after him. At the front corner of the headquarters building Saunin turned and looked back, then moved on around out of his sight. He was ascending the steps when Rhone reached the corner. At the top Saunin spoke to a soldier, then they both went inside.

Rhone was gasping for breath by the time he reached the steps. He met the soldier coming back out the door and kicked the AK-47 from his hands as he was swinging it up to fire. His second kick landed on the soldier's locked, right knee. Rhone heard the snap as it dislocated, heard his agonized cry, and saw the pain that contorted his face as he went down.

Saunin, standing in the open door of Senchenko's office, had also heard the cry and now turned, watching with awful comprehension as Rhone drew the knife from his boot.

He was on him in three leaping strides, stabbing upward through Saunin's outstretched hands and between the folds of his greatcoat, into his solar plexus and far up beneath his ribs. The big Russian groaned as if the breath had been knocked from him and grabbed Rhone with both his powerful hands. Rhone lunged against his big, barrel chest, shoving the blade higher, turning it and twisting it, digging the blade and the handle and even his own fist up into the folds of the fat as the larger man clung to him, moving him about in slow, labored steps as though in a final, eerie waltz.

Rhone watched the twisted face slowly relax, watched the

eyes go blank. He turned the blade, digging for the heart, but it seemed Saunin clung to him for a moment even after he was dead. Then suddenly Saunin released him and Rhone drew the knife back out of his chest and out of the heavy coat and, relieved finally of the terrible weight, stepped back away as Saunin collapsed in a heap on the floor.

Through the open door of the office Major Senchenko trained a Makarov semi-automatic on him from behind his desk. Rhone dropped the bloody knife and it stuck in the wood floor at his feet. Behind him he heard the groans of the injured soldier. The door opened. He heard the boot-steps of more guards coming in.

Senchenko rose, still holding the pistol on him, and walked slowly around the desk. He looked at the dead man, and back up at Rhone. "What was he going to tell me?"

Rhone said nothing.

"He had only time to say that he was an agent of the KGB, working undercover inside the camp. Is that true?"

"I don't know."

Senchenko sighed. "And I guess I will never find out. I have had a phone call from Moscow. You are going back to the Lubyanka."

23

Moscow, January 1979

Colonel Ilin was seated at the head of the table when they entered the green-painted office. His uniform was wrinkled and he had a dirty shadow of beard on his face. He appeared exhausted and pale, somewhat like a prisoner himself.

He nodded at the chair at the opposite end of the table and Rhone went over and sat down. The two civilian KGB men who'd brought him from the airport waited just inside the door. It was midnight, perhaps later. The high, barred windows were dark and Dzerzhinsky Square was silent.

"I received a report that you killed a man this morning."

"Yes."

One of the plainclothed men came and took a seat halfway along the table. The other remained at the door, behind Rhone.

"Did you know who he was?" asked the colonel.

"Just another *zek.*"

"He was a KGB major assigned to your old friend Yaroshenko on Semipalatinsk security. Why did you kill him?"

Rhone said nothing.

Ilin mashed out a cigarette in an ashtray already full of butts and immediately lit another. "He'd been planted there in

171

the hope he would learn something from you that would help Yaroshenko. What had he learned? What did he know that compelled you to kill him in full view of the commandant of the camp?"

"Word was he was an informer. I drew the job of getting rid of him."

Ilin rose and started down the table. "You are lying. But then you have lied to me all the time you were here." He stopped, halfway along it. "Your name and your purpose for coming to Moscow?"

"My name is Andrei Petrovich Davilov and I came to Moscow to visit my sister and—"

"Your name is not Andrei Petrovich Davilov! And for all I know you do not even have a sister. Andrei Davilov is dead. He was found, after an anonymous phone call, by our London Embassy personnel, hiding on an estate in the English countryside. He killed himself on the flight back from London in the custody of the KGB."

He walked back to the head of the table and resumed his seat. Rhone sat stunned as the significance of what Ilin had said sank in. He glanced back at the man behind him, then brought his left hand up to scratch his head, drew it down over his face, and covered his eyes as though to seal off the world around him. He placed his left elbow on the table and rocked forward, leaning on it, at the same time reaching up under the table with his right hand. He found the cross-brace that supported the leg and withdrew the cut-out photo section of Andrei Davilov's face from the top of the leg. By the time he'd removed his left hand from his own face, straightened up and looked again at Ilin, the photograph was tucked safely into the right sleeve of his underwear.

Ilin glanced at his watch. "I'm going to give you until dawn to think things over." He looked up at the door. "Boris!"

His aide came in.

"Take him to his cell." As Rhone rose and started toward the door the Colonel picked up the telephone and began dialing a number. "Bring me Alisa Belova."

Rhone suddenly turned back. Ilin had been waiting for his reaction and he hadn't prepared himself to conceal it.

"You thought she had left the country?" He shook his head. "She did contact your friend Brown to make the arrangements. But she did not follow through."

He nodded at the big plainclothed man, who grabbed Rhone's arm and jerked him out into the hall.

He took him across into the Old Lubyanka and they rode the elevator down into the inner prison. He marched him to a cellblock and the guard inside escorted him to a cell almost identical to the one where he'd spent his first weeks in the Lubyanka. Lying on his narrow bunk staring up into the glare of the 200-watt lightbulb, he saw clearly the gambit that must have appeared elementary to Remick the instant he got the message from Carruthers. And in his mind heard the echo of his own voice that night after he'd first arrived in Moscow, telling Alisa that no matter what happened she must never forget to act exactly as if what had happened to him had happened to her own brother. And now she would have nothing but that cover story, already irrefutably blown, to cling to.

Boris held her gently by the bicep in his big stubby hand. Her graceful ballerina's body was lost beneath the folds of the shapeless prison smock. Her face was pale, somewhat drawn, and her eyes were glazed and red. But the rarity, the classic sculptured beauty of her face, almost transcended the wretchedness. And the defiance remained in her eyes.

"We know the man who came from London as Andrei Davilov last October is not your brother," said Colonel Ilin.

Her eyes did not waver. "But of course he is my brother."

"No, Alisa Petrovna. He is not."

He studied the face, which in the months since the trial had come to haunt his dreams, as the face of the impostor who'd claimed to be her brother had never ceased to haunt them.

And now, if he wanted, she was his. "Leave us alone, Boris."

He watched the big hand gently relax on her arm. Boris

turned and went out the door. Eyes unwavering, Alisa Belova waited.

"I did not want to be your interrogator," he said. "I could have had you arrested that night at the Café des Artistes. Or even before that. We have the tapes of your telephone conversations with Brown. That you *didn't* leave the country was inconsequential. It was still a crime merely to *conspire* to leave. But I didn't arrest you. I didn't want this. But now I have it."

"So what will you do? Torture me?"

"I have never tortured anyone in my life! But I will learn whatever it is you have to tell me." He rose. "But first . . ." The words, which already he'd rehearsed time and time again silently in his mind, caught in the dryness of his throat. "First I am going to make love to you. To let you know I can do with you as I please."

And not just to let her know it, he thought as he went over to lock the door, but to let the man who'd masqueraded as Andrei Davilov know it too. For though he could never have tortured her, Ilin knew it was imperative that her shame and despair should be genuine when again they met. And planning that, he'd tried to tell himself, this way, really, might be the most humane.

He walked back and faced her. "Take off your things."

She stepped out of the canvas shoes. She pulled the smock off her head. She peeled off the undergarments, prison undergarments the same as a man's, and nothing underneath. Naked, she was still unashamed. Looking into her cold, hating eyes he was briefly afraid that his scheme would not work and afraid, in spite of his lust, that he would not be able to do it. He walked her to the couch and laid her down on her back. He felt her body, felt between her legs, and all the time she lay unmoving, watching him with the same, unchanging eyes. He left his shirt on, unbuckled his belt, and lowered his trousers. On the narrow couch there was barely room for her to spread her legs. She was dry and she groaned when he entered her but after that she made not a sound. She lay still with her arms at her sides, watching him always with her changeless eyes. He stopped as

174

he was nearing orgasm and withdrew, promising himself he would find a whore when he left the office in the morning.

He stood up and pulled up his trousers.

"You didn't finish. Why did you stop?"

He said nothing. That would truly have made the triumph hers.

She reached for the blanket and started to wrap it around her, but he took it from her hand, folded it, and set it back at the end of the couch. She looked at the smock and the prison-issue undergarments on the floor in the middle of the room and he shook his head.

"The man who claimed to be your brother has just been returned here from a labor camp near Archangel. He was tried in closed court and sentenced to ten years, a few days before I last saw you at the Café des Artistes. Who is he?"

"He's my brother. I told you."

"No. He is not your brother. Your brother is dead."

He'd slept two hours on the couch after he finished her interrogation. He could see that the prisoner, whoever he really was, as he was led back in at first morning light, had slept even less.

"Your 'sister' has been very cooperative."

"Then you can release her."

"No. But *you* can spare her. And spare yourself."

"Spare?"

"No one can save either of you." He was silent for a moment. "Perhaps you would like to see her?" He clapped his hands and the door opened. Boris hulked in the corridor. "Bring me the woman."

He closed it.

Ilin met the prisoner's angry glare. "You were having an affair with her, weren't you?"

No response.

"I knew that, yet I failed to see the obvious. We had it on tape and I thought it was incest. I even accused her of it, at the Café des Artistes." He laughed and rubbed his cheek. "She slapped me but even that was just an admission it was true."

"You saw her at the Café des Artistes?" Though it was obvious he hadn't wanted to speak, he couldn't hold it in.

"Yes. I met her there . . . several times. Even after you were sent to camp." He waited, pacing it. "She offered to sleep with me, if it would help you."

Andrei Davilov, the impostor, took a slow step toward the table. Beneath the table Ilin unsnapped the holster and slipped the Makarov silently out.

He waited, watching the prisoner trembling with rage before him, brought the Makarov up into his view, and drew back on the slide, saying: "Last night, during her interrogation, I did have intercourse with her."

He came forward two steps and stopped only as the Colonel leveled the pistol at his waist.

"You can hardly stand that, can you?"

He was silent, almost bursting with rage.

"You knew her but a short time. Three days, was it? She's admitted she never saw you before you arrived in Moscow this time. Yet now I believe you think you love her." He waited, pacing it. "Her fate is in my hands, you know. I decide whether she is tried, whether she goes to camp. And only you can help her."

The door opened. She stood in it in the shapeless gray smock, looking even paler and more exhausted than she had a few hours before, no longer concealing her fear, no longer proud or defiant, looking months or years older than she had a few hours before.

He lowered the Makarov, clicked on the safety, and slipped it back into the holster. She tried to move forward toward the prisoner already moving toward her but Boris held her back lightly with his big hand on her bicep. Then at the colonel's nod he released her and she rushed sobbing into her lover's arms. Watching them kiss and hug, listening to the loud wails that rose in her throat, Ilin hated himself and hated life.

She ceased the wailing and drew back, rubbing her eyes, shaking her head. "He says Andrei is dead. I told him. I couldn't help it."

He was trying to touch her and she was pulling away.

"I told him everything he wanted to know!" she screamed.

"It's all right. Whatever you told them, none of it matters anymore."

"I let him fuck me!" she screamed.

He tried to say something and was at a loss for words. He glared back at the colonel and turned again to her.

Ilin rose and walked around the table. "For the record," he said to the woman, hating his role, hating the words in the script, "tell us again what you told me last night."

She shook her head.

"Tell us."

"No!"

"Do you want to come back here again tonight?"

The prisoner whirled on him viciously. Boris moved through the door. By the time he had turned back to the girl her face had changed. She looked him in the eye and when she spoke it was in a changeless monotone:

"I am an agent of the CIA. I never saw this man until he arrived in Moscow a few months ago. I do not know his true identity and I do not know . . ." She faltered. "I do not know what his mission was, but I believe he got himself imprisoned here intentionally."

She bowed her head. Ilin nodded at Boris, who stepped through, took her again by the arm, and started to urge her out. But for a moment she stood resolute and looked at the man who had claimed to be her brother as if she knew it was for the last time, and knew she could not afford the luxury of regret.

24

He purchased a forty-gram tin of black caviar, a bottle of imported wine, and a package of melba toast at the KGB Club across Dzerzhinsky Square. As he passed through the check stand he saw the fat prosecutor Zverev, selecting chocolates for his children or perhaps his mistress. Though he was sure Zverev had seen him too, their eyes never met and the prosecutor did not so much as nod in acknowledgment.

Back out on the cold street, in his civilian suit and knee-length fur coat, Ilin walked past the Dom Plakata poster shop and turned down through the square. At the monument to Ivan Fedorov he stopped and looked back. The two men from Surveillance, whom he'd first noticed before he'd entered the club, were just entering the square. And now he realized it was not the first time he'd seen them, or others like them. As he continued across the square toward the line of taxis outside the Hotel Metropole, he tried to recall when it had begun and tried to figure out why.

There were eleven taxis in front of the hotel. The first six were occupied by the drivers only but in the back seat of each of the last five sat single women. Reaching them, he walked along the sidewalk and peered through the window of each vehicle. From inside the women looked out at him: a leggy blonde who appeared almost Scandinavian, a couple of plain, Russian girls out of place in their western fashions, an attractive Oriental, Mongol or Manchurian. The woman in the fifth cab was brunette in her mid-thirties, with features not quite classically Russian, the face not quite flat, the eyes not so wide apart. Ten years ago, he thought, she must have been very lovely. As he put his hand on the door handle she smiled.

He got into the back beside her and gave the driver the address. As the taxi pulled out of the line he saw the two men from Surveillance, rushing to get into the first of the empty cabs. The woman took a furtive peek into the bag at the wine and caviar and smiled at him again. In the rearview mirror Ilin watched the other taxi pull out into the traffic behind them.

"My name is Tina."

He looked at her again. She took his hand, took his glove off, and lay the hand on her lap. Though his inclination, for some reason, was to remove it, he let it remain there for a few moments. Through her skirt he felt the warmth of her thighs. Thinking of Alisa Belova's thighs, tight around his waist, remembering her silence and the changeless look in her eyes, he loathed himself. And his lust, so urgent before, was now but a dull throb. And he knew, suddenly drawing his hand away from the woman's lap, that he would not be able to do it with her, that she could not substitute, that no one could substitute, that today, perhaps tomorrow and the next day too and for how long he could not guess, he would have to live with the throb.

She touched his face and asked him what was the matter. He took out his wallet, gave her a twenty rouble note, and told the driver to take him to the Lubyanka. The driver met his eyes briefly in the mirror before he made the turn. The woman, clutching the note, regarded him with awe and, he thought, a curious pleasure.

TOP SECRET

Science and Technology Directorate
Charged Particle Beam Weaponry: Definition and Analysis

Charged Particle Beam Weapon focuses and projects

atomic particles at near the speed of light from ground sites into space to intercept and neutralize re-entry vehicles. Both U.S.S.R. and U.S.A. have investigated placement of beam weapons in space to eliminate beam propagation difficulties and magnetic field deflection. Full-scale deployment of space-based charged particle beam weapons by either side could in the event of nuclear war result in total destruction of the enemy ICBM force. Technologies Applied to Beam Weapons Production:

1. Explosive or pulse power generation through fusion or fission to achieve peak pulses of power.
2. Capacitators capable of storing extremely high levels of power for fractions of seconds.
3. Electron or proton capable of generating high energy pulse streams at high velocity.
4. Collective accelerator to generate electron pulse streams or hot gas plasma necessary to accelerate other subatomic particles at high velocity.
5. Flux compression to convert energy from explosive generators to energy to produce electron beam.
6. Beam propagation technology.

Problems:

1. Beam instability.
2. Magnetic field deflection, creating pointing and tracking difficulties.
3. Beam must be propagated and bent to intercept incoming warheads.

Current Research Status: U.S.S.R. (Semipalatinsk) Solutions:

1. Explosive generation (Andrei Terlelsky and Andrei Sakharov).
2. Electron beam fusion (Rudakov).
3. Flux compression to convert energy from explosive generation to electrical energy for accelerator power.
4. Transfer of energy with pressurized gas lines (developed by Pacific Gas and Electric Company, California, U.S.A.).

5. *Water capacitators with pressurized water to 100 atmospheres.*
6. *Switching energy from storage capacitators to electron injector (process patented by American Electronics Co., data supplied by T Directorate).*
7. *Electron Injector (Novosibirsk Institute of High Energy Physics, technology developed by Alexander Terekhov).*

He'd read enough.

Ilin closed the folder and returned it to the clerk. Out in the corridor he lit a cigarette and smoked it on the ride up to the third floor. General Drachinsky greeted him by his name and patronymic but beneath the façade Ilin thought he detected a venom.

"What brings you back so early today? Your investigation, of course. Which we all *thought* you had conducted so brilliantly before."

He let it pass. "I want to go to Vladimir to interview Yaroshenko again. I have just been reading an analysis by the Science and Technology Directorate and I have concluded Semipalatinsk has absolutely nothing to do with this affair. It is, as they say, a red herring. Yaroshenko must know that. He must be using it, just as my impostor used it."

The generals' mood had soured. "Yaroshenko has suffered a stroke. He can neither move nor speak."

"Then I must talk with Gorsky."

"This stroke was suffered last night," said the General. "While he was under interrogation."

"And Gorsky?" Ilin whispered.

"Gorsky . . . is gone."

Inside for the first time he felt the panic he'd somehow held at bay ever since he'd watched Yaroshenko at the highest court of the Supreme Soviet, sneering at him from the dock. He turned and walked slowly and silently toward the door.

"Colonel!"

He looked back.

"What have you learned from your prisoner?"

"Really almost nothing. I know that he is not Andrei Davilov."

"But you did not learn that from him!"

"No, Comrade General." He swallowed hard. "From him I have gotten nothing but the red herring of Semipalatinsk and the mythical American agent Yaroshenko was sacrificed to protect. I don't even know his real name."

"And the methods you are using?"

He hesitated. "General, I do not believe he is the kind of man who will respond to the *methods* you are referring to."

Drachinsky smiled. "But you must try, Valeri Pavlovich. You must try everything you can. For all our sakes, as well as your own."

He went out, the conversation echoing in a jumble in his ears, and crossed over into the Old Lubyanka. Downstairs in the inner prison one of the guards let him into the cellblock. The unarmed guard inside opened the door of the cell. The man who was not Andrei Davilov stared hatefully up from his bunk.

Ilin nodded at the guard, who moved a discreet distance away down the corridor, and looked back into the cell. He took out a pack of Winstons, shook one out and held it through the door, then withdrew it when he saw the prisoner would make no move to take it.

He lit it for himself. "I have come to ask you something. I am not . . . I am not a torturer. I have come to ask you to save the girl. And save me from that."

After a moment the man got up and walked to the door. Ilin did not stop him as he reached up and took the cigarette from his mouth. There was something almost hypnotic about his eyes, locked with the eyes of the colonel. He took a slow, deep drag on the cigarette and removed it from his mouth. He pressed the glowing tip to his hand. His eyes still boring into Ilin's eyes, his face as changeless as Alisa Belova's, he mashed it out.

He walked back to the bunk and sat down. When he looked back at the colonel, his face was still unchanged. But there was something uncanny to the eyes. Ilin thought that he did not even see him. That he looked right through him.

Back in his office the colonel ate the caviar and toast and drank some of the wine he'd bought at the club. Though he knew the roe was exquisite, for him it had no taste. Afterwards he lay down on the couch and drifted into a feverish kind of sleep.

He awoke at three, to the sound of Boris coming through the door.

"I am sorry to disturb you, Colonel. I thought you might want to know. There has been a suicide in the women's block."

25

The pain from the burn came and went like a pulse. The throb of his mind in and out of his body. Ilin's pale, frightened face. In that moment while I had him hypnotized. By now he should have been dead. Alisa.

The door opened. He hadn't even heard the peephole drawn. Standing in it was a young guard with a familiar and incongruously unmalicious face, which now appeared oddly sad, sympathetic. Without speaking he motioned him through the door.

Walking beside him on the bullwalk, Rhone remembered seeing him before. Before Archangel, the kid who'd whistled and bounced on his toes, and tossed and caught the coin. The day he'd first been transferred to the communal cell, when he had somehow gleaned a sense of hope from the kindness in those pale blue eyes and the innocence of the young beardless face. He whistled *Swan Lake*. Alisa dancing naked beside the bed. And now, though still kind, the face was drawn and lined and there was a tired, old sadness in the eyes. The kid had aged like a *zek*.

They went out the door, the kid with him, contrary to normal procedure. "My name is Yuri," he said as they started along the corridor. "I am your friend. You can believe me."

They boarded the elevator and rode up two floors. It stopped and they got off and marched to the door of another cellblock. Inside was a matron in a khaki skirt and a blouse with the blue shoulder-boards of the KGB. She led Rhone along it with Yuri beside him. Hearing sobs from behind one of the olive doors, he stopped. It was a woman's voice.

"I'm sorry," Yuri said. "We wanted you to see for yourself. So you would have no doubts how it happened."

He'd already left them, running and stumbling along the bullwalk. He stopped outside the open door.

The floor was awash with blood. There was more blood on the table and the bed and it had splattered over the white-painted wall like oil splattered on a painter's canvas. She lay just inside the door, wrapped in a sheet from head to toe. Two medical orderlies had just rolled her onto a stretcher. One arm lay free of the sheet. There was a deep gash in the wrist, cut by a razor blade that lay not far from her body.

He started through the door. One of the orderlies lunged upward, driving his shoulder into his stomach and pushing him back into the bullwalk. Then Yuri and the matron were there, grabbing him, holding him back. The orderly released him and went back into the cell. They lifted the stretcher and came out and started back up the bullwalk.

Though he'd ceased to struggle, Yuri and the matron both held him. "Please," the kid whispered. "You do not want to see the face."

The door at the end of the bullwalk opened, and closed with a clang after they had carried her through. Yuri and the matron released him. He looked back into the cell. Written in blood on the wall in big cyrilliac letters was the diminutive:

"ANDRUSHA"

He went through the door and stood staring at the big, red letters. Him? Or her brother? He'd never know. Silently he wept. Then he heard the boots on the parquet floor and turned.

Ilin stood at the door, looking grimly in. "The difference between you and me, Andrei Petrovich, is that I have never had a choice in this affair. I do what I do because I must do it." He drew a long sigh. "You have made your choice and now she is dead." He turned and started back up the bullwalk.

Rhone moved through the door and stared after him.

At the cellblock door he stopped and looked back. "Now we have both lost her." He nodded at Yuri. "Take him back downstairs. Take him to the punishment block."

Weak and trembling, he was led up the stone steps. He did not know how long he'd been there. Hours or days. The door had never opened. He had not seen a flicker of light until they'd come for him. In the bare closet of the cell there had been no heat, no room to straighten out his legs. No covers. No food or water. No latrine bucket. No handy squares of *Pravda*.

The colonel was waiting for him inside a bare, gray-painted room. At his nod the guard went out and closed the door, leaving them alone. "I wanted to give you some time to think."

Rhone said nothing.

"If you could see yourself." He sighed. "What you have become."

But Rhone had seen himself. Shivering in the pitch dark of the stone cell, he had seen it as though his own eyes stood apart, the miserable wretch he'd been shaped into. And there was a time, just before his body separated from his soul, when he would have told the colonel anything he wanted to know, if he'd only come to ask.

"The girl is dead. Yaroshenko is speechless and paralyzed. You are going to be charged with murder." He smiled. "Yes. I know about that too. But that murder is not why you came to Moscow. What is your mission here?"

"I need water first," he whispered.

"You may have water after you talk."

He tried to organize it in his mind. It had come to him in the cell as he'd tried to block out the bloody vision of Alisa. And it could work if Ilin already knew enough to make it credible. "My mission was not in the Lubyanka. I don't know why Yaroshenko brought me here, unless it was to try to make me his scapegoat." He fell silent, stepped toward the Colonel, and leaned into his face. "Heroin! Yaroshenko was the main supplier of heroin for the Moscow market and was also smuggling heroin from Afghanistan through Moscow to the West."

Ilin sighed and stepped away from him. "We know about that. And we are not interested in heroin."

Rhone stalked him, intent. "And do you also know that Remick, the man I knew as Ross, was his Western buyer? Do you know that Andrei Davilov's sister, who you lapped after like a dog at the Café des Artistes, was his distributor here in Moscow, using her connections among the artists and dissidents?" He paused. "Don't you see? Yaroshenko's heroin operation was merely a cover, a means of conveying Semipalatinsk data to the West without the risk of contact with American Embassy personnel or to the Western spy network inside the Soviet Union."

He fell silent.

The colonel smiled, intrigued. "You fascinate me. Did Remick give you that or did you make it up yourself?"

"I've got to have water."

Ilin brushed past him to the door, opened it and shouted for a guard to bring water.

They waited, not speaking, until it came. Rhone took the bottle, poured a little into his hands and dashed it over his face and lips. He poured out more, drank from his hand, savoring.

"You were saying?" said the colonel.

He tried to formulate the fabrication's natural extension. But his mind wouldn't focus. The vision of the dead girl in the bloody cell. If only he'd looked one last time at her face. Looking back over the months of his own extended charade as Andrei Davilov he knew that he, finally, was responsible for her death. He had bargained her, as surely as he had bargained Yaroshenko and bargained her brother Andrei Davilov, for himself and for Remick's operation. *What he had become.* It was not the torture or hunger or degradation that had reduced him to such, but the bargaining process itself.

He twisted his lips into a smile. He held the bottle up drank as much as he dared, took several additional swallows, and held

187

them in his mouth. He leaned toward the Colonel and spewed the water into his face.

He laughed. "Heroin as a conduit for classified military information? If you are willing to listen to that, you are getting desperate, Colonel. As desperate as I was to say it."

Ilin removed a handkerchief from his uniform coat and dabbed at the water on his face, walked over and opened the door. "Take this piece of human excrement to his cell!" He looked back at Rhone. "Yes, we are both desperate. And still you do not believe me, though I promise you it is the truth: since the beginning, since I first thought I was getting to know you, it has been my desire to help you."

26

He felt oddly light-headed, almost giddy. The colonel stood in the fringe of the bright spot of light beamed on the prisoner, who was seated with his eyes closed in the center of the otherwise pitch-dark room. Ilin was impressed by a certain cinematic surrealism to it all. Curls of smoke wafted through the beam of light and at its edge, along the table, the tips of their cigarettes glowed. Drachinsky. The fat prosecutor Zverev. Several other civilian KGB. A colonel from the GRU.

He whacked the truncheon into the open palm of his left hand. "Open your eyes, Andrei Petrovich."

The prisoner opened his eyes to a squint. Ilin remembered the way Davilov's look had held him as he put the cigarette out on his hand. The light, as foolish as it made him feel, at least protected him from that.

"We know that's not your name, but you don't mind, do you? We have to call you something." Again he whacked his open hand with the truncheon. In the dark, against the wall, Boris stood a solemn, loyal shadow. Ilin walked toward the prisoner, still whacking his open hand, and stopped just before the chair. "Tell me who you are and why you came to Moscow." He put his hand on his shoulder and then drew it back as he saw, even through the squint into the bright glare of the light, the loathing that filled the prisoner's eyes. "I told you I wanted to help you. I still do."

"You're not here to beg him, Valeri Pavlovich."

The general. Ilin turned on him, enraged at the position he'd been shoved into, and found himself blinded by the very light that was supposed to help him. He turned back to the prisoner, mocking him with his squinting eyes, and lashed out suddenly with the truncheon.

He heard the crack as it landed on the side of Rhone's neck.

Though his head was turned sideways by the force of the blow, the prisoner did not flinch, hardly even appeared to blink, and waited still, watching him through the squint.

Ilin felt light-headed, limp in the legs, as though it were a dream in which he were being chased and found himself unable to run. He hit Rhone again, on the shoulder, and found he already needed to catch his breath. In the chair the prisoner hardly seemed to move.

"Like a father spanking his child."

The general. Again he turned to glare back and was blinded by the light. When he looked again at the prisoner there was a trace of a smile on his lips.

"Boris."

The shadow of the big man came forward toward the light. Ilin nodded toward the floor. Boris grabbed the prisoner and started to pull him out of the chair. He started to go peacefully and then without warning drove his knee up into the bigger man's groin. Boris grunted, seizing him by the neck and pulling him out of the beam of light. For a moment they were two shadows, wrestling almost silently in the darkness. Then the man who had passed himself for so long as Andrei Davilov hit the floor almost at the colonel's feet and Boris was instantly upon him, rolling him face down, seizing both wrists to draw his arms out taut, his jackboots planted hard on both his shoulders.

Ilin waited as the light was adjusted downward slightly. Trembling, he knelt. He remembered the training film. *"The sciatic nerve is just at the base of the spine, so the pain is per-*

ceived not at the point of impact but as an explosion in the brain." He'd watched that film with Vasily Yaroshenko.

He raised the truncheon. The prisoner, who moments before had struggled, now lay still and panting, his head turned back over his shoulder to look the colonel in the eye.

With a grunt Ilin swung the truncheon. He heard the thump and saw the shudder that went through the body, but unless it had been simultaneous with his own, the eyes had never blinked.

He swung again. The shudder was more pronounced. The eyes, staring up at him in the light, were glazed. Boris smiled in encouragement and shoved down on the shoulders with his jackboots and stretched back on the arms with the full weight of his torso. He looked back at the table. The general, smiling like a proud father, inserted a cigarette into his holder and one of the civilians promptly lit it.

Ilin turned back and hit the prisoner again on the base of the spine. This time the shudder became a contortion. And each time he hit it became easier, until the blows followed rapidly, one after another, rhythmic as the fall of an ax. He watched the glazed eyes turn moist with tears, watched the body twist and jerk, listened to the moans become cries.

Then he stopped, panting and trembling, and stood and nodded at Boris. Boris released the arms and also stood. Ilin took out his handkerchief and wiped the sweat on his face. The prisoner lay still for a moment on the floor. He moved slightly, as though in restless sleep. With great effort he got to his hands and knees and crawled to the end of the table. He reached up with one hand and grabbed the corner for support, lifted himself half up, lost his hold, and collapsed back to the floor. He gasped for breath, again reached up and caught the table and pulled himself up to his knees so he could peer down it at the faces that lined the edge of the light.

He looked back at Ilin. "Who are they, Colonel? Are they here to observe me? Or to observe you?"

His hand slipped from the table and he fell back face down on the floor.

191

Ilin lay the truncheon on the end of the table. He took out a cigarette, lit it and took several, rapid drags.

He looked at the general. "I told you. I could kill him and he would not talk."

"But you must make him talk, Valeri Pavlovich. You must."

"Then I will try questioning him under sodium thiopental."

"That might be a good idea," said the general. "Perhaps I should question him myself."

Ilin shook his head. "No, General. I will question him. It's my investigation. My career. My life."

Two orderlies strapped him to the padded table as the doctor prepared the injection. The prisoner frowned as it was administered, then slowly his face relaxed. The doctor nodded and the orderlies removed the straps. The doctor moved away from the table and Ilin, aware of the general behind him like a great hovering bird, approached.

He looked silently down at the prisoner. There was a slack smile on his lips and a glog of spittle had formed at one corner of his mouth and was slipping slowly down his cheek. Ilin put his hand on Rhone's shoulder and this time the gesture was not greeted with revulsion.

"Will you talk to me now?"

He nodded.

"We know you intentionally got yourself incarcerated here. Would you like to tell me why?"

"Yes."

He waited. The prisoner, silent, stared up at him.

"Then tell me."

"I can't tell you."

"Why can't you tell me?"

"I don't know." He appeared momentarily bewildered. "There was a hypnotist at Staffordshire. They must have known you would try this sooner or later. All I can tell you is I came because of Duffy."

"*Duffy?*" Behind him, Ilin could hear the general's angry, wheezing breath. "Who is *Duffy?*"

192

"Duffy was my commanding officer in Vietnam."

There was a hush over the little room, but in it Ilin thought he could perceive the patter of the crumbled falling sky.

The doctor touched his shoulder and eased back up to the table. "What is your name?"

"My name is Edward Rhone."

"You are an American?" the general asked. "You were an American soldier in the Vietnam war?"

Rhone nodded. No one knew what really had happened. Jackson and Perry knew he'd done it but they didn't know the real reason. And though Remick might have suspected he'd pulled the trigger he couldn't have known for sure. And Rhone had told no one about it since then.

Now these men standing around the table were his confessors. He wanted to tell them. He had to tell them.

27

Duffy didn't show him the sword until they were touching down on the lz. Seeing it and knowing he'd already seen the scabbard where it fit, Rhone said nothing.

Two days later Duffy ordered Perry's squad out after the snipers at dusk and only Perry and Jackson made it back. The next night Rhone caught them drawing straws, matches, in a bunker. They were both surprised when he told them he wanted in.

He lost. But then that must have been the way he'd wanted it. After he held up the short match Jackson asked him if he'd zap Duffy on patrol in the morning.

"No," he told him. "I'll do it now."

He crawled out. The night was silent.

He found Duffy out by the wire staring off into the trees. He said he was trying to draw some fire.

Rhone asked him if the V.C. he'd zapped in Cholon were drinking tea.

"Yeah man, they were all drinkin' fuckin' tea."

Duffy didn't ask him how he knew. He just looked around at him in the dark with his wild, crazy eyes beneath that black silk bandana, and then he looked back out through the wire into the bush. Rhone already had his holster unsnapped, and as he took

out the Colt, brought it up, and pointed it at the back of his
head he couldn't imagine Duffy didn't know, hadn't been wait-
ing for this ever since he'd first shown him the sword.
  But he never moved. Never tried to resist.

In the dusty stacks at Archives and Registry Ilin found the
NKVD dossier on an Albert Rhone, who'd been attached to the
American Embassy in Moscow from 1947 until 1950. He knew
without having to consult the files that Avery Remick had also
been at the Moscow Embassy at that time. Rhone's dossier
stated that he'd been involved with the wife of a military attaché at the Embassy during the first few months of his tenure
in Moscow, but since his own wife was aware of the affair and
the husband of the woman in question had been transferred
back to the United States, the information was probably of no
value to attempted recruitment. Rhone had one child, a son
Edward.
  He closed the folder and walked out.
  Back in the infirmary he looked through the open door of the
room at the prisoner Edward Rhone, now fully conscious and
sitting up on the table. He wondered what kind of a man it was
who could be convinced to get himself intentionally incarcerated in a place like the Lubyanka. But whatever he was,
whoever he was, Ilin envied him. His courage. Alisa Belova.
She was everything *he* would never have. Rhone was everything that he would never be.
  He stepped past the guard through the door and Rhone
looked up. On his lips the trace of a mocking smile.
  Ilin glared at him. From his days at the University he constructed the sentence word by word in his mind. "So you are an
American," he said in English with his thick Russian accent,
preconstructing the next sentence even as he spoke. "So every-
thing you have told me has been a lie. All this time you have
been trying to make a fool of me."
  "You are wrong, Colonel," the American said with a smile.
"All of this time I *have* made a fool of you."
  The words sank slowly in and Ilin knew they were true.

195

"Yes. He has made a very *great* fool of you."

It was Drachinsky, standing beside the door. Ilin hadn't realized he was there.

"But I am taking over his interrogation now and I promise he will not make a fool of me." Drachinsky clapped for the guard. "Take him to his cell. I am going out to the dacha to see if I can get one good night's sleep. Monday morning, one by one, we start breaking all his bones."

Rhone pushed the table into the corner of the cell beneath the grated vent, stood on it on his tiptoes, reached through to retrieve the cut-out photo section of Andrei Davilov's face, and dropped back to the floor. He put the photo beneath his pillow and moved the table back to the middle of the cell. When again the peephole opened he was seated back at the table.

The next time the guard looked in, it was to announce bed call. It was ironic. As evening rations were served, Rhone had looked into his sad blue eyes and been sorry.

He kicked off his boots, removed his dungarees, got beneath the blanket, and spread the dungarees over the blanket. His eyes were closed when the peephole opened again.

When it closed he tossed the blanket off and pulled on his dungarees. He retrieved the canvas boots and slipped them under his mattress. Then he stood on the bunk, facing into the corner to the right of the door.

He extended his left leg up and planted his bare foot against the door facing, extended both arms upward and outward, and pressed his palms flat against the two converging walls. Using the three pressure points, he lifted himself up and planted his right foot against the wall above his bunk, juxtaposing that pressure against the pressure of his left hand on the other wall to move his left foot a few inches higher up the door facing.

Alternating his opposite pressure points, he inched up the corner of the cell until his left foot rested finally on the top facing of the door, and his outreached hands clung almost where the walls converged with the ceiling.

Defying gravity, he waited.

196

The shutter opened, then closed. The key turned in the lock. The door opened inward beneath him. He looked back down as Yuri hurried through. Rhone released the outward pressure and dropped down behind him.

As Yuri turned Rhone thought he saw in those clear blue eyes only the vaguest inkling of his pitiful vulnerability. He hit him in the solar plexus and Yuri dropped as if he'd been shot.

Rhone knelt and rolled him onto his back. He felt at his neck for a pulse, then took the pillow from the bunk and placed it over his face. He held it down with the weight of his upper body supported by both his locked, extended arms.

After a couple of minutes he removed it and checked again for the pulse. This time there was none. Rhone looked at the pale, youngish face, stared into the pale blue eyes, now blank, open wide. He sighed and closed them, and started to unbutton the dead man's uniform.

After he'd removed his dungarees and put on the uniform, which almost fit him after his months of starvation, and put on Yuri's wristwatch, socks, and boots, he dragged the corpse onto the bunk and rolled it face toward the wall, placed the pillow beneath the head, and lay the blanket over the body with the dungarees on top of the blanket.

He put the canvas boots back beneath the table and spread the contents of Yuri's uniform pockets on top. A half pack of Astras and a few wooden matches. Some change and a few rouble notes. The identification card with the photograph of the boyish face and the pale eyes staring at him through the protective lamination. He read the name. *Yuri Ivanovich Anikin.*

He put the money in his trouser pocket, along with cigarettes and matches, retrieved the photograph of Andrei Davilov from beneath his pillow, and put that, with Yuri Anikin's KGB card, in the breast pocket of the uniform. He took a last look around the cell, retrieved the key ring from the lock, went out and closed the door behind him.

He moved down the bullwalk toward the gallery at the end,

197

pausing outside each of the little olive doors to open the shutters and look into the cells, all but a couple of which were occupied. And in each of them a man with his own terrible story to tell.

Around the gallery he entered the washroom. He took out the key ring and found the key to the supply cabinet, unlocked it, and got a razor and a box of new blades. He took out Yuri's ID card and the photograph of Andrei Davilov, removed the ID card from the open-ended laminated casing and lay the card and the Davilov photo side by side on the counter. He studied them both for a minute, then got a fresh blade from the box and started to draw it down the outer edge of Yuri's photo on the KGB card. The eyes in the picture stared up at him from the boyish face. He hesitated, his hand trembling, and let the blade slip from his fingers. He stepped back, rubbing his hands together as if they were freezing cold. There was a constriction in his throat and his stomach fluttered so that he thought he might throw up. He looked away from the eyes in the photo, held up his hand, and observed the trembling. He sucked in his breath in a series of deep, rapid gasps and waited until the trembling had ceased. When again he took up the blade and began to cut along the edge of the picture his hand was steady and it was only upon the line of the cut that his eyes found focus. The face in the photo was a blur.

He made the four cuts, pushed the square photo out of the ID card, lay it upon the photo of Andrei Davilov, as a pattern, and cut that to an identical size. He fitted the Davilov photo into the framed open square that had been left in the ID card by the removal of the original photo, smoothed the joining edges with his thumb and slipped the card back into the sheathed laminated casing. He tore Yuri's photo into tiny pieces, dropped it into the open hole of one of the toilets, returned to the counter, and studied his work. The Davilov photo fit perfectly in the frame he'd cut into the ID. Unless it were removed from the casing no one should ever suspect it was not legitimate.

He washed his face over one of the wash basins, put a fresh blade in the razor, and shaved. He returned the razor and all

198

but one of the blades to the supply cabinet, locked the cabinet, put the blade and the ID card into the breast pocket of the uniform, and started out. As he emerged onto the bullwalk he heard the steel door open at the end of the cellblock.

"Prisoner back from interrogation."

He tilted the bill of his uniform hat down over his forehead and started toward the door, where an escort guard waited with a haggard old man.

The guard pushed the prisoner through as Rhone got to the door, and Rhone took his arm as the door clanged shut behind him. He walked beside the prisoner, half-supporting him, along the bullwalk to the first empty cell, found the key, unlocked it and ushered him through. He closed the door behind him and stopped to look through the peephole.

Inside, the old man, looking as sickly and emaciated as Alexander Terekhov the night he'd visited him in the infirmary, stared dully back. His face was a mask of agony and despair. Just below his knees his dungarees were caked with dried blood so the rough material adhered to the flesh beneath.

Rhone found the key again and turned it in the lock. The old man gawked at him as he stepped inside. He took out the pack of Astras, shook out a cigarette, and handed it to him. The old man sat down tiredly on his bunk, looking at Rhone with wonderment. Rhone smiled sadly and went out.

He moved along the bullwalk, stopped outside the door of his own cell, and looked in. Yuri lay facing the wall, peaceful and still.

At 11:45 he went back into the washroom, stopped at the end of the radiator, and removed the cotter pin from the steam release valve. He bent one prong back out of the way, placed the end of the other prong against the side of a metal wash basin, and bent it at a right angle half an inch from the tip, making another slight short bend just at the tip. He dropped it into his pocket and removed his right boot.

He placed the sole of the boot against the edge of the wash basin so the heel overlapped it and with several downward

199

hammer blows of his fist against the reinforced back of the boot, knocked the heel loose from the sole by a quarter of an inch, then slipped it down over the edge of the basin and pried it open a little farther.

He put the boot back on and looked at the watch. It was 11:57. Walking tiptoe on his left foot, he went back out around the gallery and down the bullwalk halfway to the steel door. He removed the boot and got down on one knee, facing the door, and held the boot up by the toe, poised to strike the floor.

The key turned in the lock and the door opened inward. Beneath the bill of the cap he saw the new cellblock guard come through, visible only from the waist down, and in the open door the boots of the two table guards now ready to go off shift. He swung the boot down, striking a hammer blow with the heel on the parquet floor.

"Anikin," one of the guards said from the door. "It's time to go."

He struck another blow. "You go on. I'll catch up to you."

Pretending to inspect his shoe, he watched the boots of the cellblock guard moving toward him. The two table guards turned from the door and started away. It shut with a clang.

Rhone struck another blow with the boot and waited, head still bowed, as the guard came up and stood just beside him, then took another short step, almost past him.

He checked the heel again, and without ever lifting his face, raised himself up on his right leg, balancing in a half crouch, and tugged the left boot back on.

His foot slipped in with a pop and still in his half crouch he tested it once against the floor. Without ever looking around at the guard he started away down the bullwalk.

"Anikin."

He stopped and turned halfway back, his face still in the shadow of the bill of his cap.

"Keys."

Rhone took out the keys and pitched them to the guard. He saw a big stubby hand catch them but still did not see the face. He turned and continued on.

200

At the door he opened the shuttered window. The two guards were already seated at the table with their weapons resting across their laps. They already looked bored and neither of them looked particularly familiar. What he could see of the corridor appeared deserted, though beyond the first bend he could hear a bustling.

He took a fifty kopeck coin, one of Yuri's, from his pocket. He knocked once on the door and closed the shutter as the guards were looking up.

He heard one of them slide his chair back, heard the click of his boot heels and the jangle of the keys. He stepped to the left edge of the door, pressed almost against it, and as it opened outward he moved with it. When it was barely halfway open he flipped the fifty kopeck coin, made a slapping motion to catch it and sent it bouncing along the floor, past the table and away from the door.

He muttered a soft curse and stepped quickly past the standing guard and the one still seated without ever looking back. He hurried after the coin and caught it where it rolled ten paces along the corridor.

He straightened up slowly, his back still to the guards, and pursed his lips. He stood still for an instant, his mind a sudden blank. Then it came back to him.

He whistled a phrase of the theme from *Swan Lake*. The door clanged shut. Tossing and catching the coin, he started away down the corridor, bouncing on his toes.

28

A narrow passage led off the main ground floor corridor to an "L" bend. He stopped at a small door just before the bend, tried the handle, and found it locked. He produced the cotter pin from his pocket, slipped it into the keyhole, and probed for the tumblers. He withdrew it and making a slight adjustment to the bend, tried again.

The door opened onto a small janitorial supply room filled with cans of disinfectant, brooms, mops, brushes, and stacks of washcloths and aprons. He stepped back out and closed the door without locking it.

Around the bend two armed guards sat at a table outside the cellblock door, a short, wiry Russian with a thin moustache and a fat, broad-faced Mongol. They looked up as he approached. The Russian's machine gun stood against the wall directly behind his chair. The Mongol's lay across his lap.

Rhone stopped before the table. "I've come for the prisoner Terekhov. Interrogation. Orders of Colonel Moiseyevaite."

The Russian frowned. "Colonel Moiseyevaite? It's Sunday."

"I know it's Sunday. And Colonel Moiseyevaite knows it's Sunday. He was not pleased to be called back here this time of night."

The Mongol shrugged and rose. He slung his weapon over his

shoulder and took out his keyring. The Russian reached for the phone.

Rhone stepped closer. He placed his left hand on the table and leaned forward as the guard began to dial. "I wouldn't."

He hesitated after two numbers. Rhone was staring into his eyes but at the same time he was taking stock of the position of the Mongol.

The Russian dialed another number slowly.

"He's on a rampage," Rhone said.

He hesitated, his finger still poised at the dial.

Rhone leaned closer, smiling. "He smells like vodka and French perfume," he whispered. "I don't think it was his grandchildren he had with him at the dacha today."

The Russian laughed and Rhone laughed with him. He replaced the receiver and nodded at the Mongol. The keys rattled as he unlocked the door. The Russian pushed a ledger and a ballpoint pen across the table. Rhone took out Yuri's ID card, placed it down on the table, and signed the ledger *Yuri Ivanovich Anikin* as the Mongol shouted for the cellblock guard to bring out the prisoner Terekhov.

Rhone retrieved the ID card and stepped over to gaze past the Mongol, through the door and down the narrow enclosed bullwalk. The lights were dim and he could feel a draft of cold air. The guard unlocked a door halfway along the hall and shouted inside. After a moment he muttered a curse and stepped in, emerging momentarily holding a trembling old man by the arm.

Slowly they walked toward the door. Alexander Terekhov's head was bowed, his shoulders slumped. He blinked, shuffling his loose canvas boots along the floor. He looked up at Rhone as they reached the door, but in his weary eyes there was no sign of recognition.

The Mongol helped him out the door.

"Hands behind the back!" said Rhone.

Terekhov's eyes focused on him for the first time. He looked as though he'd seen a ghost.

"Hands behind the back!"

He crossed his hands suddenly behind his back. Rhone seized his bony arm, pulled him through the door, and shoved him away along the corridor. He nodded at the guards and swaggered after him.

Around the bend the old man turned to look at him again. When Rhone nodded, his eyes lit up and his withered face broke suddenly into a smile. Rhone opened the door of the supply room and motioned him inside.

"I'd given up hope," Terekhov whispered.

Rhone closed the door, found the cord, and switched on the light. "It's still a long way to Helsinki." He took out the razor, handed it to Alexander Terekhov, and told him to shave. "Leave the moustache."

He reached for the door to go. Terekhov was beaming at him. Rhone smiled into his withered face, then looked past him at one of the shelves. On the end of it there was a flashlight.

Rhone took it, told the old man he would be back for him soon, went out, and closed and locked the door behind him.

The straight, wide corridor to the north exit was almost deserted, though there were still a few stragglers filing past the guard table and through the heavy steel doors to the courtyard, and a few more milling about the locker room.

Rhone entered and looked around. In the open door of one of the lockers he could see a military overcoat. The guard at the locker closed the door and went out. Four lockers along the row another guard removed his coat and hung it on a hanger. He wore shiny new boots. A pair of older, worn boots lay in the bottom of the locker. Rhone watched him close the door and start out. Then he crossed toward the toilet in a path designed to intercept the guard.

They collided halfway between the lockers and the door. Rhone jammed his boot hard into the man's shin and brought his hands up as though to stop him from falling. His left hand caught the guard's shoulder and his right hand brushed lightly over the breastpocket of his jacket.

"Comrade! My apologies." Rhone stepped back from him, executing a gesture of obeisance.

The guard glared at him, smoothed down his jacket, and stalked on toward the door without a word.

In the little toilet Rhone removed the ID card from the sleeve of his jacket, glanced at it briefly, and slipped it into his shirt pocket.

There was a mirror above the washbasin and an unprotected 100-watt bulb above the mirror. He stood for a moment looking at his face before the mirror. After a few weeks of Archangel's noonday sun he had gotten some color back, but there were lines he had never seen, and in the eyes that stared back at him the look of a total stranger.

He reached up to his jacket pocket and ripped off one of the metal buttons, then took out the flashlight and flicked it on. He unscrewed the lightbulb and fitted the button in. He positioned the bulb over the socket and clicked the flashlight off. In darkness he screwed it back in. The light didn't come on and from the curses outside he knew the entire circuit had been blown the minute the dead short to the ground had been established.

He stepped back out. The locker room and the passage outside were pitch dark. He dropped the flashlight back into his pocket, removed the cotter pin lockpick, and made his way in the darkness to the first of the two lockers he'd selected.

As men bustled about in the darkness all around him, he picked the lock and retrieved the heavy coat, on its hanger, and the uniform. He moved to the second door, picked that lock, took out a second overcoat and the old pair of boots. He rolled the boots up in the second coat, made his way to the door, and started out. At the steel door that led to the courtyard he could hear a guard talking excitedly on the phone. He went the opposite way, back up the wide corridor that led into the inner prison, in the direction of a flashlight that came bobbing swiftly toward him.

"Has something happened?" Terekhov asked him as he stepped off the lighted passage back into the closet. "I've heard a lot of men running by."

"The lights went out at the north exit. They'll have to check

205

the whole circuit before they find it, and when they do, they'll be sure that's the way we went."

He handed him the uniform and told him to get dressed.

A few minutes later they emerged and started back toward the main corridor. Terekhov, now in uniform and clean-shaved except for a thin gray moustache, carried one of the greatcoats over his shoulder. Rhone had the other, still on its hanger. They walked back to the staircase, ascended one flight, and emerged out onto the corridor.

The elevator arrived just as they got there. The accordion door slid open and a guard with a weary prisoner stepped off. In the cab were two more guards, one of whom held the door open for Rhone and Terekhov. Rhone signaled they were going up rather than down and after the guard released it, the door swung shut. The electric motor whined and the cab descended on toward the ground floor. Terekhov was staring after the prisoner with a dazed, far away look. Then he looked down, fascinated, at his own blue epaulets.

Rhone took the coat off the hanger, straightened the hanger out, and then bent one end back to form a hook. He looked up and down to make sure the corridor was clear, then slid the hook-end of the hanger into the crack near the upper left corner of the sliding door. He probed for the lock carefully. When he found it he slipped the hook over the catch and lifted it out of the contact box, pulling the door open by hand.

Holding it back, he leaned in for a look down the dark shaft at the top of the cab, then used the sleeve of the coat to insulate the hanger, which he thrust into the opening in the contact box to allow the cab to move. He pushed the button to summon it. The motor whined and the cab started up with a lurch.

When the top of the cab was a foot below floor level he removed the hanger from the box to break the circuit and stall it.

He put on his coat and motioned for Terekhov, still staring down the corridor, to do the same. "Sir. Come on."

The old man looked back at him and looked at the open door to the shaft. Inside the cab someone cursed and Rhone held his fingers to his lips to signal Terekhov to be quiet. Rhone used hand signals to indicate he wanted him to take hold of the cable to balance himself and step down onto the steel cross-head where the cable connected to the cab.

Terekhov came back to the open door slowly. He stared into the shaft as though it were a dark abyss, though the step down to the cross-head was but a foot. Rhone took his hand and guided it out toward the cables. Terekhov grasped one of them, then grasped it with his other hand and planted one foot cautiously down on the cross-head. Rhone squeezed his arm, urging him, and he swung down, caught the cross-head with his other foot and hung there, teetering precariously. From inside the cab a Russian mother oath was heard.

After Terekhov had regained his balance Rhone motioned him around to the other side of the cables. Slowly and clumsily, he went. Rhone bent the hanger double and pushed it into his coat pocket, seized one of the cables, and dropped silently onto the cross-head, letting the accordion door slide shut behind him. As the mechanical hook-lock slipped back into the contact box the circuit was restored and the cab started up with a jerk. Now, except for the little lines of light from the halls that shone through above and below the doors, the elevator shaft was dark.

The cab stopped again at floor level in response to Rhone's summons. Then the motor whined and once more it lurched upward.

Rhone took out the flashlight and beamed it up the shaft. Running up one wall was a narrow access ladder. The cab and the stack of rectangular counterweights now descending toward them on Terekhov's side were each supported by a set of two heavy steel cables. Far above them a layer of fine mesh wire with an opening in the center for the cables was stretched across the overhead at the top of the shaft. Above that, resting on two steel girders, was the big electric motor.

The counterweight passed them going down and the cab continued upward without further interruption to the fifth floor, stopping with a jolt. Through the thin metal roof of the cab they heard the door open and close. Then there was silence and the cab remained still.

Rhone looked at the ladder. It was fifteen feet from where they stood to the overhead wire, but he could see no opening access for the ladder through the wire and he knew that in any case Terekhov would not have had the strength for the climb.

The door opened and shut again and to the loud whine of the motor the cab started back down the shaft, opposite the direction Rhone had wanted to go.

It stopped on the third floor, level with the counterweight. Rhone directed the flashlight beam over the stack of metal plates, six inches deep, a foot wide, about three feet in length, with about a square foot of the potential standing space given up to the cable connectors. Then the cab resumed its descent and with the flashlight Rhone followed the ascending weight. The cab stopped on the ground floor. The weight hung but a couple of feet below the wire across the overhead. The steel girders that supported the motor were a couple or three feet above that.

The cab started upward again, then stopped with a jolt halfway between the third and fourth floor as the motor suddenly went silent.

Rhone clicked off the light and looked up at the bottom of the next accordion door. Now no light was visible beneath it. The shaft was pitch black and he could not even see Terekhov, standing directly before him on the cross-head.

"What has happened?" the old man whispered.

"The electricians have shorted out the whole system. Now they'll try the auxiliary generator and that will probably go too."

"Then we are left here?"

"No. The primary system will still function once they replace the fuses." He reached out and touched Terekhov's shoulder. "Are you all right?"

"Yes. I am all right." He hesitated. "Do you still think we will get out of here?"

"Yes. We'll get out."

They heard the generator motor. The thin line of light appeared beneath the door of the next floor. The cab lurched, instantly stopped, and again all was silent and dark.

Twenty minutes passed before the current was restored. The electric motor whined and the elevator lurched suddenly upward. In the near darkness Rhone heard the old man's cry, heard his bootheel on the roof of the cab, felt his struggle. He reached out to grab him and Terekhov, grabbing frantically for him, hit his hand and knocked the flashlight loose. Rhone heard it rattle off down the shaft. He caught his own balance and felt for the old man on the other side of the cable.

But Terekhov was no longer there.

29

Awakening at midnight from nightmarish slumber Ilin was haunted by the memory of the first time he'd seen Edward Rhone. He remembered the look in his eyes, unafraid, even undismayed, without apology, refusing to accept the wretched cloak of the miserable role in which he'd found himself cast, just as he refused to grant the Colonel the status of the part to which he'd been assigned. He remembered how he'd opened the Davilov folder and examined the pictures of Rhone, as Andrei Petrovich Davilov, with Avery Remick in London, and remembered clearly his thoughts as he'd compared the face in the photographs with the face of the man before him: *though the two men looked like strangers, they also looked the same.*

In an instant he was wide awake. He left Katusha, softly snoring, slipped from beneath the covers, and put on his robe. Out in the kitchen he made himself a strong cup of instant coffee and spiked it with a stiff shot of brandy. That afternoon, even after the general had informed him he'd been removed from the case, he'd gone back to Registry and Archives and spent two hours combing the files and put a couple of technicians through an exercise of almost equal duration on the computers. And nowhere had he been able to find any record of

Edward Rhone, under that name or any attributable alias, performing any service for the Central Intelligence Agency or any other Western intelligence network. Back in his office he'd looked through the photos again. Something had bothered him, but he couldn't quite figure what it was. Exhausted, he'd finally come back to his apartment. He'd told Katusha merely that it was over. He hadn't had the heart to tell her that in its ending he had been doomed to permanent oblivion.

And now suddenly he knew what it was that had bothered him about the photos, knew it must have been the imminence of the revelation that had woken him in the first place. Edward Rhone, as he stood before him that morning in the Lubyanka, was not the man in the photographs. The man in the photographs was Andrei Davilov. They'd looked that much alike. And that different.

Breathless, he rose, his mind boggling as he grappled with the significance of the revelation. Up Drachinsky's ass. The grandfather clock above the mantel in the living room said 12:10. In London it was eight o'clock, perhaps nine. He wasn't sure. He singed his tongue on the coffee and lit a cigarette, went to the living room for the telephone, and dialed the Lubyanka switchboard. He identified himself to the operator and told her to put through his call and ring him back there when she had a connection.

He'd been waiting ten minutes when the call came through. "Valeri Pavlovich? Yuri Fedorov. How can I help you?"

"Avery Remick. You were in charge of his surveillance last fall in London?"

"Yes." The voice crackled on the line.

"You made the photographs of him and the expatriate Andrei Davilov. Was it always the same?"

A brief silence. "I don't understand."

"Was Andrei Davilov always the same man? Or could it have been two men of similar appearance?"

Another silence. "It was the same man. I'm sure."

"Did you ever see Remick with anyone else of a similar appearance?"

"No. He rarely left the Embassy except for his meetings with Davilov."

Ilin paused to think. "And Remick arrived in London directly from Washington?"

"No. He arrived on a flight from Paris."

"Paris!" He was breathless. "Who had him in Paris?"

"I think Samarin had him in Paris. Yes, Samarin."

The colonel thanked him and started to hang up.

"Valeri Pavlovich? It was too bad about Vasily Yemelyanovich, wasn't it?"

"Yes, Ivan Stepanovich. It was too bad."

He hung up. He'd forgotten Fedorov had been Yaroshenko's closest friend at the Academy.

He dialed the Lubyanka switchboard again and told the operator to reach Samarin in Paris. This time it took almost half an hour before the call came back.

"Samarin? Colonel Ilin, Moscow. I want to know about Avery Remick in Paris last October. I understand you had him."

"Yes."

"Tell me about it. Everything."

"There is really very little. He landed at Orly on a TWA flight from Washington. He was met by a limousine that took him straight to the embassy. He only left it once and the next day he was on a flight to London."

"And the time he left?"

"That was curious. He went to the Isle de la Cité. There was a performance on the bridge and a large crowd had gathered to watch. I observed from the cathedral. Notre Dame, if you don't know Paris. It was an escape artist who had himself handcuffed, put into a chained box, and lowered into the river. But there was a student demonstration in the Place St. Michel, across the river, and by the time he came up it had broken into a full scale riot. The boat that was supposed to pick him up did not come and he had to swim to the quay of the Isle de la Cité. Avery Remick pulled him out of the water."

Ilin hung up. Katusha, red-eyed, was standing in her nightgown in the door. "So it's not over," she said. "It's not really over at all."

The cab climbed up the dark shaft. It seemed a long time before it stopped. Peering down, Rhone could see nothing. They'd been halfway between the third and fourth floors when he'd fallen. So that was it for Alexander Terekhov too, on top of all the others. And all of them for nothing.

He struck a match. The overhead wire was but a foot above his head, with an opening cut into it for the cables and the steel girders a couple of feet above the wire. In the flickering light he could just make out the walls of the engine housing. At the end of one of the girders was a door just large enough for a man to crawl through. From his observation in the exercise pens he knew that between that door and the squirrel cage blower there were but ten meters of open space.

The elevator moved suddenly downward. The match burned down and went out. He rode down in darkness, then lit another match and peered over the side of the cab, where the counterweight, shrouded in shadow, climbed up the shaft toward him.

Gradually, in the little flame's uneven flicker, the uniformed figure took shape. They passed without stopping at the third floor level. The cab continued downward. Alexander Terekhov, standing on the flat surface of the rectangular weight, his bony hands rigid on the cables, rode upward into the shadows.

The cab stopped on the first floor, then jolted almost immediately back up. Rhone struck another match and squinted up the shaft. The cab passed the second floor without interruption. Gradually the weight appeared and Terekhov came into view, staring with his bulging eyes at Rhone and at the flickering light. At the third floor the elevator and the weight jerked to their simultaneous stops, even.

Terekhov stood directly before him, not three feet away. The door opened and several men entered the cab. Rhone held the match toward the frightened old man and motioned for him to step back over onto the cab. He tried to offer him his hand. Terekhov wouldn't move. His knuckles were white over the

213

cables and when Rhone tried to pry his fingers loose they would not budge. Then the door slid shut and the cab started back down and the counterweight, with Alexander Terekhov frozen on his precarious perch, ascended back up into darkness.

The cab stopped once more on the first floor. Rhone listened to the accordion door open and close. He struck another match and held it up to the dead guard's watch. It was 12:58.

The motor whined and the elevator started back up. The cab passed the descending counterweight without pause. Terekhov's face, illuminated briefly in the flicker of the match, was unchanged. His hands were still frozen on the cables.

The cab stopped on the fifth floor. The door opened and closed but still the cab remained. The dark shaft was silent. Rhone struck a match. After that only one remained. He was looking at the ladder, fading into the shadows above. Then the silence was shattered suddenly by the jangle of an electric bell. Though it was a sound Rhone had not heard during his entire time in the Lubyanka, he knew it had to be an alarm. The elevator started down. He made a snap decision and jumped.

For a brief instant his stomach seemed to rise toward his throat as he found himself falling free. Then he caught one of the metal bars with his hands and found two lower rungs with his feet.

He climbed rapidly in the dark. Above him the whine of the motor stopped and started. His hands found the overhead wire. He pulled but it held fast. Beneath the whine of the motor he could hear the rustle of the cables; he seemed to sense the presence of the counterweight, rising toward him. Then the motor stopped. In the silence, just across the shaft, he could hear Terekhov's wheezing breath. From where he stood he could have reached up and touched the girders.

"I'm here," Rhone said. "I'll climb the wire to the girder. You'll probably go back down before I get there. The next time you come up I'll light a match. Give me your hand."

The motor started and Terekhov, giving no sign he'd heard, was gone with the descending weight back down the shaft.

214

Rhone reached his fingers back into the fine mesh of the wire and pulled harder. It held. He clung to the mesh with one hand, to the ladder rung with the other, and let his feet swing free. Supporting half his weight, the mesh still held. He removed his other hand from the ladder rung and reached out to the wire. The motor stopped and the shaft again was silent. Hanging suspended from the wire he walked forward with his hands. The motor started up. He continued along the wire, stopped, extended one foot out and felt the cables brush his boot, only three feet away. The cable stopped and he hooked it with the boot, continuing his hand-walk on the mesh of the wire.

He was about to reach out for the cable when he heard the ripping of the wire.

He fell two feet, down and away from the cable, and lost it with his boot. He swung his legs up and again reached for it with the boot but merely brushed it with the toe. The wire ripped again and he fell another foot farther away. He waited, dangling, for the tear to continue, but now it held. He swung his legs backward to try to catch the ladder, but it was still beyond his reach.

The motor started and again there was the rustling of the cables. He swung his legs back and forth and turned loose of the wire. Again his heart seemed to be leaping into his throat as he fell freely down the shaft. His boots brushed the moving cables and he caught them with his hands, feeling the skin of his palms tear before he was able to break his slide with his feet. The motor stopped and the cables were still. He hung to them, gasping for breath. It started again and the cables rustled, moving up the shaft.

He worked his way around the ascending cables until he was between them and the other two going down, held on with his feet and one hand, and extended the other hand out to feel for the girder. He heard the wire brush the cables as he went through the overhead, felt the girder, took hold of it, and released the cable just before it would have run him through the wheel. He chinned up and clambered onto the girder, lay him-

215

self out belly down across it, and fumbled in his pocket for the last match.

He waited until the motor had stopped and started again before he struck it. Gradually Terekhov, still on the counterweight, ascended into his view. When again the motor stopped, the cab, lost in the darkness below, was on the ground floor and the counterweight was on the sixth, as high as it could go. Terekhov, his fingers still frozen around the cables, was but a foot below Rhone's outreaching hands.

"Give me your hand."

"I ... I can't."

The old man stared up at him, paralyzed. Rhone eased forward across the girder, lying in precarious balance over it. Far below he heard an accordion door slide open on the shaft.

"They're entering the shaft. They'll be shining lights. Riding the cab up."

Down the shaft a light played over the roof of the cab. Terekhov stared at it. With an apparent tremendous effort he tore his right hand free of the cable and extended it upward. Rhone grabbed it with his own bloody left hand just before the match burned out. The motor started back up, the counterweight dropped from below Terekhov's feet, and Rhone reached back with his right hand to steady himself on the girder. As the cab started upward and the flashlight beam played up the walls of the shaft, Rhone lifted the old man up through the opening in the wire.

Then Terekhov's left hand was on his shoulder, clutching desperately at the collar of his coat, and Rhone hoisted him onto the beam. He stretched out straight atop the girder and pulled the old man's legs up so Terekhov lay straight upon it before him. A moment later the flashlight was beamed up through the wire along the bottom of the girder. The light explored the engine, the housing, the locked door at the end of the steel beam. A voice shouted in Russian that there was no one there.

The motor whined briefly and the cab stopped again with its roof at the level of the sixth floor. The door slid open and the guards, whom Rhone still hadn't seen, left the shaft and let it slide back shut behind them.

In the utter darkness Rhone coaxed Terekhov along the girder. At the end he felt for the little tin door, stood up, and waited for the motor to start up again.

When it did he kicked. The hasp for the padlock on the outside broke free, and the door flew open onto the snow-covered roof of the Lubyanka.

Rhone pulled it almost shut, and peered out through the crack. The spotlight from the guard tower swept back and forth across the snow. He heard voices, unintelligible. Across the short open space he could see the door of the blower-housing, also locked with a padlock. He told Terekhov he would go first, to follow on his signal.

The beam of light played across the snow before him and continued its exploration. He pushed the door open and dashed across the no man's land. Reaching the blower-housing he crouched outside the door. He dug his hand into his pocket, got the cotter pin, and fitted the hooked end into the keyhole. He searched blindly for the tumblers with frozen fingers instantly numb. When it caught he didn't even feel it. It was merely his continued probing effort that coincidentally threw them.

He ducked inside as the light played back across the snow. He waited until it had passed again in the opposite direction and motioned Terekhov over.

The scientist emerged like an animal from a lair. Half-walking and half-crawling, he traversed the open space and stuck his head through the open door as the light came sweeping back across the snow. Rhone pulled him through by the shoulders. After he'd shut the door they were again in utter darkness.

In the hot wind rushing off the paddlewheel fan they crawled along a narrowing shaft descending at a forty-five degree angle. When it leveled off and branched out they stopped. Rhone conjured an overview of the Old and New Lubyankas, selected one of the narrow horizontal passages, and whispered for the old man to follow him. By the time he'd seen the light ahead, reached the vent, and looked in on what appeared to be an interrogator's empty office, his uniform was damp with sweat beneath his heavy coat.

He inspected the vent briefly. It appeared to be a little more than a foot wide and about nine inches high. The cover was hinged at the bottom and, he determined by reaching his finger through the grating, was fastened at the top by two screws into the facing.

He tested one of the screws with his finger and found it held firm. He took out a ten-kopeck coin from his pocket, balanced it on the index finger of his left hand, and inserted the finger through the grating near the upper right hand corner of the vent cover. At the same time he inserted his middle finger through another mesh and grasped the coin between them, fitting the edge of it into the groove at the head of the screw and twisting it to break the hold.

A key turned in the lock on the door to the room. He dropped the coin and withdrew his fingers. Lying motionless, he watched through the grating as a pair of jackboots crossed the carpeted floor to the desk. A drawer was opened. There was the sound of shuffling papers. It closed and the boots moved back toward the door. Then they stopped, turned, and started back toward the vent.

Rhone held his breath as a hand appeared to retrieve the ten-kopeck piece. In a moment the boots returned to the door. Behind Rhone, Terekhov muffled a cough. The boots went out. The door was closed and locked. Terekhov was immediately racked by a violent coughing.

Rhone reached through the vent and twisted the screw loose with his finger, using another coin to loosen the one on the left. When it dropped he pushed the vent cover down by its hinged bottom, extended both arms into the opening, doubled his shoulders in toward his chest, and pulled himself through. Still on his hands and knees, he turned to help Terekhov.

Rhone stood and helped the old man to his feet, then stooped and closed the vent cover and replaced the screws. When again he straightened up, Terekhov looked composed, almost unafraid. The light Rhone had seen before was again shining in his eyes.

They dusted themselves off. Terekhov drank from a water pitcher on the desk. "I'm afraid I have humiliated myself."

"What?"

"In the elevator shaft. I must have appeared such a coward."

Rhone touched his shoulder gently and shook his head.

"It's ironic," Terekhov said, laughing softly. "If they had only known."

"Known what?"

"If they had put me through that, I would gladly have answered all their questions. Even the questions they didn't know to ask. All my life it's been my greatest fear. I have acrophobia."

Rhone smiled. "Can you tell me how to get to your interrogator's office?"

"I think so. It's on the fifth floor."

They walked to the door and Rhone opened it and peered out onto the shabby corridor. It was deserted, the same familiar corridor he'd been led along so many times on his way to Ilin's office.

He stepped out and Terekhov followed him. He took out the cotter pin and turned to lock the door. He'd just felt the tumblers catch when he heard the door open down the passage. He glanced up, quickly averting his face.

Colonel Ilin was walking hurriedly down the corridor toward him.

30

He didn't throw the tumblers. He hit the colonel hard across the back of the neck as he was going by and caught him as he started to fall. Terekhov looked on gravely as Rhone dragged Ilin back to the door, opened it, and took him through. The old man followed him and closed it.

Rhone pushed the colonel into the chair behind the desk. He unbuckled Ilin's holster belt, with its Makarov, and lay the holster with the pistol on the desk. He undid the colonel's tie, removed it from around his neck, and used it to bind his hands to one of the legs of the chair. Sitting down on the edge of the desk, staring silently down at him, Rhone trembled with welling emotion. He picked up the water pitcher and sloshed it over him.

Ilin shook his head, still only half-conscious. Rhone watched the water drip down his face. He slapped his interrogator hard across the cheek as a means of bringing him around, counted a couple of beats, and came back with a backhand to the opposite side.

Ilin recoiled. Over his face with his returning consciousness spread a dreadful awareness of the significance of the utter reversal of their roles. Then he recognized Terekhov.

"Now you know why I'm here," Rhone whispered.

"Terekhov?" He was incredulous. "Why?"

"The Helsinki Accord. The president's way of sticking it up Brezhnev's ass." He glanced briefly at Terekhov. "Snatching Mother Russia's most celebrated dissident from the clutches of the KGB. A real feather in his cap." It was the explanation Remick had given him at Staffordshire. But he could see Terekhov didn't believe it for a minute. And neither did Ilin. And Ilin knew of course, as well as Rhone, that he, the operative, would never be allowed to know what really lay behind his mission.

He looked down at the Makarov. He could feel the sweat on his face. The dead were lining up in his mind, the ones he had killed, the ones who had been killed because of him. The back of William Duffy's head had disintegrated a thousand times and still he could see it now. He'd done his job of killing and indirectly so had Remick. All a means to an end. And Ilin was no different really from Remick except that he had more to fear from failure and perhaps something worse to fear than death.

Rhone picked up the holster and strapped it around his waist. He glanced around the room. Against one wall was a cot with a pillow and a blanket. He went over and took the pillow case off the pillow and came back toward the colonel. He sat down on the desk, watching Ilin's reaction as he began to comprehend.

"You're not going to leave me alive?"

Rhone thrust the pillow case across his mouth and tied it behind his neck.

"Yes, Colonel. I'm going to leave you for your friends here. They'll do a better job on you than I ever could."

He lingered for a moment, milking his victory for all its hollow satisfaction. Then he got up and started toward the door.

"He was your interrogator?" Terekhov said as they were going out.

Rhone looked back one last time. "Yes. He was my interrogator." He closed the door and locked it with the pick.

* * *

Briefly the colonel struggled, not to free himself, for he knew that was impossible, but merely as a rebellion against brutal irony. As he felt the tie cut painfully into his wrists, he relaxed and heaved out a long slow breath and let his body sag in the chair. It was no use, he told himself, to think of how close he had come. On his own he had found the truth and found it only moments too late. If he had phoned ahead he might have been in time. But he had not wanted to phone. He had wanted to see Davilov-Rhone's face when he told them.

Now almost certainly it *was* over for everyone but him. Softly he laughed. And as he laughed he remembered what he'd been thinking when Boris first brought him the news of Yaroshenko's arrest. The time he'd gone with his father to the Carpathians. Standing on the side of the green mountain, gazing across the rolling green hills of Rumania, where a murderer would flee. His father, a history professor, had been dragged from their house in 1937 and was never heard from again. Ilin remembered the tears in his eyes that day on the side of the mountain. Now he thought he understood what had eluded him that day. His father must have envied the murderer his freedom, as Ilin envied the American.

Tears streaming down his face, he laughed.

He envied Rhone. He hated him and loved him. He hoped he made it.

Rhone left Terekhov in a cubicle in the toilet across from the stairs and walked down one flight and along another hall, where uniformed and plainclothed KGB and an occasional clerical worker moved back and forth in all directions. Around a corner he found the door Terekhov had described.

He paused outside, listened, and heard nothing. A girl with a thick stack of papers emerged from the next door down and started away without a glance. Two uniformed KGB officers passed behind his back and entered the door at the end of the corridor.

Rhone tried the doorknob and found it locked. He took out the cotter pin, probed with the hook, and opened it. He stepped into the dark office and closed and locked it behind him.

He turned on the light. It was almost identical to Ilin's office, with a big table and file cabinet against one wall and the photograph of Lenin on the other. He went over to the file cabinet, where each drawer was labeled in alphabetical order, picked the lock on one of them, and found the file labeled *Terekhov*.

He opened it on the table and thumbed through it, found a stack of photographs, and selected one that had been taken after his arrest in which the face was the right size. He sat down at Terekhov's interrogator's desk, took out the razor blade and the ID card he'd lifted off the guard in the locker room, and removed the card from the laminated casing. This time, as he drew the blade along the edge of the photo, his hand did not tremble and he executed an immediate perfect cut. He removed the picture and used it as a pattern to trim Terekhov's photo to size, fitted it into the cut-out frame in the card, and returned the card to the laminated sheath. He put the guard's photo into his pocket, put the rest of the Terekhov data and photos back into the folder, and returned the folder to the file cabinet. Remick would have loved to have seen it. But that wasn't part of their bargain and he didn't owe Remick any favors.

He'd just closed the drawer when he heard a key turn in the lock. The door opened. Through it came an old man with a mop and a bucket and a cleaning rag draped over his shoulder. Silently the two of them stared at each other. A sheepish smile played on the old man's face and he mumbled an apology and started to back out the door.

"*Nyet!*" Rhone's firm voice stopped him. "Clean it up."

He passed him and went out the door, walked back to the stairs, ascended them, and crossed to the toilet. A fat civilian KGB man in the standard drab business suit was washing his hands at the lavatory. Beneath the saloon door one of the cubicles Rhone could see Terekhov's boots. He entered the cubicle next to it. He shredded the photo from the ID he'd taken from the guard and dropped it into the toilet. He waited until he heard the fat man start out before he flushed it, then tapped lightly three times on the cubicle wall.

"It's me," he said. "Here." He handed the identification card to Terekhov under the partition. "I'll go out first," he said. "You count three and follow. We'll take the stairs down."

He stepped out of the cubicle. The door opened and a uniformed captain entered and took his place. He ran the water in the lavatory, then went back out into the hall. A moment later Terekhov emerged. They crossed the hall and went through the door to the stairs.

They descended the six flights, encountering no one but a pair of night-shift secretaries who'd slipped out of their offices to share a smoke. On the ground floor landing Rhone opened the door to a crack and peered out over the spacious foyer. On the opposite wall was an enormous hammer and sickle banner, beneath it a guard table with a sign that said *Reception*. One uniformed guard was seated behind the table and another, with a submachine gun, stood just to the side. He recalled the day he'd been summoned there to discuss Andrei Davilov's years abroad. Then there'd been no weaponry in evidence.

Three civilian KGB men emerged from an elevator, presented their cards at the table, and went out. Rhone took out Ilin's Makarov, pulled the slide, and threw off the safety. He took off his coat and wrapped it around the pistol.

He looked back at Terekhov. "You go first. If they recognize you I'll have to kill them, so stay out of my line of fire."

The old man stepped through the door and started briskly across the foyer. He stopped at the desk and fumbled for his identification card, found it, and laid it before the seated guard. The elevator doors opened again and two more uniformed KGB men emerged. They walked toward the table, stopped just short of it, and waited as the guard compared Terekhov's picture to his face. After a moment he handed it back to him and waved him by.

Terekhov pocketed the card and started toward the wide steps that led down to the main exit. The two officers who'd gotten off the elevator stepped up to the table and presented their passes, but the guard there was still staring after Terekhov, now going down the steps. He sighed, glanced briefly at the men's cards and waved them by as Terekhov went out the door.

Rhone unrolled the overcoat from around the pistol, clicked the safety back on and returned it to his holster. He stepped out the door and started across the foyer, putting on the coat as he went. He gave his ID to the guard, who examined it briefly and handed it back.

He went down the stairs and out the door onto Dzerzhinsky Square.

31

Valeri Pavlovich Ilin squinted against the morning sunlight that poured through the high barred windows of General Drachinsky's office. Across the desk the general spread his marmalade carefully over his toast and took a delicate bite. The prosecutor, Zverev, had already cleaned his plate and was looking at the colonel's untouched breakfast enviously.

Ilin sighed and pushed it toward him.

"You might regret that later," Drachinsky said with a mean smile.

Numbed, the colonel smiled back.

"How is the circulation?" the general asked, aimiably as if he were inquiring about a cold.

"It's coming back." The colonel massaged his wrists.

"Well. We have the tape of their call to Moscow Station. They were picked up by an American limousine on the Moskvoretsky Bridge just after they left the Lubyanka. No doubt they are in a safe house somewhere near the city now. We can assume there will be an attempt to get them out of the country through one of the Embassy's safe channels. We can only hope we will be fortunate enough to stop them."

He looked at the colonel as if he expected him to say something, so Ilin said, "And if you do, what effect will that have on my situation?"

"It hardly changes the fact that you've committed a terrible blunder. Really," the general sighed, "I'm afraid it will have no effect at all." He paused. "What might help is if you could offer an explanation. Why all that trouble for one worn-out old physicist?"

"The American said it had something to do with the Helsinki Accords. The president's way of sticking it up Brezhnev's ass." Ilin watched Zverev flinch and experienced a twinge of secret enjoyment. There was a freedom, he thought, in having nothing left to lose. A day ago, he could never so casually have repeated the remark.

Across the table the general seethed. "Do you believe that?"

He laughed. "Of course not."

"Would you care to tell us what you do believe?"

He'd had the whole night to think about it. "I have nothing concrete with which to substantiate this. It's just a suggestion."

"Yes?"

"Terekhov must have some scientific information they want, or information they want to prevent us from obtaining."

"Perhaps. What kind of information?"

"Something to do with our particle beam research project."

Now the general laughed. "I find that suggestion preposterous. A couple of days ago you yourself told me you were convinced the whole Semipalatinsk angle in this affair was simply the . . . as you said . . . red herring."

"There is another American expression I remember from my university days. *Not seeing the forest for the trees.* I think using the herring to divert us from the herring would be typical of Remick."

"And I think, Valeri Pavlovich, you are, as the Americans also say, grasping for straws."

The colonel shrugged. Perhaps it was true. Somehow he no longer really cared. He was, as the Americans said, simply going through the motions. "I want to remind you, General, of one thing: when you congratulated me on obtaining the Davilov confession, a confession we all now know was carefully contrived to mislead us, I was the one who was dissatisfied. I was the one who wanted to continue the investigation. I was the one who was sure the prisoner had falsely revealed himself. It was your decision, and yours Comrade Prosecutor, to press for a hasty closure of the matter." He fell silent, meeting the general's furious gaze, sighed, and started to rise. "Now, if I am free to leave, that is all I have to say."

The general shook his head. "You are not free to leave, Valeri Pavlovich." He pushed the telephone across his desk. "Perhaps you would like to phone your wife yourself and tell her you will not be coming home . . . now."

"No." How could he tell Katusha that? "I am under arrest, then?"

"Yes."

"You cannot arrest me for being a fool, General. You must have a charge."

"I have a charge. Interference with the organs of state security. After the girl Alisa Belova conspired to leave the country illegally, you prevented her arrest. An arrest, I might add, that most certainly would have led us to the fact that her brother was an impostor and prevented this entire disastrous outcome."

The colonel lit a cigarette. His hand, he noticed, was quite steady. Steadier than it had been in days. This was the worst of all he had feared. Yet now that it was happening he was no longer afraid. He thought of the hundreds and the thousands that he'd seen go through that arched gate before him. He saw the day of processing rolling out like an unending carpet before him. The searches. The physical examination. The shaving. The probing of his rectum. The confiscation of all he had, all he'd come to take for granted. His reduction from name to number. Then the months or years ahead. The changeless, tasteless meals. The cells. The interrogations.

For so long it had been the source of his greatest dread and fascination. Yet now that it was upon him he no longer feared it.

And he hardly regretted anything, unless it was the whole sum of his life.

32

Helsinki, January 1979

It was mid-afternoon, twilight, when the Aeroflot jet banked and began its descent toward Vantaa Airport. Beneath them the city spread white over the island-ringed peninsula. Rhone's Soviet diplomatic passport said his name was Nikolai Denisovich Sirokhin, newly attached to the Russian Embassy in Helsinki. Another card in his wallet identified him as a captain in the KGB. He wore a dark suit hardly more fashionable than the one which had been tailored for his trial. The passport said he was fifty-one years old and a make-up artist at the safe dacha in Peredelkino had given him the gray hair and the lines to prove it.

The older man with the dark goatee beside him had passed through customs at Sheremetevo under the name of Anton Yevgenyevich Nivagres. His passport said he held the same diplomatic rank as Rhone. His KGB card listed him as a colonel. There were tears in his eyes as they boarded the plane.

They carried their bags unopened through Finnish customs, bypassing the metal detectors so that the Makarov each man wore in a shoulder-holster beneath his arm proved no embarrassment.

A Russian Embassy limousine was waiting for them outside the arrivals terminal. Parked behind it was a Volvo sedan with a driver and three passengers, their civilian KGB escort to the Embassy. The chauffeur of the limousine got out, loaded their bags into the trunk, and held the door open for them. After they'd pulled out of the airport, Rhone remarked to him that he was thrilled to see Helsinki, and asked him if he would detour down Mannesheim Avenue to give him the chance to get a feel of the city before they reported to the embassy.

They'd spent one night in an American Embassy safe house in Peredelkino, on the outskirts of Moscow, where Brown's replacement, an Ivy League type named MacMahan, had badgered Rhone for a preliminary debriefing. After soaking in a hot bath and having his bruises and lacerations looked at by an embassy physician who also treated Terekhov, Rhone had sat down at the dining table with the dissident and shared a feast of Georgian hors d'oeuvres, chicken Kiev, French bread, cheese, and wine. Afterwards they drank real coffee and French cognac from elegant tumblers.

"When you were talking about your acrophobia?" Rhone had asked the Russian. "The question they didn't know to ask. It was about a new accelerator principle?"

Terekhov nodded. "We were just talking, passing ideas back and forth, and it started coming to us. A revolutionary concept. But we realized if either side got it the balance of power would be destroyed. We vowed to keep it secret. But I suppose when he learned of my difficulties with the KGB he decided he had to tell them what I knew." He paused. "Do you know where he is? Erich Reisinger?"

"He's dead," Rhone said gently. "Several months ago."

"I don't believe he would have revealed to them the actual principle," Terekhov said gravely after a silence.

They turned onto Mannesheim Avenue, lined with trees. In his rearview mirror the chauffeur watched the Volvo make the turn behind them. A crowded trolley rattled along the tracks in the center divider. Finns, bundled against the cold, hurried along the sidewalks. Night was falling and the streetlights were already lit.

Rhone counted the blocks, the names of the cross streets clicking off in his mind. After they'd gone a couple of kilometers he slipped his hand into his coat and unsnapped the shoulder-holster. His fingers curled around the Makarov and beside him Terekhov shifted in his seat and looked back at the Volvo close behind them. The driver's eyes met Rhone's in the mirror.

He drew the Makarov, showed it to him in the mirror, and pointed it at the back of his head. "Three blocks ahead. The light will be red. Don't stop for it."

The driver was automatically slowing down, veering momentarily half out of the lane so that a Volkswagon with horn blaring swerved to avoid them. He again met Rhone's eyes in the mirror and accelerated.

They passed through another green light. The Volvo closed the distance behind them. Rhone still held the pistol on the driver's head. Terekhov turned in his seat and looked again at the Volvo. They approached another green. The Volvo followed them through on the yellow.

The next light turned red as they reached the middle of the block. A milk truck lurched forward and sputtered to a halt in the middle of the one-way cross street, its nose protruding into the intersection.

"Slow down," Rhone said. "Then give it gas when you get there."

The driver slowed the limousine. His frightened eyes met Rhone's in the mirror. They were pulling almost to a stop.

"Now!"

The driver stepped on the accelerator. The limousine shot forward past the milk truck. Belatedly, the Volvo also accelerated behind them. At the same time the milk truck started forward. Rhone glanced backward as he heard the impact.

The milk truck had broadsided the Volvo. Tires spinning, the truck pushed the car sideways across the intersection as from all directions traffic was screeching to a halt.

"Straight ahead," Rhone told the driver. "After the fourth light, pull over and stop."

In the rearview mirror he could see their KGB escorts climbing angrily from the demolished Volvo. From somewhere he heard the donkey-bray of an old Gestapo-style siren. Already he could see Remick's American Embassy limousine parked on the right, just through the intersection now three blocks ahead.

The driver had seen it also and was looking nervously about.

"Stop behind it when we get there," Rhone told him. "Do as you're told and you won't be harmed."

They passed through another green light, then another. The rear door of Remick's limousine opened and Remick got out, looking like a Russian in his black overcoat and fluffy fur hat. The driver slowed and started to ease over to the right. The light turned yellow and he pulled to a stop, still one vehicle short of the intersection.

"When the light changes continue straight ahead." It was Terekhov beside him.

Rhone heard the safety click and turned to find himself staring down the barrel of the other Makarov.

He shook his head, his own weapon still aimed at the chauffeur. "Yours was loaded with blanks."

Terekhov's hand was as steady as his gaze. "I suspected as much. Last night in Peredelkino I switched them after you were asleep." He paused. "Now drop yours. I don't want to have to harm you."

The light had turned green. The driver was looking back, waiting. Rhone shook his head and tossed his own weapon to the floorboard.

"Go!" Terekhov commanded.

The driver hesitated for another instant and Terekhov swung the pistol barrel toward him, a gesture, then pointed it again at Rhone.

The driver hit the accelerator and swung the steering wheel to the left. The tires squealed. On Remick's face caught in the headlights the smile turned to befuddlement as the limousine shot through the intersection back out into the traffic lane and left the parked limousine behind.

In the rearview mirror Rhone saw Remick stare after them for a second, then rush to the door of his own vehicle. Rhone looked back at Terekhov, who'd retreated far over on his side of the seat.

"I cannot betray my country. And that is what they would force me to do."

Rhone nodded. Through the rear window he saw the American limousine pull out into the traffic, seven or eight cars behind them. "So what are you going to do?"

The Russian pondered for a moment as the driver weaved through the flowing traffic. "I am going to the Yugoslav Embassy. Take me there."

The driver swung over to the left lane and passed a small delivery truck.

Terekhov looked back at the American limousine racing through the traffic, gaining on them. "Turn left at the next street."

A trolley was approaching on the center divider. The light turned yellow. The driver started to slow.

Terekhov waved the gun at him. "Do not stop. Make the turn in front of the trolley."

The driver looked back at Terekhov, hesitating. The trolley was bearing down on the intersection. The traffic light had turned red but the trolley light was still green. He decided the gun scared him worse than the train. He hit the accelerator and spun the wheel. Rhone watched it racing toward them. There was a screeching of metal on metal just before impact. Rhone's head hit the window and the shattering of the glass was loud in his ears.

They had stopped, the limousine half on its side, resting against the engine of the derailed trolley. Rhone shook his head to try to clear out the cobwebs. He could feel the blood pouring down the side of his face. The driver was unconscious, slumped forward on the steering wheel. Terekhov, still holding the pistol on him and clinging to the arm rest to keep from sliding across the seat, was unhurt. Up and down Mannesheim Avenue, traffic had come to a stop and already a crowd was converging upon them.

Terekhov pondered nervously. "Get out. You will be my hostage."

Rhone shook his head. "I'm expendable now. It's you they want, one way or the other."

Terekhov absorbed this. Somewhere, another siren brayed. He pondered for a moment longer, nodded as a means of saying goodbye, and climbed suddenly out of the car, swinging the pistol in an arc to stop the converging crowd. Then, running and stumbling, he started alongside the tracks down the first crowded passenger car. At the end he climbed over the coupling.

Rhone's door was jammed, so he had to climb out the other side. He started along the tracks in the same path Terekhov had taken. He was just reaching the end of the first car when he heard the gun discharge. At the coupling he looked across and saw Terekhov standing in the alcove entrance of an office building on the opposite side of the street, the gun still in his hand, pedestrians fleeing in panic in either direction along the sidewalk.

Rhone scrambled across the coupling. Terekhov fired again, up the street in the direction from which they'd come, where he saw Remick and another armed man crouched behind a stopped car.

Now the siren was deafening and, half a block up the street, weaving its way slowly through the stalled traffic, Rhone could see the Finnish police van approaching. Hearing it, Terekhov stepped out of the alcove and fired a wild shot toward it. The windshield of a stalled car beside it was shattered and from inside there was a scream.

He stepped back into the alcove, utter panic in his eyes. He looked back at Remick, peering over the hood of the car. He looked at Rhone, standing unprotected before the trolley couplings. He raised the Makarov slowly and placed the barrel against his head.

"*Nyet! Nyet!*" It was Remick, who'd thrown down his own gun and was running toward him at an angle across the street.

And Rhone was running also, weaving through the stalled

235

cars, shouting for Remick to get back. Then he stopped. Terekhov's brightened eyes were upon him as he pulled the trigger and his bloody brains exploded out of his skull and the muffled discharge echoed.

Rhone got there first, Remick a step behind him. Alexander Terekhov lay dead on the floor of the blood-splattered alcove.
"Damn," Remick said. "Damn, damn!"
Rhone turned away, the months passing before his eyes, which had only come to this. The police were closing in on foot, pushing back the crowd. Remick showed one of them a document he'd gotten from the Finnish government and said he could vouch for Rhone. Rhone pushed into the crowd and started away up the street.
He was half a block along it before Remick caught him and fell into step beside him. "He was supposed to have blanks."
Rhone walked on in silence.
"Why did he do it?"
Rhone stopped and turned and stared at him. "Why the fuck do you think he did it? He was a dissident, not a traitor."
He walked on. The blood was still oozing down the side of his head and some of the passers-by stopped to stare after him.
In a moment Remick caught up. "He was supposed to have blanks."
"He switched them."
"*He* switched them?"
"I guess I let him switch them."
"You what?"
Rhone stopped again, looking down at him. "Andrei Davilov. You gave him to the KGB."
"It was the best way to get you back to the Lubyanka. Hell, I thought that was why you sent the message."
"He's dead! His sister is dead!" Rhone walked on.
Remick followed, shrugging. "It's just one of those things."
"You didn't take any chances, did you. Just one of those things. And the two thugs you had jump me on Komsomolsky Prospekt?"

"No. That wasn't my doing."

Rhone looked at him silently. They continued along the street.

"It was Yaroshenko," Remick said. "He knew Davilov had been sent to set him up for the slaughter and he knew there was no way Davilov was going to kill both of them with his own bare hands. So you had to be someone else." He took out his handkerchief and tried to dab at the blood on the side of Rhone's face.

Rhone shook him off and started across the intersection.

"It's not a complete failure," said Remick, hurrying along at his side. "We *wanted* him alive, but at least the KGB doesn't have him. Come on, we'll get a cab back to the Embassy."

"Fuck you."

Rhone turned and started out into the street. A cab was approaching. He raised his hand to hail it, but the light turned and it stopped short of the intersection.

Remick started out after him. The light changed, and again Rhone raised his hand.

"We've still got your debriefing," Remick said, stopping just short of the curb.

The cab pulled up and Rhone started to open the door.

"She's not dead."

He froze, turned, started back toward him. As horns blared behind it, the cab pulled away.

"What did you say?" Rhone asked him as he reached the curb.

"She's not dead. She's in Vladimir Prison."

Rhone grabbed him by the shoulders and shook him furiously, shouting at the top of his lungs: "Vladimir! What the fuck are you talking about fucking Vladimir? She killed herself in the Lubyanka! I . . ." He stopped, deeply thoughtful, and went on in a whisper, ". . . saw her."

"I *could* trade for her," Remick said. "We've got a man they want. It's no deal from our point of view but I could do it."

"You do it, Remick. Goddamn you do it."

"It's you."

"What?"

"The man they want. It's you. General Drachinsky has apparently taken this whole thing personally. But he's agreed to free the girl if you go back."

33

Berlin, April 1979

From the quay where Remick's chauffeur parked the limousine he could see the fenced pedestrian bridge, translucent in arc light, and the overhead railway on its tall concrete pillars. On the near side two West German policemen stood smoking behind the sandbags. Across the deserted span of the bridge a *vopo* with an automatic rifle slung over his shoulders found the limousine with his binoculars.

"It's early," Remick said, looking at his watch.

Beside him, Rhone said nothing.

The *vopo* lowered his binoculars and walked back to the East German booth. Beyond the booth, rising up in domination of the dreary scene, was a wooden gun tower manned by two more *vopos*. The river below the bridge, wide and slow, was also bathed in theatrical light; gradually, upstream and downstream moving away from the bridge, the light faded to misty darkness.

He'd set his conditions in Helsinki, the day after Alexander Terekhov had died. In Paris, where he'd gone to wait for Remick to make the arrangements with Drachinsky, he'd gone to the hospital to pay a final visit to Jean-Pierre Duval. He was old, withered and blind, yellowed by jaundice, and said he'd been told he was dying. Rhone had told him what he had done and what he had to do. The old Frenchman had listened until he had finished and then shook his head. "Do not go. There is no way to do it. Besides, I have had a dream about you last night. If you try it, they will kill you."

"Who will kill me?"

"Either one of them. Or both of them together."

"Why will they kill me?"

"The Russian general will kill you for vengeance, though certainly he would rather have you alive. And the American cannot risk letting you go back to the Russians because he can never be sure what you may have learned from the dissident. I am sure they already have it planned. Otherwise, what would either of them have to gain by making this arrangement?"

The question had been rhetorical, but even if it had demanded an answer the old man's feverish eyes had been closed before Rhone would have had time to reply.

The next day he had flown to London. He had been arrested at Heathrow airport and taken to Scotland Yard. In his cell the next day he had read in the *International Herald Tribune* the account of the arrest of the Russian expatriate and former Russian language broadcaster for Radio Liberty, Andrei Davilov, charged with conspiracy to sell secret CIA documents to the KGB.

"They're coming," Remick said.

Two headlights wound through the desolation that lay beyond the bridge and all along the wall. A Russian Zil materialized into the lights around the East German checkpoint. Remick's chauffeur got out of the American limousine, walked around, and opened the trunk. Across the bridge one of the *vopos* came out and opened the back door of the Zil.

"Ready?" Remick said.

"The gun."

"Yes." He smiled. "I stick by my word. You know, I *could* screw you."

Rhone, impassive, said nothing.

He pulled it out of his coat, a Smith and Wesson "body-guard" .38, and handed it to him.

Rhone waited, impassive.

"You know my ass will be in the sling in Washington," Remick said. "Not just the gun. You know this is all my own initiative. Don't you wonder why?"

"I know why," Rhone said.

Remick took a cartridge out of his shirt pocket and held it up. "One cartridge."

Rhone took it.

"Just one? I hope it's not for Drachinsky," Remick said. "You wouldn't want to start World War III."

Rhone loaded the revolver and rotated the cylinder until the cartridge was in the chamber. He slipped the weapon beneath his coat and into his belt behind his back.

"For yourself?" Remick smiled.

"You'd like that? It would save trouble for both sides."

"Or me?" He laughed.

Rhone was impassive.

Beaming, Remick held out the handcuffs. Rhone turned on the seat and placed his hands behind his back. Remick clapped them on. The chauffeur, carrying an Uzi submachine gun and a doubled "L" clip, came back around and opened the rear door on Rhone's side. He got out and Remick slid across the seat and got out behind him. He took the Uzi, attached the clip, and slipped it up under his overcoat.

Drachinsky, in his KGB uniform and military greatcoat, got out of the Russian limousine and stood waiting by the open door. Rhone and Remick walked along the quay toward the sandbags at the Western checkpoint.

"You can still change your mind," Remick said. "You know once you're out there there's nothing I can do to help you."

Rhone said nothing.

"There are some men," Remick said, "men like you, who will test themselves to the limit, when there are men like me to let them."

"Like you," Rhone said. "And Drachinsky."

Remick scowled. They reached the sandbags. One of the West Germans scanned the bridge with his binoculars. Remick took them from him and lifted them to his eyes. Across the bridge Drachinsky looked at his watch and snapped his fingers. The *vopo* handed him his binoculars and he lifted them to his own eyes. Each of them, Drachinsky and Remick, looked across at the opposite checkpoint for what seemed a long time. Then, as if through some secret unspoken communication, they both lowered their binoculars together.

A West German policeman raised the barricade. One of the *vopos* raised the barricade opposite. Rhone and Remick started forward. From the opposite side, Drachinsky and Alisa Belova walked toward them. Then Remick stopped and Rhone, walking on, left him behind. On the far end of the bridge Alisa, walking toward him, also left Drachinsky.

In the middle of the bridge they stopped, facing each other. Her face was ashen, drawn. Her hands, like his own, were cuffed behind her back. Facing her halfway across the bridge over the precipice that separated two sides of the world, he wondered if, after all that had happened to them, there could ever have been anything again between them. They waited, eye to eye and silent. Then she whispered:

"You're giving your life for me. How can I take it?"

She started to walk on, but before she'd quite passed him he stopped her with a look. "Before you get to Remick, stop and look back at me. When I move, fall. And remember afterwards: *I was your brother.*"

She walked on, toward Remick and the West German sector, and Rhone, his fingers finding the lock-pick sewn into the material in the back of his coat, walked on toward Drachinsky's gleaming eyes.

He was ten meters short of Drachinsky when he felt the click of the tumblers. Above the overhead railway the shadow of a *vopo* paced the small circle of the gun tower and was suddenly still. Drachinsky, smiling at him, eyes gleaming, turned suddenly, and started back toward the East German booth. A train whistle screamed and the bridge seemed to shudder as it came

242

hurtling across the tracks. On both sides of the river and the wall, save for the arc lights on the bridge, the city seemed asleep. Rhone turned, looking back up the bridge at Alisa, who'd also stopped ten meters short of Remick, and was looking back at him. Beyond her, Remick observed with lurid fascination.

Rhone shed the cuffs and drew out the pistol as Alisa fell to the bricks. He shot Remick, in spite of the distance, and in spite of the terrible odds, almost directly between the eyes.

They said you never heard the bullet that hit you. No one had ever told him that sometimes, even when it did not instantly kill you, you also did not feel it. Remick, reeling on the bridge, perceived it as a skip, a moment of blackness and awesome silence and oblivion slashed out of the march of time, that could have been death itself already but was not. And as oblivion faded, the bridge, translucent and shimmering, and the roar of the train, deafening, returned with his sudden angry awareness and a stultifying headache. Enraged, he clutched under his coat for the Uzi. Across the bridge he saw Drachinsky rushing for cover behind the East German barricade. He saw the *vopos* in the guard tower fanning their automatic weapons across the bridge. He saw the Russian woman running, screaming, toward him. She was past him by the time he had the Uzi out of his coat. His finger sat hard on the trigger. Nine milimeter shells sprayed the bridge, ripping the Allied fencing, peppering the sandbags at the East German barrier and the dark pocked wall beyond.

When the clip was empty he dropped the weapon and dropped to his own knees on the bricks, reeling, his vision fading again, coming and going like a weak memory, and finally gone for good as Remick, dead in a pool of blood, was gone. But not before he had seen, had known beyond a shadow of a doubt that the bridge, from where he stood all the way to the East German checkpoint, was empty.

Edward Rhone was gone.

* * *

Falling toward the misty flowing water as the gunfire rattled overhead he waited for the snapping tight of the rope, the snapping of the noose at his neck. Waited for the dream to end. But by the time he hit the water it had not. He sank into the murky dark depths, holding his breath until he thought his lungs would burst, and started the swim, struggling in the cold in his heavy clothing, knowing that, having survived his moment on the fence, when death had been his most reasonable probability and he had been as prepared for it as ever in his life, if he drowned here and now he'd already lived a few seconds longer and traveled a few meters farther than his gambit could ever have been reasonably expected to allow.

Houdini performed an illusion in which he caused an elephant to disappear on stage. The animal was led into a square curtained enclosure with two doors that opened outward, like wings, toward the audience. The doors were closed behind it, then immediately reopened to reveal the enclosure, empty. The elephant had been led directly through the rear curtain and was standing at the back of the enclosure, concealed from the audience by the spread of the open wings. Houdini worked on stage but Rhone had not been allowed that luxury. Though there was probably not a person on either end of the bridge who had not been alerted to the fact that he would attempt to escape, what no one, not even Remick—his own remark notwithstanding—would have dreamed he would do was turn and shoot the very man who'd just relinquished his custody. Shock had bought him the blink of an eye.

He swam with the gentle current, dominating second by second the angry longing of his lungs. Above him on the East German side lay the shadow of the hull of a patrol boat, bobbing on its mooring. He felt the shock as its engines were started and perceived the violent fanning of its props. He felt the patter shocks of the gunfire still pelting the surface. His lungs screamed for air and still he swam, now deeper, stronger and swifter, into the darkness downstream from the misty light. Alisa. Her eyes as she looked at him on the bridge. Somewhere, he wondered, far down the metaphorical stream of his life, would she run out to greet him as the wife of the hanged man, in the story he'd been thinking of before Remick pulled him from the Seine, had greeted him? Of the people on the bridge, only she and Drachinsky and Remick had known he was not the Russian expatriate Andrei Davilov. If he could swim far enough, stay submerged long enough, it was not an impossible vision.

Swimming, hard and deep, he silenced the screaming of his lungs one lost breath longer at a time, and waited for the moment when they above would conclude that there was not a chance he could have survived so long. And the gunfire would stop and the sweeping lights go dark.